MW01245892

Della B's

Bleu Glo

J. Stewart Willis

Author's Tranquility Press
ATLANTA, GEORGIA

J. Stewart Willis/Author's Tranquility Press
3800 Camp Creek Pkwy SW Bldg. 1400-116 #1255
Atlanta, GA 30331, USA
www.authorstranquilitypress.com

Ordering Information:
Quantity sales. Special discounts are available on quantity purchases by corporations, associations, and others. For details, contact the "Special Sales Department" at the address above.

DELLA B'S BLEU GLO/ J. Stewart Willis
Hardback: 978-1-962492-18-8
Paperback: 978-1-962492-20-1
eBook: 978-1-962492-21-8

Contents

Prologue in Bleu iii

Part One: The Rise

Chapter One 1

Chapter Two 3

Chapter Three 6

Chapter Four 10

Chapter Five 14

Chapter Six 16

Chapter Seven 18

Chapter Eight 21

Chapter Nine 23

Chapter Ten 27

Chapter Eleven 31

Chapter Twelve 33

Chapter Thirteen 38

Chapter Fourteen 40

Chapter Fifteen 44

Chapter Sixteen 48

Chapter Seventeen 52

Chapter Eighteen 55

Chapter Nineteen 61

Chapter Twenty 66

Chapter Twenty-One 70

Chapter Twenty-Two 71

Chapter Twenty-Three 74

Chapter Twenty-Four 77

Chapter Twenty-Five 78

Chapter Twenty-Six 80

Chapter Twenty-Seven 83

Chapter Twenty-Eight 86

Chapter Twenty-Nine 89

Chapter Thirty 92

Chapter Thirty-One 95

Chapter Thirty-Two 98

Chapter Thirty-Three 102

Chapter Thirty-Four 107

Chapter Thirty-Five 108

Chapter Thirty-Six 109

Chapter Thirty-Seven 114

Chapter Thirty-Eight 119

Chapter Thirty-Nine 127

Chapter Forty 131

Chapter Forty-One 133

Chapter Forty-Two 136

Chapter Forty-Three 138

Chapter Forty-Four 142

Chapter Forty-Five 145

Chapter Forty-Six 150

Chapter Forty-Seven 154

Chapter Forty-Eight 159

Chapter Forty-Nine 161

Chapter Fifty 164

Chapter Fifty-One 167

Chapter Fifty-Two 172

Part Two: The Dream is Stolen

Chapter Fifty-Three 175

Chapter Fifty-Four 177

Chapter Fifty-Five 180

Chapter Fifty-Six 182

Chapter Fifty-Seven 184

Chapter Fifty-Eight 187

Chapter Fifty-Nine 189

Chapter Sixty 190

Chapter Sixty-One 193

Chapter Sixty-Two 195

Chapter Sixty-Three 197

Part Three: The Dream is Reinvented

Chapter Sixty-Four 200

Chapter Sixty-Five 205

Chapter Sixty-Six 207

Chapter Sixty-Seven 212

Chapter Sixty-Eight 214

Chapter Sixty-Nine 220

Part Four: Cathy's Dream Slips Away

Chapter Seventy 230

Chapter Seventy-One 234

Chapter Seventy-Two 240

Chapter Seventy-Three 242

Chapter Seventy-Four 244

Chapter Seventy-Five 249

Chapter Seventy-Six 252

Chapter Seventy-Seven 254

Chapter Seventy-Eight 257

Chapter Seventy-Nine 260

Chapter Eighty.. 262

Chapter Eighty-One... 267

Chapter Eighty-Two 271

Chapter Eighty-Three 273

Chapter Eighty-Four 278

Chapter Eighty-Five 280

Chapter Eighty-Six 283

Chapter Eighty-Seven 294

Chapter Eighty-Eight 298

Chapter Eighty-Nine 301

Chapter Ninety.. 305

Chapter Ninety-One 312

Chapter Ninety-Two 316

Chapter Ninety-Three 320

Chapter Ninety-Four 326

Chapter Ninety-Five 328

Chapter Ninety-Six 334

To All Who Write Indies and Dream

Other books by J. Stewart Willis

Gestation Seven

Deadly Highway

Three Degrees and Gone

One Vote

Requiem for Geraldine Gerbil

The Johnson Place

Tent City Convoy

Prologue in Bleu

Della B sits at the head of the table like an African queen glaring down at her minions. She is a formidable woman, both in size and in presence, and a three-time Grammy award-winning superstar.

Today the subject is her presence. Like her money, Della B can never have enough of it. She leans forward, with her bosom low over the conference table, arms stretched out, and palms down. It's as if she's ready to pounce. "Where's the lab guy?"

The others look around.

Etienne Mallet of Mallet Pharmaceuticals answers, "Do you mean the inventor?"

"Yeah, the twitchy guy."

Mallet has never met or seen Les Warin. "I don't know whether he's twitchy or not, but Mallet Pharmaceuticals owns the patent, so he's irrelevant."

Della B grimaces. "You telling me you bought him out?"

Mallet turns to Andrew Boudreaux, his attorney, who answers, "Mallet Pharmaceuticals owns the patent and all rights."

Della B glares. "Who the hell are you?"

"Er, Andrew Boudreaux, the attorney for Mallet Pharmaceuticals. And yes, you might say we bought Mr. Warin out."

"Might say? Does that mean you twisted his arm, waterboarded him, or something?"

Boudreaux's face flushes. "Everything was above board."

Della B glares at Boudreaux. "So everything we do today is legal?"

Boudreaux smirks. "We only deal in legal."

Della B scans the others at the table. "Let's see. I've met Vincent Raby and Georgina Makoff before, and I've now met Mr. Mallet of Mallet Pharmaceuticals and his attorney. And the other two, who are you?"

The two look at each other, uncertain who should speak first. Finally, the woman says, "I'm Debra Holly, Ms. Makoff's attorney."

Holly extends a hand to the other unknown.

"Larry Wygel, representing Vincent Cosmetics."

Della B nods. "A damn lawyer's convention." She pats the arm of the man sitting next to her. "And this guy with his white hair swept back in a ducktail is my attorney, Barney Edelmann. So, as Mr. Boudeaux says, we do it legally."

She reaches down into a briefcase sitting on the floor beside her and pulls out a jar containing a glowing blue material. She sets it on the table. "This is the subject for today. This is a jar of paint that has been colored with a glowing blue dye. The dye is going to make us all millions." She looks at the group around the table. "As I understand it, Vincent and Georgina, you've signed contracts with Mallet Pharmaceuticals to use the dye in cosmetics and ceramic jewelry. Is that right?"

Raby and Makoff both turn to their attorneys who nod. Mallet Pharmaceuticals' attorney says, "Signed, sealed, and delivered, and we're ready to go. We're putting the dye factory together as we speak using an existing building. We'll be producing in a month."

Della B puckers her lips in thought. "Georgina, you ready to produce if you start receiving dye in a month?"

Debra Holly glances at Makoff for approval and replies, "Georgina has signed contracts with twenty-seven other ceramic jewelry manufacturers and is ready."

Della B looks at her attorney who is checking the hair at the back of his head. "You checked the contracts, Barney? They good?"

Edelmann quickly brings his hand down. "They're good."

Della B turns back to Holly. "Well, sister, I'm glad to hear your client is ready, but I'm going to slow you down. You see, Mr. Raby here wants to do testing to make sure his cosmetics are safe. So we need to schedule things. I want you to start by making earrings and jewelry for navel piercings. I've already signed a contract to have low-cut jeans made with decorative stitching in glowing bleu thread. There are going to be a hundred million exposed navels showing in this country, and eventually, I want a hundred million pierced navels displaying Bleu Glo jewelry— that's Della B's Bleu Glo Jewelry. I don't care if the women are skinny, curved, or fat. I want them all glowing belly buttons bleu. But not yet. I want the jeans and the jewelry available in February, Valentine's Day maybe, no sooner."

She next looks down at Raby. "You testing the dye, Vincent? I know you said you had to test. You had to be safe. So do it, but recognize that once a fad starts, we all have to get on the bandwagon. Get it done before the world passes you by. We need the products out there—lipstick, rouge, eyeliner, mascara, nail polish, hair dye, the works, products for men and women. In a few months, I don't want any blonde surfers coming out of the water. I want them all with glowing blue hair."

She looks pensive for a moment. "Damn, that's a good image. Use it in your ads." Again, she eyes Raby. "Take all the time you want, Vincent. But understand the Grammys will be given out at the end of March next year. Understand further that I'm featured. When I get on that stage, I want to be wearing Bleu lipstick, Bleu eye shadow, Bleu earrings, etc., etc. Is that clear, Vincent?"

Raby nods nervously. "Yes."

"You going to do it, Vincent? I want to hear it."

"We'll do it, Della."

"Good to hear. And, Georgina, when I look at the audience, I want to see young women dancing with their arms up and glowing navels gyrating to the music. You with me?"

Makoff laughs. "I'm with you, Della."

Della B laughs back. "It'll be a party."

Next, Della B turns to Edelmann. "Time for you to do your thing."

Edelmann fingers some papers in front of him. "I've already passed these contracts out for everyone to read. In them, you agree to pay Della B 2 percent of the cost of all items you sell, with a further agreement to use Della B's name on your products—Della B's Bleu Glo Jewelry and Della B's Bleu Glo Cosmetics."

Holly asks, "That's 2 percent of the wholesale price, right?"

Edelmann nods. "That's what the paper says. Just jack your sales price to cover it, sweetheart." He looks around the table. "Are you ready to sign?"

Wygel says, "Already have." And he passes the contract down to Edelmann for Della B to sign.

Della B grins and signs the papers with elan. She then raises her glass of water. "To a Bleu tomorrow."

PART ONE

The Rise

Chapter One

Blue! It's glowing out in the darkness of his lab.

His name is Les Warin. He's lying awake in the dark, thinking. His wife, Cathy, is breathing softly beside him. Thoughts race through his mind: Should I be excited about it, or at least curious? Yeah, I'm curious. How could I not be? I'm a chemist, after all. I'm trying to discover things … new medicines … medicines to make money for Mallet Pharmaceuticals.

So what is this stuff? It's supposed to be the residue of the research, the waste spun off by the centrifuge. Why does the damn stuff glow? Can I try to find out what it's about? That's not part of the job. My time belongs to the company. I wonder if I can sneak. It'll be hard, with Godfrey working in the same lab always asking questions. Curiosity. Damned curiosity. It gets me. It gets Godfrey. It's what our lives are about.

Les's mind begins to wander. He turns on his side, facing the back of his wife's neck. Her auburn hair cascades over her pillow and shoulders. He loves it when he can run his fingers through it. It feels like silk. He feels a need to reach out and touch her, to run the tip of his finger down the vertebrae of her spine. His body stirs, and he quickly turns onto his back. She doesn't like spontaneity.

He feels her body adjust to the motion of the bed. He sighs. What else can he do? He's always amazed at having her wonderous body lying next to him. Wondrous and smart, and she knows it. She doesn't understand what I do. Organic chemistry isn't her world. She doesn't understand it … isn't interested in talking about it. Hell, I'm smart too.

He turns away from her. I must stop thinking about her. I wish

I could talk to her about the blue glow. I know she'd laugh my thoughts off. She'd probably say that she remembers high school chemistry with test tubes of liquid bubbling up and overflowing. She'd said it before, "Bubble, bubble, toil, and trouble." She views what I do as a game … pouring things together and watching them bubble. But how can I care? Who'd have thought a woman like this would marry me.

Chapter Two

The following morning, Les does his usual morning run. Sometimes it's through Parkfairfax in Alexandria, Virginia, where he lives, doing the circle that runs through the apartment complex on Gunston Drive, or when he wants variety, it's taking a lap through the adjacent ninety-year-old housing complex of Beverly Hills. Today it's the latter along Cameron Mills and N. Overlook and, finally, the struggle up Chalfonte.

He then returns to his apartment, breathing hard and wiping his forehead with his handkerchief. Cathy is in the living room, gathering herself together for her day at work. Les tries to kiss her, but she turns her head away. "You need a shower."

He nods in resignation and notices how she's dressed. "New suit?"

She looks down at her clothing. "Yeah. What do you think?"

"The suit looks good. The woman looks beautiful. The damn brass tag makes it look like a uniform."

"Well, it is. Everyone at work has to wear one."

"It doesn't say your name. Hell, they're all the same."

"It's for the public. Gets the name Pleasure Hotels out to the world."

Les stands back and looks at her. "I think pleasure on you gives the wrong connotation … presents a graphic image."

Cathy grins happily. "And you're full of the Irish today."

"No, just leering. Nothing sophisticated about it."

Cathy turns to pick up her cell phone. "Well, enjoy it while you can."

"Before I turn you over to the general public?"

She smiles at him. "You think they leer too?"

"They'd be fools not to."

"The women too."

"A flow of jealousy green."

"Malarkey."

"Yeah, and since when has my Frenchie wife started speaking Irish?"

"Since being sweet-talked in the morning."

"Morning, noon, and night."

She kisses him. "Ew, sweaty," and goes out the door.

Les takes a deep breath and heads for the shower. He feels like he's done a second morning run. He works at his romance. Sometimes it's hard. He knows it shouldn't be, but he always worries that Cathy will vanish in a puff of smoke.

He and Cathy have been married since late June, a month after they graduated from college. That was six months ago. At the time, he had already accepted a job with Mallet Pharmaceuticals in Sterling, Virginia. Cathy had been excited about living in Washington.

When she had seen Sterling and how far it was from the city, she had refused to live there. They had settled on Parkfairfax as a compromise. After looking at apartments in DC, she had understood that living in the city was too expensive. Even Parkfairfax had been expensive.

She said they would pay for it, that she would get a job, and she had. She had gone to work as a receptionist for the Pleasure Hotel Chain, which was headquartered a few blocks from the railroad and Metro stations in Alexandria.

They had quickly realized that Parkfairfax didn't fit the Metro Rail Network very well. They had then considered Cathy's new paycheck and had bought a second car on time.

After six months, Cathy had done very well in her job. Without a hospitality degree, she was soon making more money than her husband. She had moved up from being a receptionist in the hotel chain's flagship hotel in Crystal City to a manager in charge of conference rooms, managing their use and bookings.

All this goes through Les's mind as he's showering after his run.

Somehow, he has the feeling he's been left behind. It's easy to tell Cathy, she's beautiful. She is incomprehensibly so, but saying it constantly out of some inner feeling of uncertainty is getting old. At times when he holds her, feels her body against his, it's worth it. He can't think of enough words to say. At other times, when he senses her mind is elsewhere, it's an effort—pure labor. But he does it. Anything's worth keeping her.

It's highs and lows. It's ecstasy and pain. Obsession and self-loathing.

If the world knew, they'd call me a fool. I probably am. Sometimes it's worth it. More than worth it.

Chapter Three

My life for the first twenty-two years was indifferent. I guess that's the word for it. No one paid much attention to it—not my father, my mother, or my sister. When I think back about it, I don't remember much of significance.

My father sold Fords. He didn't run the dealership. He simply sold the cars. The cars upgraded from year to year, but he didn't. If he'd sold Maseratis, it might have been different. Faroom! Faroom! Faroom! But there was no Faroom … just holidays with heavy sales and long stretches of medium but steady sales. That was probably better than once-in-a-while luxury car sales.

My mother was a housewife. That was in the late 1990s when the word was antiquated, even reviled by some. You might say she was born thirty years too late. She wasn't even a soccer mom. Neither my sister nor I were much in the way of being athletes. Sure, I played Sandlot games with my friends, but I was never on a high school team. When she was little, my sister was taken to piano and ballet lessons, but she hated both. That was as close as Mom came to being the proverbial soccer mom.

I did go to school dances, though I didn't really dance until junior year in high school. That was also the year I kissed a girl for the first time. It was a girl I'd gone to grade school with. She kissed me back a lot harder than I'd kissed her. It surprised me. After all, I'd gone to school with her for eight years. It made me eager to date her again. It was amazing how easily it turned me on.

I graduated from high school reasonably high in my class. I wasn't valedictorian. I would guess I was in the top twenty out of the 307 students in my class. I really don't know exactly. The school authorities didn't make a list. They feared it would affect our psychs, although I suspected they didn't know what the word meant. The people at the bottom of the class didn't have to be told. They knew they had been given a pass to get rid of them.

Anyway, I was high enough in the class to obtain admission to Purdue University, where I became a chemistry major. My parents were suddenly a little proud of me. My sister even bragged about what I'd done, but she was always more outgoing than I was. I didn't brag about it to anyone.

So, back to my love life, I didn't have sex until my first year in college. I think that was still sooner than some guys but much later than others. Some of them talked about it, some a lot. I wondered how much was true. I guess I was a little jealous. Some of the girls they talked about were good-looking, some of the most glamorous on campus. I wondered if what they said was really true or if the guys were just trying to feel important. Still, I knew that there were girls on campus who were willing. They had reputations. They were talked about. I dated one once, but nothing happened.

The girls I dated were not beauties. Still, some were very nice. They weren't ugly. They were experimenting with life too. Nothing seemed real. Sometimes it was convenient … sometimes exciting … sometimes disappointing. There was no great romance. Does that sound indifferent? Well, it was. God, it was. And I think the girls thought the same.

Anyway, I met Cathy Carmichael DuChant the summer before my senior year. I was doing an internship in a chemistry lab my professor trying to encourage me to stay for a graduate degree. Cathy was home from Indiana State University for the summer.

Two friends of mine and I were at a local bar. We were, as usual, drinking beer. The hard stuff was too expensive. Besides, it always got us high too quickly. Cathy walked in with a girl I had been intimate with a week before. The girl, Brigit, spotted me and headed over. Our previous encounter didn't seem to bother her. She introduced Cathy and asked if they could join us. All the guys scurried to make room. There was no way they were going to miss this.

Cathy was something. And, I say "thing" because there was no way to describe her as simply a girl. Her hair was luxurious. Her eyebrows were just right. Her sparkling brown eyes were framed with the longest eyelashes I had ever seen. I wasn't sure if they were real. They were amazing. Her cheekbones were what all the books describe. Her lips were full and wide. Her neck was slender and vulnerable. And her breasts, well, when she breathed, we all watched.

When we three walked back to the dorm that night, not walking quite straight, we had no doubt of our memories. Cathy was all we talked about that night and for several days after that.

I had never pursued anyone. It was too much effort. That was fine if a girl was willing to go on a date. If she wasn't, I'd ask someone else. I didn't make a big deal of it. Some of the girls didn't either. I wasn't ready for a commitment. If girls started calling me back, I moved on. Still, I was a little shy with beautiful girls and girls in demand. Cathy was beyond beautiful. I didn't know if she was in demand. I couldn't imagine that she would not be. What I knew was that I suddenly had no control. With what little money and time I had, I was going to pursue Cathy DuChant.

I phoned Brigit. I had expected her to be annoyed, blow me off, or be downright angry. Instead, she had broken out laughing. She had called me crazy, insane. When I had asked if she meant there was no use in my pursuing Cathy, she had said, "Shit no, Les. If you have a death wish, join the competition. You have nothing to lose but your sanity, maybe your life."

I hadn't been discouraged. I told Brigit she had to be exaggerating. I told her she made Cathy sound like something from a fantasy movie… something not real.

Brigit told me Cathy was every man's fantasy. She said Cathy was even her fantasy, and she wasn't into girls, at least not since grade school. She gave me Cathy's phone number, wished me good luck, and asked what she should sing at my funeral.

I said, "Ha ha."

She snickered.

I phoned Cathy. I had to remind her about meeting at a bar with Brigit. It took her a minute, but she acknowledged me. She agreed to go to a movie. I was surprised. It seemed too easy.

We shared popcorn. After we finished it, she held my hand, sought it, and took it. When I got home, I licked the salt off the hand.

Was that stupid, or was that stupid?

On the third date, I picked her up at her parents ... old fashioned. I like them. I worked on them over the balance of the summer ... got them to like me ... hoping it worked on Cathy ... hoped it worked for the future.

On weekends during my senior year, when Cathy wasn't home in West Lafayette, I was in Terre Haute. I asked her to marry me in March. I hadn't been able to wait any longer. But she had made me wait.

I grew frustrated ... then angry. It was cruel and humiliating. I almost came to hate her. I suffered like a damned fool.

Final exams were a struggle. My mind was elsewhere.

Finally, she accepted my proposal two days before our graduation ceremonies while drinking at the bar where we had met. Amazement and relief replaced my frustration. I was still being a fool, but a happy one.

Cathy immediately went back to Indiana State for her graduation, and ok I didn't hear from her again until she came home three days later. She had been to New Jersey, to the beach. Evidently, I wasn't the primary thing on her mind.

After her return, I had been afraid to ask too many questions. My engagement had come slowly, and to me, it seemed tenuous.

We got married the end of June.

To this day, I don't know why she said "Yes." I sometimes wonder if she hadn't planned to ... that she had had too many drinks at the bar that night, and the "yes" just kind of came out of nowhere ... maybe even surprised her. Anyway, she stuck with it ... went through with the marriage ceremony. The whole bit.

Chapter Four

As Cathy had promised, right after she and Les moved to Parkfairfax, she was interviewed at the hotel in Crystal City, not at the corporate headquarters in Alexandria. She was relieved she didn't have to still wear a mask. That requirement had eased a year ago, although boosters were still being supplied.

While waiting for her interview, she wondered if it was a mistake. She had already avoided being interviewed at the hotel's corporate headquarters, afraid that her college degree in sociology would not qualify her for any job there. She hoped that the hotel itself might be less discerning. She was soon met by the HR person, Jean Stapleton, who apparently was from the headquarters. Stapleton led her to a table in the hotel's dining room, which was unoccupied between the breakfast and lunch shifts. Cathy was surprised. She had assumed the hotel office area would be extensive. She had expected an office or a conference room.

Stapleton was very formal. She introduced herself using her full name. There were no smiles. Cathy introduced herself as Catherine. Stapleton nodded, checked her folders, presented Cathy with forms and a ballpoint pen, and set her to work.

As Cathy filled out the forms, she felt Stapleton was studying her. It made her feel uncertain, uncomfortable. She looked up and gave the woman a brief smile and, in return, received a half smile through a crooked mouth.

Cathy wore a silk blouse through which you could faintly see the lace of her bra. She was beginning to sense that it had been a mistake. She felt the woman's eyes were boring through with a disapproving appraisal. She learned in time that most of the HR people were women. If she'd known, she would have dressed differently.

Finally, Stapleton led her into an office suite behind the reception area. "Mr. Wigram will interview you."

Mister, Cathy had thought, Thank God. There's hope.

Stapleton knocked on an office door frame and led Cathy in. "Mr. Wigram, this is Catherine DuChant, who is interviewing for a job at reception."

Wigram looked at Cathy for a moment, with his mouth slightly open, and turned to Stapleton. "That will be fine, er, Jean. It is Jean, isn't it?"

"Yes."

"Yes, thank you. I'll take it from here."

Stapleton looked taken aback, as if she hadn't expected to be dismissed before she could say a few more words about the applicant. She gave a slight nod, turned, and left.

Cathy, with a condescending smile, watched her go. I'll be damned if he's not going to forget my name.

When Cathy turned back to Wigram, he was walking around the desk to greet her. He put out his hand. "Catherine, huh? I'm Stanley Wigram. I'm pleased to meet you."

She smiled her broadest smile and took his hand. "My friends call me Cat."

Wigram laughed a little nervously, hesitating as if deciding what to say. "Cat, huh? Are you feral?"

Cathy wet her upper lip with her tongue. "When I want to be."

Wigram then grinned lasciviously. "A real tiger, huh."

He waved his hand for her to have a seat while he sat back on the edge of his desk.

Cathy sat. Her skirt hadn't seemed short. She had tried to be conservative with a skirt just above her knees. Now, as she crossed her legs, the hem rose to mid-thigh.

Her legs obviously caught Wigram's eye, and she saw him jerk his head up to look her in the eye, with his face transitioning to a more formal and serious state. "So, Cat, tell me about yourself."

While he was doing that, she gave him a quick study. Not bad looking … slender build … maybe thirty … not too old … blonde hair bordering on red … pocked face, but it's been worked on. I wonder if the scars ever go away. She then said, "Well, I just graduated from college, from Indiana State University."

"Ah, Larry Bird territory?"

Cathy was dumbfounded. Christ, that was forty years ago. "Right, he's still a deity there."

"Yeah, I come from Boston. He's a legend up there too. So what did you study?"

"Er, Sociology."

"Sociology, huh. So what do you do with that?"

Cathy smiled awkwardly. "Hopefully work in the hotel business."

Wigram corrected her. "Hospitality industry."

"Right. I always thought it should be a service, not an industry. Sounds too much like factories."

Wigram chuckled. "You're right, Ms. Cat. We're in the hospitality service."

"Ms. Cat sounds formal."

Wigram's face then became serious. "I'm trying to forget the 'feral' business."

Cathy looked down with a small smile of satisfaction on her lips.

When she looked back up, Wigram was going back around his desk. As he sat in his desk chair, he asked, "Can you work on a computer?"

She almost laughed. He thinks the game is over. As she answered, she stretched out her legs as if trying to adjust her comfort. "Of course. You can't survive college without a computer."

Wigram moved some papers around his desk, trying to avoid watching her.

He chuckled. "Well, I know you can smile warmly. I know you're comfortable with people. The computer is a benny. When can you start?"

"Uh, whenever. Tomorrow if you want me."

"How about Monday?"

"Okay, what time?"

"Come here to my office at eight. I'll show you around ... break you in." Wigram leaned across the desk.

Cathy quickly stood and shook his hand. She then turned and tried unobtrusively to pull down her skirt as she walked to the door.

"And, oh, Cat."

She turned back to him at the door.

"Try to wear something more subdued."

She looked down. "This is just a simple skirt and blouse."

"No, it's not."

Looking back, Cathy laughs about the whole thing. Wigram was easy. Most men are.

Chapter Five

Stanley Wigram closed his office door after Cathy left. He wanted to be by himself and think about her, feeling a strange excitement running through his body. He had never interviewed anyone like her.

His mind had been excited by the lace partially exposed by her sheer blouse. He had walked around his desk so he could view the full extent of her body and the legs so completely exposed. Unfortunately, he had also felt exposed and had to return to his position behind his desk.

He had brought up the "feral" and tried to play games with her, but he had quickly felt overmatched.

He wondered what his boss, Bill Sturges, would think. Will he think I've been blinded by Cat's looks ... that I've hired foolishly? He knew a woman like Cathy could be a distraction; could create a loss of efficiency among the male workforce, their finding excuses to walk through the lobby; and could create annoyance among the women who'd think she'd only been hired for her looks. Hell, she's got a college degree. How many times do I get to hire a woman for reception who has a college degree ... never? It's never happened. Mostly high school graduates ... young wives ... some cute ... some even pretty, but no one like Cat.

He looks at his watch. Damn, time's flying. I need to get myself together ... get to the gym.

Each day he's at work, he goes to the hotel gym in the late morning. He goes when it's unlikely hotel guests are there. The timing is critical. He has to be finished before the managers have lunch together. He feels he has to be there when Sturges is there.

On days off, he goes to Golds. He feels he can't miss a day. He's in terrific physical shape. He believes he has to compensate for his pocked face, his overly reddish-blonde complexion, his watery, pale blue eyes, and his almost invisible beard- for his feeling of inadequacy.

God, how did I banter with this woman? Did she see my build?

… Hell no, not in my suit. All she saw were the pockmarks … a bumbling fool who hired her with virtually no knowledge of her abilities or experience … without recommendations … without even a resume. She just comes in and says, "Look at me," then stretches her legs and says without actually speaking, "What more could you want?" … says, hire me.

And I did. Women like Cat are few and far between. You don't pass up a woman like her. I can't wait for her to see me driving my Mercedes convertible. No one working at the hotel can afford to drive a car like that. I'm one of a kind. Takes every cent I have and then some. The maintenance is a killer. But it gets the girls' interest. Makes them know I'm more than a guy in a suit. Maybe it will make Cat notice.

For the next several months, Wigram knows he'll spend more time walking through the lobby than usual.

He will need to admire his find—his prize. Damn, I won't be able to help myself.

Chapter Six

After the interview, Cathy sat in her car, which was parked on the street three blocks from the hotel. She hadn't known if an interview entitled her to park in the garage under the hotel.

There weren't many times that Cathy felt unsure of herself. The insecurity hadn't lasted long. When she heard Stapleton being dismissed from Wigram's office, she had almost laughed. She had known she would now be in charge at least with Wigram.

Now, she could only smile.

Hell, it's been that way since I was fifteen. Before that, the boys had the lead, but it didn't take long for me to learn. They were like puppy dogs with their tails wagging or folded between their legs. I was the one who controlled the tails. It could be fun. Uncle Charley had made me nervous, but he had stopped visiting. I think that was Aunt Betty's doing, but that's between them. I had no interest. I had enough on my plate.

When I met Les, I didn't have a second thought. I was just going to a bar with a friend. It didn't dawn on me that I'd ever see him or his friends again. But, like some others, he didn't go away. He soon became another puppy. I could take him or leave him, but my parents learned to love him. He was clever that way.

Still, I never would have thought of marrying him. Proposals were nothing new. The trouble was that I was going to graduate from college and had to do something. My parents expected it. My friends expected it. They were getting jobs. They were getting married. What's worse is they were staying in Indiana. The guys who proposed were staying in Indiana. I didn't dislike Indiana. It just didn't seem exciting. If I had gotten the exposure, I know I could have escaped.

Then I learned Les was going to Washington. It wasn't New York, but what the heck? He was a nice guy … not spectacular … but nice. It wasn't like sex was important. I'd had plenty of that. It was the future that was important—the future and opportunities.

Heck, marriage doesn't have to be forever. This is the twenty-first century. You have to start somewhere. So I said yes to Les, fucked the hell out of myself with Indiana State buddies on the New Jersey shore, graduated from college, gave my mother the big wedding she wanted, stopped worrying my poor father to death, and moved to Northern Virginia. Now I have a job. It's just the damn beginning. I'm going to do whatever I have to do.

Cathy pounded on the steering wheel of her four-year-old Corolla. "Wake up, you fucking little car. You're going to grow big. It'll just take time."

Chapter Seven

Cathy learned her job almost instantly. The computer was nothing to her. Hell, if the high school graduates she worked with could do it, she could do it. She soon learned that checking people in and out could be done by rote. That was the easy part of the job.

It was interacting with guest complaints that was the hard part. Her smile came naturally. It always had. Generally, dealing with the men was easy. She tried to accommodate all their wants and needs. The women were more problematic. Many seemed to respond to her with instant distrust, as if she had been put behind the reception desk solely to ensure the hotel would win any arguments, as if someone who looked like her was there to distract them from their rights as guests. She often turned these people over to the other receptionists or called Wigram for help. She didn't like doing the latter. She wanted to prove her efficiency. Nonetheless, she often dropped into Wigram's office on her breaks to discuss trivial issues. She liked to see his discomfort.

Cathy liked walking by Bill Sturges's door during these same periods. She'd take off her suit jacket when she walked around the executive offices. She was sure Sturges noted, although she never dared to enter his office on some silly excuse.

Sturges was in his early forties. He was not tall, but he was clearly masculine. His body was thick but not fat. She was sure he would be considered to weigh too much for his height, but it was the build, not fat. He kept his sleeves rolled up when he wasn't in public. His hairy arms led to Cathy picturing a hairy body. She wondered what that would be like. Les didn't have a hair on his chest.

Cathy brought in cookies, sometimes doughnuts, and left them in the coffee area. She tried to buy cookies that looked homemade. She wanted credit. She always made a show of carrying them past the office doors. Sometimes when she did this, Sturges would look up, "Hey, Cathy the Cat strikes again. More sweets for us old guys. Many thanks, pretty lady."

Not too misogynistic, not "Thanks, babe," not "Thanks, gorgeous," maybe borderline. It was fine with Cathy. She wasn't a hypocrite. She was dealing with fools. She knew what she was doing.

So it wasn't unusually late one Thursday afternoon when she popped open Wigram's door without knocking. She sometimes didn't knock. She never did when the door was open. When it was closed, she sometimes thought about it, but Wigram never complained when she just walked in. Usually, he just turned a little red, which was different, a little strange, on a pale man with pockmarked skin. Today, his response was unusual. He was immediately in motion, sweeping things into his desk drawer. Cathy caught sight of some money being hidden away—cash. Remaining on his desk were printouts of the day's receipts.

She quickly looked him in the eye, as if she hadn't seen the things on the desk. "Working late, Stanley? Do you need any help?" She was the only receptionist who addressed him by his first name. He never corrected her.

"No, Cat, just closing down things for the day. I'll be out of here in a moment."

"Okay, you're putting in a long day. I've got things under control for the evening."

"I know you do, Cat. I just need a few more minutes. I'll let you know when I leave."

Cathy went back to the reception desk. She'd only been gone for half a minute, and there were already a couple of guests waiting to check in. "I'm sorry. I hope you haven't been waiting long."

The big man grinned. "Nah, just got here." He rocked back and forth from one foot to the other.

"Be fine when I get to the bathroom."

Damn, men. Why can't he hold it like prune face who's looking me up and down with disdain, looking a little embarrassed by her husband's display. "I'll have you checked in seconds. Do you need help with your luggage?"

"Nah, just point the way. I'll leave the luggage in the car until we've checked out the room."

Cathy sighed when the couple was in the elevator with the door closed. She looked around the lobby. It didn't look like anyone needed to be served at the moment. She sighed again and thought about Wigram. What was with the reaction? Why'd he try to hide the money? There's nothing wrong with going over the receipts. He's in charge. He deposits the money. Why hide it? Strange as hell.

Chapter Eight

After a few months, Cathy's success at being a receptionist results in her promotion to running the banquet areas. She has no allusions that efficiency is the only thing that earned her the promotions. She has used all her assets to get ahead.

Cathy the Cat loves being a manager. Cathy the Cat is what the general manager, William Sturges, calls her. She likes it.

She's worked on Wigram to get him to commend her to Sturges. Maybe Sturges will have selected her anyway, but she needs to use all her cards. Wigram is easy. He's been funny ever since she found him going over the receipts, especially amenable to supporting her in almost anything she wants to do. Something is off. She keeps it in mind. Maybe she can use it more than she already does.

As a manager, Cathy often has lunch with Sturges and Wigram. She enjoys being part of the hierarchy. Sometimes Maureen Davidson joins them. She's the head of housekeeping. Most of the time, Maureen's too busy. Lunchtime means there are lots of rooms to service. On those days, Cathy likes being with just the men. It means she can take off her suit jacket and let the men's eyes warm her.

She especially likes it when Billy Covington, the head of maintenance, joins them. Even in winter, he rolls up his sleeves and exposes his arms' muscles and dark hair. He has the build and the square jaw that belongs on the cover of a romance novel. She can picture him ripping off her bodice. She's sure he pictures it too. The only trouble is the gold ring on his finger.

God, she always thinks, I've got to get sex off my mind. I've a gold ring too, even if I don't wear it. Besides, who the hell wears bodices these days.

When she returns to her office on days those thoughts have gone through her mind, she always feels guilty. I've got sweet Leslie at home. The guy works so hard … treats me like a damned goddess. I can turn him on just by touching him. He'd do anything in the world for me.

And then she thinks of Billy Covington's body. She knows he'd be easy, wife or not.

If I ever messed with Covington, she thinks, Davidson would know it first. Damned women. Then what would Wigram and Sturges do? I'm their entertainment. Would they fire me? It might be fun to find out. Could I do that to Les? Damned if I know.

More importantly, I'm moving up in this company. I'm already way ahead of my husband. The poor idiot is just laboring away in his little white coat and getting nowhere. I'll bet he's making the same money a year from now. Sweet words and intense lovemaking only go so far. We've got to make something of our lives.

Chapter Nine

After a little over six months into his job, while driving to work after his morning run, Les finds his mind returning to the beaker with the blue glow. He is suddenly afraid that his lab partner, Godfrey Trainham, may have moved it or dumped it before he gets to the lab. He worries that he should have come earlier. He decides to hurry. He wishes he had hidden the beaker, put it in a cabinet, or something.

Last night, he left the lab late. As he turned off the lab lights and headed out the door, something caught his eye. From the back corner of the lab, a blue glow came from the far side of a cabinet. Les flicked the lights back on and went to the counter where a beaker was sitting. He picked it up and looked at the blue liquid. Then he carried it back to the door and flicked out the lights. Sure enough, the liquid glowed blue. With the lights on, it only looked like a shimmering blue, but in the dark, it was obviously fluorescent or luminescent. He wondered which.

Now he rushes through the lobby of the Mallet Pharmaceutical lab building, and out of breath, he unlocks and pushes open the door to his lab room. He is relieved that Godfrey is not there. In the dark lab, he rushes to the back corner. The beaker is still there, but it's different. It's brighter. In relief, he picks up the beaker, studies it in the dark, and thinks, if it's fluorescent, it needs another source of radiation to set it off. He knows of nothing in the lab that would fit that bill. He looks up at the fluorescent lights and thinks, Maybe, but the lights are not on. He sets the beaker back on the counter and looks around. There are no other lights. All the equipment but the desiccator is turned off. If there's no other radiation source, the beaker's material must be luminescent. I'll check the desiccator later.

He turns the lights back on and hurries back to the beaker. Now he knows what is different. The blue material has settled to the bottom of the beaker, leaving clear liquid on top. He suspects the liquid is the distilled water left over from the suspension he had initially made to be used in the centrifuge to separate the light pharmaceutical material he was studying. When I extracted the waste material from the centrifuge, I must have stirred it up. Looks like the blue stuff was in suspension, not dissolved.

Fearing Godfrey's arrival, Les picks up the beaker and hurries to the locker where he keeps his things, trying not to slosh the liquid and throws the blue material back into suspension. He doesn't really know why he is being careful. After all, the material had settled out overnight and would no doubt do it again. Still, it's an unknown, and he doesn't want to do anything wrong.

He sets the beaker at the back of the cabinet, takes the sweater he hung on a nearby coat rack, balls it up, and puts it in front of the beaker to hide it. As he closes the cabinet door, Godfrey comes into the lab.

"You're here early, my lesser friend."

Godfrey's comment annoys Les. "Cut it out, Godfrey. The 'lesser' is getting old."

Godfrey sneers, "Hell, I didn't give you a girl's name that you must hide by calling yourself Les. You know we have to go through the morning banter. Tell me, if I had a nickname, it would be 'God,' and I'd tell you that will be appropriate when I invent the great cure."

"Yeah, the 'great cure' from our current work on a safe Zantac."

Sadly, Godfrey concedes, "Well, we have to go where the money is. We work on indigestion today and on arthritis and real diseases tomorrow."

"You hope, Godfrey. We need to deal with stomach gas first."

"So you're not going to call me 'God'?"

Les guffaws. "Not till you earn it."

"Even if I do, I don't think I'll share it with Mallet."

"Share it? They'll own it."

"Saddest part of our job."

Less agrees, "Yeah, well, this is not computer stuff. For that, you can buy all the equipment you need and stick it in a garage. Not so with a chemistry lab."

"Yeah, but if I had the money, the financing, I could build my own lab."

"But if someone financed you, they'd own your discovery. You know you can't win."

Godfrey desolately sighs. "It's all a dream anyway. Mother Mallet owns us."

He turns to the counter. "How late did you stay last night, my diligent partner? You were sitting, watching the centrifuge when I left. Did that stuff separate?"

"Yes. The lighter stuff is in the desiccator now. I had it there all night. You think that's long enough?"

Godfrey tries to stare through the glass window of the desiccator. "Can't really tell. Looks like there might be some moisture left. Let's wait until this afternoon."

***

As he eats his home-packed lunch, Les thinks about the secrecy—all the effort to hide his discovery from Godfrey. He wonders if it is worth it. He thinks it might be so much easier if he just shared the discovery with his lab partner.

He mulls the idea.

Godfrey is such a hustler. How can I trust him? He's a finagler. He'll probably figure a way to take all the credit. Besides, it's mine. It's my accomplishment. It could make me important ... make Cathy realize I'm not just a lab nerd ... make me a man of consequence.

***

That afternoon, they pull a white powder from the desiccator.

Godfrey frowns as he studies it. "Not much for a quart of liquid. If we keep this up, we will have to buy distilled water in fifty-five-gallon drums. What do you think we should do next?"

"I think we need to make more. This is hardly enough to work with."

"Yeah, okay. Sounds like work for tomorrow. I'm out of here."

Les protests but knows it won't affect Godfrey's leaving. "Gosh, Godfrey, you're going to miss the fun."

"Fun? What fun?"

Les wants to stay and needs an excuse. "I'm going to spread this stuff out in a Petri dish and see if it hydrolyzes."

"Geez, Les, you just separated it from water. That doesn't make sense. It had to be a suspension. If you've got to stay, see if the stuff dissolves in alcohol or something. Feed it to the rats. Do something useful."

"Okay, I'll try something useful. See you tomorrow."

As soon as Godfrey is gone, Les heads for his cabinet. He stands in front of the open door, waiting a minute to make sure Godfrey doesn't return, and then gently removes the glowing beaker. He tries not to disturb the material at the bottom. He carries it to the counter and checks the pH of the fluid. He compares it against the distilled water they had used in the original experiment. The pHs are the same.

Les is pretty sure that nothing remains in solution. He then carefully pours off the water and puts the blue residue in the desiccator.

I'll skip my morning run and be in early tomorrow.

Chapter Ten

After the third day of Les being gone, when Cathy wakes in the morning, she demands to know what is happening. "Les, what the hell is going on? You're gone before I get up, and you come home late … later and later each night. Have you got another woman on the side?"

Les has just gotten home carrying take-out Italian. He stands back, looks at his wife up and down, and laughs. "Damn, look at yourself in the mirror. If I chased other women, I'd be certified. They'd just put me away."

"Well, you're full of baloney. What's going on?"

"You're a fine one to talk. Ever since you got the job as a manager, you stay late for banquets, weddings, and I know not what. Even if I stay late, I beat you home most of the time."

"Yeah, you know the functions at the hotel keep me late. It's the job. But what's with you? And what's with skipping your morning run and going in early?"

"I've got something going at work that I don't want Godfrey to know about."

"Something more interesting than me?"

"Gosh, beautiful, I wish I could patent you. I'd make a killing."

"Patent, huh? That would be a first. Can't they duplicate things that are patented?"

"That's an idea. I'd make every man in the world happy."

"Hey, I like being one of a kind."

"Damn, I like it too."

"So what's going on in the wee hours?"

"I've made Blue."

"You've made blue. That makes no sense. What are you talking about?"

"I've made a blue powder. It's a glowing, blob-like material I can grind up."

"So what are you going to do, make a better crayon?"

"Maybe … yeah, that's an idea."

"Les, you're talking crazy."

"No, I'm not. This stuff glows … puts out blue light. Can you imagine a crayon that writes on paper, and the writing glows with blue light?"

"One of those things you shine ultraviolet light on, and it glows."

"No, it does the light all by itself. You can see it in daylight, but in the dark, it really beams."

"Yeah, what's your company going to do with it?"

"The company doesn't know about it."

"Yeah, how about your partner, God or whatever?"

"He doesn't know about it either."

"How are you keeping it from him?"

"That's why I'm going in early and staying late."

Cathy studies Les incredulously. "Les, this all sounds crazy. Do you really think this stuff's important? Could you make money or something with this stuff? It sounds like blue smoke … a blue pipe dream."

Les looks down and mumbles, "Yeah, money. I think it's possible."

They eat dinner in silence, with their thoughts whirling in their minds.

Finally, Cathy looks up from her empty plate. "Do you really think there's money in this, Les? I always pictured you at work in a white lab coat with a pestle and mortar, grinding stuff into powders and mixing them into gooey stuff to make cough syrup. Is this blue stuff supposed to cure something?"

"No, it's not medicinal. It's a byproduct, something that's left over. Normally, we'd just throw it out."

"It's waste?"

"It would have been if I hadn't seen it glow."

"So what are you going to do? Sneak it out the back door."

"No. If I want to take it out, I'll probably do it in a baggie in my briefcase."

"A baggie?"

"Yeah, I only have a few ounces."

"And you think it's going to make money?"

"Millions."

Cathy stares at Les. "You're either nuts or a genius."

"Neither. This has to be industrialized … scaled … scaled big."

"Hey, I don't know what that means. It seems like a lot of exposure … a lot of involvement by a lot of people. How is Mallet going to let you get away with that?"

"I don't know for sure. I need to keep the whole thing a secret as long as I can, but I also must keep using Mallet's equipment for a while to firmly understand this material. Then I've got to build a case that this stuff was not something I was trying to produce for Mallet, and that it was waste. That maybe it wasn't even developed at Mallet. After that, I'll quit my job and wait a while … maybe take an interim job not associated with pharmaceuticals … try to distance myself from Mallet."

"Can we afford that?"

"I don't plan not to work."

"Yeah, well, you'll have to separate yourself from working as a chemist. What are you going to do … sell mattresses?"

"Maybe. You have a great job. We can survive."

"Are you serious? I'm supposed to support you?"

"Hey, beautiful, do you want to be a millionaire?"

"Well, how long do we have to distance ourselves?"

Chapter Eleven

Les allows himself a month. He preaches patience to himself.

Cathy's harder. Each day, she becomes more involved. To Les, it is both a relief and a plague. He has always wanted her engaged in what he is doing—always wanted to be able to talk to her about his work and what he is accomplishing. Being able to do so is exciting at first. However, she soon becomes bored with the details of the work and only wants to talk about the potential, how they're going to get the seed money or bring people in as the producers, how they're going to make money.

Les forces her to wait. He wishes to learn details of the material he has discovered. He wants to find if it is stable as a suspension in various materials—in water, in base materials for cosmetics, in latex and alkyd base mixes of paints, in waxes, in oils, in all kinds of things.

He wants to find out why it luminesces. He knows it must be an instability, something that spontaneously corrects itself over time. He finds implications of a half-life. With only a month to work, he's unable to pin the half-life down but estimates that it is in the range of twenty years. Half the emitting molecules would spontaneously change to a more stable configuration in twenty years, three-quarters in forty years. Heck, he thinks, that's a lifetime for a technology.

He works to learn the structure of the material and learns it's an organic molecule, roughly in the shape of a centipede with various radicals and phosphorous atoms extending as legs. Eventually, he learns that the molecule coils upon itself—joining radicals at either end, apparently reducing the instability, lowering its energy, and emitting light in the blue wavelength.

He isn't sure of the implications. Clearly, the number of molecules emitting the light will reduce in time, but with a half-life of twenty years, that seems a trivial problem, and the material can be replaced with newly manufactured materials from centrifuges whenever it needs to be.

The future seems wide open. If only Cathy will wait.

Chapter Twelve

Cathy sits on a stool in Morton's Bar and Grill a few blocks from her hotel in Crystal City. She often goes to bars in the evenings when Les is working late in his lab, and she has nothing going on at the hotel. It gets lonely at home. She wants to be with people. She goes to various bars. She prefers not to stay at the hotel. She doesn't want to be hit upon by hotel guests. It could be awkward.

When she's alone, she likes bars with mirrors behind the bottles. She can see the guys coming. They always do. She prefers to sit with empty bar stools next to her so that she can move as soon as they sit. It usually makes the point. If it doesn't, she says clearly that she wants to be alone.

Sometimes Wigram goes with her. He's a nice guy and unmarried. She knows he has a thing for her. Lots of guys at work do. But he doesn't push. She knows he must have told Sturges about her calling herself Cat. That's how Sturges named her Cathy the Cat. Let them both dream.

She even went with Maureen a couple of times. She is a little, pugnacious woman. It was nice to be out with someone who wasn't thinking about bedding her. But then she found out that Maureen was thinking about bedding her.

She had thought, It's a crazy, damned world. She tried to be gentle but made it clear to Maureen that she was only interested in men. As she walked away from Maureen, she had looked back at the woman. I wonder … nah, just men.

Tonight, as she sits while stirring her gin and tonic and pondering life, she feels someone slide onto the stool next to her. She hasn't been alert. She starts to move. "Summer drink on a winter night?"

She looks over at Eddie Chisholm, settles back on her stool, and says, "G and T's all year round. Not sophisticated enough for a working man?"

Eddie orders a Johnny Walker Black over ice with a squirt of water. "Not when the wind is blowing, and I'm chilled to the bone."

"The air-conditioning man, chilled to the bone? Can that be real?"

"Hey, I'm human. How you been? We've missed you on the loading dock. Your britches gotten too big for us low lives?"

"Nah, Eddie. I'm just playing the game. Want to move up in the company."

"You don't miss what we have to offer. It's always available. Just visit now and then."

Cathy chuckles. "You always willing to help me out, Eddie?"

"Always, gorgeous. Just don't get too big for us."

Cathy's mind flashes back to when she was a receptionist. During breaks, she would go to the loading docks behind the hotel where others hung out on their breaks. Eddie was often there with other maintenance personnel and some cleaning staff. He was in charge of mechanical maintenance—air conditioners, soda machines, kitchen refrigeration, and the like. When he was with some of the others, he smoked. Cathy would stand away from them when she first went to the docks.

Eddie had looked across at her, trying to get her attention. To him, she was too juicy to ignore.

"Hey, what are you doing standing over there? You too good for us?"

"I don't want to smell like cigarette smoke."

"Ah, you just swig a little mouth wash, and you're okay."

"Not true. I've been on the elevator with you. It gets in your clothes."

"You noticed me, huh?"

"Yeah, your smell."

"Really?"

"Really."

Eddie had looked at the swimming pool guy. "You hear that, Cory? I smell."

"Wouldn't know, Eddie. I smoke too. The only time I notice it is when you smoke the weed."

"Hey, Cory. Don't let the pretty lady know about that. She might turn me in."

He had turned back to Cathy. "You going to turn me in, lady?"

"Cat."

"Cat?"

"That's my name. You smoke marijuana here on the docks?"

"Sometimes. Does that bother you?"

"No, but let me know when. I can't have that smell on my clothes either, at least not at reception."

"Really, it would be that bad … keep the customers away. I'm going to have to start washing my clothes every day."

"Either that or stay away from management."

"Easy, but they have nothing to do with me anyway."

A couple of weeks later, as she had gone to the dock, she smelled the marijuana. She made eye contact with Eddie, turned, and left.

A few days later, Eddie was alone at the dock. He held up his hands in innocence.

"Hempless day, Cat. Even have on a clean uniform. Come join me."

She spread a hotel guest towel on the edge of the dock and sat down. As she did, she knew he was watching her with curiosity. She looked at him. "Navy blue skirts are a bitch. Have to keep a clean ass."

"Such talk, lady."

"Well, some things in life aren't easy."

"Well, I'm all for your clean skirt."

"My clean ass?"

"That too, but not my words. You sound tough."

"Maybe I am tough. You're saying you don't use words like that?"

"Proper place … proper time."

"So no cigarettes today … no marijuana?"

"Got something to show you."

He had taken a baggie of white powder out of his pocket and waved it in front of her face.

"Is that what I think it is?"

"It doesn't smell. Won't get in the cloth of that fancy suit you're protecting from the dock. Ever tried it?"

"In college."

"Yeah."

"It scared me."

"Still scare you?"

"Don't want to screw up my job."

She watched Eddie take out his checkbook, open it to a plastic insert, pour the powder in a line on the insert, and inhale it through a straw he took from his pocket. He then held the insert, the straw, and the baggie out to Cathy. She shook her head.

He made an oh-well face. She got up and left.

But two weeks later, she again had found Eddie alone. She had her own straw. She didn't always find him alone, but when she did, he was ready. From the third time on, it wasn't free.

Now, as she sits at the bar, her feelings stir. "If I don't go to the dock, what do I do?"

He pulls a small notebook and a pen from his shirt pocket, tears out a page, writes out an address, and slaps it on the bar. He drains his glass, looks her in the eye, and says, "I'm there most nights at dinner time before I go out."

She folds the paper, takes her wallet out of her purse, and carefully stores the address away.

Chapter Thirteen

Les comes home to find Cathy sitting at the dining table reading the newspaper. She rises and approaches her husband with a smile. She wraps her hands around his neck and kisses him while pressing her body against his. She leans her upper body back and grins at him. "Have I got your attention?"

"God, yes. Shall we go to bed now?"

Cathy laughs and pirouettes away from him. "Save it for later, babe."

She swings back into her chair at the table. "Guess where I've been today."

Les walks awkwardly to the table and sits. "You're losing my attention fast."

"Then I better talk quick."

"It's got nothing to do with talking. What's up?"

"Took a two-hour lunch break today and drove out to McLean."

"Yeah, fancy area. What were you doing there?"

"I've been reading the paper … real estate section. You should see the houses you can get for eight or ten million. You should see the size of the places … all surrounded by trees … and just a few minutes from the shopping at Tyson's. Paradise, Les, paradise."

"What the hell, Cathy. The money is months off. I've got to separate from Mallet Pharmaceuticals and build up my own company."

"Yeah, but you said you'd make millions."

"In two or three years … yeah."

"Lord, Les, don't tell me that. I've already got it worked out in my mind."

"It'll come, sweetheart. It'll come, but we must work it right. We have to be patient, or we'll blow it."

"But you said we'll make millions. I want one of those houses, Les. Promise me you'll buy me one of those houses."

"I'll buy you the world in a few years, but you have to be patient. Can you do that?"

"Damn, Les, I guess. As long as you promise, I'll wait. How many millions do you think it will be?"

Chapter Fourteen

The following morning, Cathy sits in her office thinking about her visit from Eddie Chisholm at the bar. She is becoming more and more impatient by the day.

Damn, I know I promised, but the way Les has this blue thing planned will take forever, maybe never. I know I told him I could wait, but I can't just sit twiddling my thumbs. How do I know it's not just a dream in his head? I need more cards in my deck ... more eggs in my basket ... or whatever. I need alternatives. She considers Eddie Chisholm. Eddie's a maintenance guy ... a refrigeration guy ... a man with a mechanical mind. I bet he can help me.

At mid-afternoon, she tells her assistant Peggy Sanchez—the plain one, the one she assigns to deal with the women, the wedding parties, etc.—that she is going to check the parking lot to ensure spaces are blocked off for the wedding reception they are having that night. She actually wants to check out the loading dock to see if Eddie is there. She doesn't want to use the old route she took as a receptionist. She doesn't want people to talk about her going to the dock.

Eddie is there. So is another maintenance guy. Nonetheless, she makes eye contact with her man. He nods. Cathy goes on past the loading dock, and after a couple of minutes, she turns around and heads back.

Eddie isn't by the dock. Damn, I'll have to try another day. But as she approaches a side entrance to the hotel, she finds Eddie standing there, smoking a cigarette. As she approaches him, he drops the cigarette and grinds it out with his shoe.

Cathy looks at the cigarette. "We have a standing ash tray by the door, Eddie."

"Yeah, are you wandering around the parking lot looking for a way to give me a hard time? The grounds guys will pick it up…give them something to do."

Cathy chuckles. "Taking care of your fellow workers?"

"What the shit, Cat. Why are you looking for me?"

"Who says I'm looking for you?"

"You gave me the look as you passed me. It wasn't a look that said you love me. It said to get rid of the other guy. So what do you want … coke, heroin, what?"

"None of the above. I need a helping hand."

"For money?"

Cathy pouted. "For friendship, Eddie, for friendship."

"Shit, you're not the kind of woman a guy can easily be a friend with. You make men nervous, and I don't pretend I'm not one of them. You're to be enjoyed from a distance."

"So, friendship's not enough? How about fifty dollars?"

"Hell, can't be much of a job."

"I'm not rich. If I must, I'll find other ways. Maybe I'll do it myself."

"Okay, let's see what it's about."

"I want to put a camera in Wigram's office … record what he's doing."

"You think he's abusing himself in there?"

"I'm not a voyeur, Eddie. I want to know if he's stealing."

"Stealing? What the hell?"

"Listen, I walked into his office a few months back. I didn't knock, just walked in."

"God, with you around, a guy should learn to lock his office."

"I don't think it has a lock."

"Damn, I'd get one installed."

"Stop sidetracking me. I used to check in with him regularly to remind him I was working for him."

"He needs reminding? He's male, isn't he? Or is there something I don't know?"

"Just shut up, Eddie, and listen. When I went in one afternoon, Wigram panicked and shoved a bunch of money into his desk drawer like he was trying to hide it. He had the day's receipts on his desk."

"Yeah, I imagine he goes over them."

"Yeah, that part's all right. But why panic? Why hide the cash? Afterward, I got to thinking about it. You know, the system is set up so that the people working at the reception counter record everything— charges, checks, cash, everything."

"Yeah, makes sense."

"Except for Skeets."

"Skeets Morgan, the cute little girl, a head shorter than you."

"Yeah, sweet little Skeets. She doesn't record the cash or the checks. Just does the charges. She says she has trouble with the computer and that Wigram helped her out by saying he'd record those things for her. I caught Wigram shortly after Skeets went off duty. If Wigram hadn't panicked, I wouldn't have thought any more about it. I would have just figured, like you said, he was just going over the day's receipts. But I got to putting that together with the special way he handles Skeets and the fact that he drives a car that's beyond his pay grade. I think the guy's skimming."

"You really think so? I always wondered about that car. You think he could skim enough to buy that?"

"Six or seven hundred a month."

"Yeah, I guess he could do that. You going to document him stealing, turn him in, take his job, or what?"

"No, I don't want his job. I just want to know."

42

"Yeah, why."

"That's between him and me."

"Shit, I knew you were no one to mess with."

"So you going to help me."

"For fifty dollars?"

"I'll buy the camera and whatever else you need."

"Okay, that might be fun. You want me to install it at night? How are you going to distract the people at the desk?"

"You're going to get someone to do that ... one of the guys you sell to ... someone who owes you."

"How come you're not going to do it?"

Cathy grinned. "Because I'm going to watch you. I'm going to learn."

"Hell, no one's going to be safe."

***

A week later, Cathy follows Wigram into his office after he has picked the receipts up from reception. Skeets Morgan had worked the day shift and had just left. Cathy had been watching.

Wigram doesn't realize she is behind him until he hears her close the office door. He turns. "What? Oh, Cat, don't close the door. I don't want anyone thinking we're doing something wrong."

Cathy smiles sweetly. "Oh, no one would think that of you, Stanley. I just need a minute. Set the money down and take your seat."

Uncertainly, he does. "What's going on, Cat? What's this all about?"

She lays a flash drive on top of the cash box. "When you have time, take a look at this."

"What's this."

"Something you'll find interesting. As you look at it, think of me. Think of being my friend ... of helping me out if I should ever need anything." She feels she has added an egg to her basket.

Chapter Fifteen

Les arrives at the lab at six thirty in the morning to turn off the centrifuge. The door is unlocked. The lights are on. Godfrey is sitting in a chair in the back of the room with his arms crossed.

Shit.

"Good morning, sunshine. God's checking on you … wondering why the centrifuge is whirling at eleven at night."

"Gosh, Godfrey, what the hell are you doing here at six thirty in the morning?"

Godfrey flips his hand toward a pile of lab coats in the corner. "I slept there."

Les is appalled. "You slept there?"

"Yeah, what's your excuse?"

Les delays. "You slept on that pile of lab coats.? Why in the world would you do that?"

"I had a few drinks … well, several drinks at an oyster bar out on Route 7. My friends left me, and I had one more for the road. Shouldn't have. I could barely find the car, pulled out on the highway, and realized I shouldn't be there. Pulled my car into the industrial park and parked at the lab. Fortunately, the parking lot was empty."

"You drove down past the police station drunk?"

"Mostly coasted past, concentrating on staying centered … seemed like the best thing to do. So what about the centrifuge? The damned thing woke me up."

Les responds quickly with the only thing he can think of. "Gosh,

I must have forgotten to turn it off."

Godfrey scoffs. "Yeah, but why was it on? It looked like a sample of 722F. We finished with that two or three weeks ago."

"Huh, I thought it might work as a rodent control substance. It made the rats nauseous when we tested the stuff on them."

"Yeah, you think the company wants to get into that business … make rats puke all over the place. Now, wouldn't that be something? The rats would survive, and the user would have to clean up after them. You have a marketing gimmick for that?"

Les's mind scrambles. "I thought maybe we could make it more virulent."

"Is that why you've got all the blue stuff in your cabinet?"

"You've been in my cabinet?"

Godfrey swings the cabinet door open. "It's not locked."

"Still, it's my cabinet."

"Yeah, you're changing the subject." He motions his hand across the front of the cabinet. "You have beakers filled with the blue waste … a glob in each beaker."

"I'm just curious about it. Hate to waste anything without looking at it thoroughly … just like the 722F. Either of the separated items might be good for something."

"Okay, how come there's no 722F, the white powder, in your cabinet … only the blue stuff?"

Les sighs as if frustrated and bored with the conversation. "I just quit on the white powder from 722F. Couldn't find anything interesting about it. I threw it out. Now I'm going to start on the waste."

"The blue stuff."

"Yeah, the blue stuff. The stuff we'd normally throw out."

Godfrey lifts out one of the beakers. "The stuff in the beakers just seems to be amorphous blobs."

Les tenses, wanting to take the beaker away from Godfrey, but doesn't. He doesn't want to appear too possessive.

"Yeah, that's what it looks like when you dry it out."

"Not crystalline, huh?"

Les's mind whirls. How much should I tell him? How do I change the subject? "No, just the blobs you see."

"It precipitates out that way? Just kind of draws into itself and become a blob."

"Yes."

"Interesting the way it shimmers."

Les freezes. Gosh, don't let him see it in the darkness. "Yeah, before I throw it out, I thought I might cut a chunk and put it in a finger-ring."

"If it's not crystalline, you can't cut it like a gemstone."

"No, but someone might be able to grind it into the shape of a gemstone and polish it. I'll have to look around."

"It's not dangerous, is it?"

"You think I should buy my own rat and feed it to him? See if it kills him?"

Godfrey laughs. "You're not going to put it on a sandwich, are you?"

"No, I'm not planning to eat it."

Godfrey studies the blue blob. "Seriously, before you handle it, you need to test it on skin, check it for fumes, make sure it's safe."

Les has already done those tests but is not about to volunteer the information.

"Seriously, Godfrey, do you know anyone who might make me a ring out of this stuff?"

"Sorry, buddy. You're on your own on that. And you don't have to hide what you're doing. I'll be interested in what you learn."

"Well, I don't want to do this on Mallet time. It's just my curiosity thing. I'd hate to waste the company's money."

Godfrey chuckles. "You're using some of the lab's electricity."

"You think I should try to pay them back?"

"That'd be interesting. Power company could install our own meter to run at night. I suspect the installation would cost more than it's worth … more than the electricity. Maybe they'd be willing to charge you a flat fee."

"That's funny, Godfrey."

"Always like a laugh."

Les takes the beaker from Godfrey, nonchalantly sets it on the counter, and closes the cabinet door.

"Okay, what are we working on today?"

"725R."

***

Les volunteers to bring in lunch. He tells Godfrey to keep working, and that he'll get them some Gyros at a nearby Greek restaurant. He doesn't want the man to go out to lunch with others in the building.

He worries that Godfrey will talk about the blue blobs Les is working on. He doesn't want the information to spread. He needs the work to be concealed from other scientists and especially from management. He doesn't want the blue blobs left in anyone's memory.

He will soon be gone from the lab and the company. He doesn't even want to be history.

Chapter Sixteen

After work, Godfrey heads for his favorite watering hole. It's already the second time this week. He was there with Billy Moore and Peter Denkin last night. The two bastards left him drinking, didn't take care of him, just like the old days at the fraternity. He had been on his own.

Denkin will be here again tonight with some other guys from University of Maryland days. They've been gone from College Park for almost a year and a half and still hanging together like they had never left. He wonders how long it will last. He had thought Buzz Wladyslaw getting married would be the beginning of the end, but Devlin said Buzz would be there tonight.

Godfrey enters the restaurant, waves the hostess off, and heads for the table where he sees Denkin and Gaylord Eversham seated. He likes the bar, but four is too many for a bar conversation. He offers his hand to Peter, "How's it dunkin, Denkin?"

"It's not."

They shake hands.

"Sorry to hear it."

"You're sorry?"

He reaches toward his hand to Eversham. "Lord."

"God."

Denkin groans. "Oh, shit, here we go again."

Godfrey grins. "I see you already have your beer, Pete, and Lord's got his nectar. How come you haven't got any nuts?"

Denkin gives a sardonic smile. "Lord ordered them, but we needed

God to pick them up. Get them while at the bar ordering your drink."

Godfrey gives a thumbs up. "You need the power of God, huh?"

Gaylord snickers. "Let God wait on Lord."

Devlin looks annoyed. "Quit the shit. You know God and Lord are the same things." Gaylord draws back, offended. "Do Trainham and I look the same?"

"Well, you're both ugly bastards, if that's what you mean? Your appearances demean the real God."

Gaylord throws his fist against his forehead. "Oh, such cruelty."

Devlin picks up his beer. "More than five years of this shit. Are you through?" Godfrey sighs. "Back to earth."

"On angels' wings." Gaylord capitulates.

When things begin to settle down, Wladyslaw arrives from the bar, following Godfrey carrying a bowl of peanuts.

Gaylord beams. "The horn of plenty followed by Boris the Buzz, the Vlad, ready to partake of a little blood."

Wladyslaw slides in next to Gaylord and sets his drink down. "Scotch and water."

"Is that as good as blood?"

"Better on a winter night."

Godfrey inquires, "So Olena is still letting you out?"

"Olena's good."

"Six months pregnant."

"Yeah."

Devlin raises his beer. "Let's drink to pregnancy and Vlad's last three months of freedom."

Wladyslaw groans. "Ah, shit, guys. Life is going to go on."

Devlin nods. "Sure, it is."

Godfrey lifts his body and his rum and coke up. "Let's talk about brighter things. How about it, milord. How's the world of law? Any murders and rapes to talk about?"

Gaylord grimaces. "That's not where the money is, and the characters are not the savoriest."

Godfrey nods his head in acknowledgment. "I know. We need to keep things savory: medical malpractice; old ladies stumbling on the uneven concrete on the neighbor's sidewalk; dog bites; all the good stuff."

"Hey, insurance pays for most of it."

"You haven't bankrupted any old folks lately?"

"Come on, Godfrey. I don't try to hurt people. Just making sure people are getting the compensation they deserve."

"And the cut you deserve."

"The way life works."

"And you're the honest broker."

"Yeah, I am."

Devlin cuts in, "Hey, guys, this is too serious. Let's cut it. What about you, Godfrey? Did you cure any diseases today?"

"Hey, curing diseases is a work of art. It takes time."

"So you stand around in your white coat while things incubate in Petri dishes and flasks of stuff bubble over Bunsen burners."

"It's all carefully honed processes starting with feasible goals based on modifications on known chemicals following precepts that have worked before."

"You mix the stuff from the back room and see what happens."

"Hardly."

"Yeah, well, what happened today?"

"Today, my lab mate is acting weird. He's got a beaker of some blue blobs, the residue from an experiment, and he's hiding it in his locker. It's waste from an experiment. He's working on it at night when I'm not there. Claims he doesn't want to do it on the company's dollar because it isn't a medical thing, just something he's interested in. It seems he's been hiding it from me, pretending he doesn't want to work on it on company time ... like he's being secretive about it."

Wladyslaw is curious. "You think he's created something important and wants to hide it?"

"I don't know. I really want to keep an eye on him. It's strange."

Devlin offers, "You'd better. You don't want him to take a million-dollar idea from under your nose."

"The company will own it, so it doesn't matter much."

"Yeah, but you don't know."

And so, it goes on through the evening. This time, Godfrey is the first to leave. "Sorry, guys. I need to be up early in the morning.

Tomorrow's Saturday, but I want to check in early and see if Warin is in and what he's up to."

Chapter Seventeen

That night, Les doesn't work on Blue. He doesn't want to continue stimulating Godfrey's interest.

He goes home on time, but no one is there. He finds himself a beer and turns on the television—the local news. It's still too early for the national news. He hasn't watched the news in a while. He's been working late.

A key rattle in the door lock about 7:30 p.m. He shouts, "It's unlocked."

Cathy comes in, with her face perplexed. "What are you doing here?"

"I live here. Where have you been?"

Cathy is defensive. "You've been coming home late."

"Yeah, I've been trying to make us a million dollars."

Cathy corrects, "Millions with an 's.'"

"Yeah, millions."

Cathy sets a bag on the counter. "Dinner … Chinese."

"You're not making dinner?"

"Why should I? I never know when either one of us is coming home. If I cooked, the food would go to waste most of the time."

"So how come you're early tonight but still later than you'd finish work if you didn't have something going on in the banquet rooms?"

"No sense coming home right away. You've been working late. I'd just be by myself."

"So what did you do?"

"Why do you care? You're never here."

"I'm here tonight."

"Yeah, and how am I supposed to know your schedule?"

"So what do you do for two hours after work."

"Sometimes three or four when I've got nothing else to do. I drink, okay. Does that make you happy? I go to a bar with friends, associates. We talk and drink. What the hell else am I supposed to do?"

Les is suddenly discomfited. "I'm sorry. I missed you. I'm sorry you haven't had a place to come home to."

"Hell, Les, you can't help it. You've got a purpose. We've got a purpose. We're in this together." Cathy spreads out the food on the dining table and sits down. "Sit down and eat. Why are you so uptight?"

Les sits down, scoops some rice onto his plate, and studies it dejectedly. "I'm worried we might have a problem."

"A problem … might have … what the shit are you talking about?"

"Godfrey found out I'm working on Blue."

Cathy keeps eating. "The blue stuff?"

"I call it Blue, with a capital 'B.'"

"Okay. What's he going to do?"

"I don't know. He really doesn't know what I'm doing with it. He got drunk last night and went to the lab to sleep it off. He found my experiment running and started nosing around. He found the stuff I hid in my locker."

"Maybe you shouldn't have left it there."

"Too late now."

Cathy is growing impatient. "Damn, Les. If he doesn't know what you're doing, what's the problem? Just lay off the whole thing for a week or so."

"Damn, look who's talking. You're the one out looking at houses, trying to spend the money before we make it."

Cathy starts to clean the food off the table, although Les has hardly eaten. After dumping things in the trash, she returns to the table and impatiently throws up her hands. "Okay, okay, I'll have to wait. Just needed something to look forward to. So what's the problem with Godfrey?"

"I'm afraid Godfrey will talk. I went out and bought lunch for us both today, so he wouldn't go to the cafeteria. I didn't want him to talk to other people."

"Yeah, why's that a worry?"

"It's because when we start making money off Blue, someone will remember and tell the management or blackmail us. Things could go to hell."

"So Godfrey may cost us the money?"

"Maybe. There's no way to know. He could talk, or someone he talks to could."

"So kill the bastard."

"Do what?"

Cathy approaches him from behind as he sits in his chair. She puts her hands on his shoulders and begins to message them. "We need to talk about it."

She leans over and kisses his cheek. "Come on to bed, and let's think."

Chapter Eighteen

Les hardly has time to recover. When Cathy takes him to bed to talk about things, there's little time to think.

Cathy is out of bed and getting dressed.

She pulls the covers off him. "Get your clothes back on. Maybe jeans. It might be rough."

"God, Cathy. This can't be real."

"You like my loving, stud. Get your ass in gear, or it might become a memory."

"What are we going to do?"

"It's only quarter after eight. The night's young. Friday night, and maybe Mr. Godfrey's back out on the town. Let's go see. Do you know where he was drinking last night?"

"Probably the oyster bar near where we work."

"Let's go check it out."

Cathy drives. She follows Les's directions and stops in front of the bar. "Get out and see if he's there."

"Why me?"

"Damn it, Les. I don't know what he looks like."

"Okay."

Les gets out of the car and looks through a corner of the front window that isn't covered with neon signs and beer advertisements. Godfrey is in the corner with some other people, none of whom he recognizes, which is a relief.

He quickly returns to the car. "He's there. Now what?"

Cathy roars off, complaining, "God, Sterling's in the middle of nowhere. Now we've got to drive all the way back to Alexandria." She whips around a car in front of her.

"Damn, Cathy. Slow down, or the cops will get us."

She slows. "Just excited."

"You're excited, and I'm scared. What the hell, Cathy? Where are we going?"

"Del Ray. Eddie Chisholm's house."

"Who the hell is Eddie Chisholm?"

"Maintenance man at the hotel."

"Why do we need him?"

"Heroin."

"Heroin? What are you talking about?"

"We have to take care of Godfrey. We can't knife him, and we don't own a gun. We need to put him out."

"Okay, but how do we get him to take dope?"

"We inject it."

Les looks at Cathy, aghast. "What do you know about that?"

"I've watched the guys at work."

"They take it at work at the hotel?"

"Out by the loading dock and the dumpsters."

"Have you taken it?"

"Snorted a little, but that's all killing time while working late. Don't worry. It's just for fun."

"Jesus, Cathy. You're going to get addicted drain all the money you make buying the stuff."

"No, worry, Les. Just do it now, and then it's not a problem. I won't let it be."

Nearly a half-hour later, Cathy pulls up in front of a small two-story house. It looks as if it still has asbestos siding. Les wonders why the building hasn't been stripped. It probably requires a special license.

Cathy puts the car in park and turns out the lights. She faces Les. "How much money do you have?"

"A little over a couple of hundred."

"Good, give it to me. It might save me from having to blow him." As he hands her the money, Les gasps. "What the hell, Cathy?"

"It's no big deal. Just don't want to waste the time."

"Cathy?"

She pats his knee and grins. "Just getting your attention, babe."

With that, she's gone. The light comes on in front of the house, the door opens, and Cathy is led inside.

Les leans back in his seat, breathing hard. He thinks his blood pressure is going through the roof. He's in disbelieving shock. His wife had just talked casually about blowing a guy to get heroin.

He feels sweat coming out on his forehead and under his arms. He pounds the seat impatiently with his fists.

Cathy is suddenly back in the car. It's been fifteen minutes. To Les, it seems like forever. She opens the compartment between the seats and puts a package in.

Les stammers, "Wh-what did you do?"

Cathy gives him a semi-tolerant look. "I didn't fuck him, okay? Everything's fine."

She starts the car, drives to the alley behind the George Washington Middle School, stops, and turns out the headlights. She takes the package—a brown bag—out of the compartment, opens it, and takes out a syringe, holding it with a tissue. She pulls out the plunger and hands it to Les. "Hold this upright. Hold it steady."

She takes out another syringe, pulls out the plunger, and pours the liquid into the syringe that Les was holding. She repeats the process two more times and then takes the syringe from Les and puts the plunger back in. She wraps the whole thing in additional tissue and puts it back into the compartment. Finally, she takes the bag with the empty syringes and throws it into the back seat. "Don't want to leave it in the alley and scare the school principal to death."

She starts the car, drives down the alley, and as she comes out from behind the building, she turns on the headlights.

She looks at Les and grins. "We're on a roll now, babe."

Les sits, nearly catatonic. His wife is flying high. He wonders if it's because of what happened in the Chisholm house. Had she been snorting, or was she just on a high because they were going after Godfrey? No, she had been on another plain even before that. God help us. He shivers.

Cathy drives, staring ahead with purpose. "Okay, where's this guy living? You know what his car looks like? Let's see if we can get there before he does, get this on while life is flying."

A few minutes later, they pull into the parking lot of Godfrey's apartment complex off US 1 north of Alexandria and drive slowly past the parked cars.

Cathy's breathing fiercely. "Do you see the car? Is he here?"

Les chokes, "No."

"Good, good, good," Cathy intones. She pulled the car into a space between two parked cars. "What'd you say he drives?"

Les responds in a hoarse whisper, "A white Camry."

"Headlights like slanting eyes."

"Yeah."

Cathy shakes the steering wheel with her hands. "Come on, slanting eyes." After half an hour, Les can feel Cathy losing her energy ... her excitement. "Where are you, you son of a bitch?"

Finally, Godfrey's car turns into the parking lot. Unfortunately for him, a streetlight at the parking lot entrance makes it easy to identify him even before his headlights turn to face the lot.

Cathy has instructed Les as to what to do. She has put the syringe in his hand, with the cap removed.

"Don't stab yourself."

Then she quickly studies herself in the rearview mirror, unbuttons the top buttons of her blouse, and pulls the collar open wide.

As Godfrey pulls into a space four cars down, Cathy and Les get out of their car. Cathy goes around the front and Les the rear. Cathy passes the front of the Camry as Godfrey opens the car door. As he gets out of his car, she moves down its side to the open door. She spreads her collar, as if nervous. Godfrey gapes and suddenly feels a stab to the side of his neck. His hands reach up in defense, but it's too late. "What … what are you doing?"

He whirls and tries to attack his assailant whom he suddenly recognizes. "Le … " He drops to his knees, gasping for breath, and then falls over.

Les looks down at the man, as if in a trance. "Shit, Godfrey, I'm sorry."

Cathy barks, "Sorry, hell. He was a threat, Les. Your biggest threat."

Just then, another car comes down the road. Les and Cathy hunker down, pushing the body under the side of the vehicle and pushing the driver's door the rest of the way closed. "Shit," Cathy whispers, "I hope they didn't see the car's interior light."

The car parks on the passenger side of Godfrey's car. Its doors open and close, and footsteps walk away, down a sidewalk that didn't require going past the front of Godfrey's car. Cathy and Les listen to a couple chattering as they walked away. Les feels like he will never breathe again.

When the interlopers are gone, Cathy stands up. "It's clear. Give me your handkerchief."

She takes the handkerchief, wipes the car's door handle, and then reaches down to grab Godfrey under an arm. As she does so, she surreptitiously pulls the syringe out of Godfrey's neck with the handkerchief and puts it in her blouse pocket. "You grab him under the other arm. We need to get him into our trunk before someone else comes."

They moved quickly. In Cathy's excitement, she seems to have enormous strength, and they soon have the body in the trunk of their car. Cathy goes back toward Godfrey's car and uses her foot to feather out any drag marks from the pavement.

When she gets back behind the steering wheel, Les is already seated, staring blankly. His arms are clutched across his chest. She pats him on the thigh and grins. "We did it, big boy. Let's go home. I'll give you a morning ride. Man, we'll fly, fly, fly."

She practically dances to their apartment door when they get home. As they enter the apartment, he asks, "What are we going to do with Godfrey when he wakes up? Are you going to kill him? Don't we need to do it before he wakes up?"

Cathy smiles and taps Les on the nose with her index finger. "Don't be silly, babe. He won't wake up. You killed him."

Chapter Nineteen

Cathy's promised morning ride dissipates through Les's evolving sense of realization, self-incrimination, and horror and Cathy's reactive feeling of frustration and anger.

Instead, Les finds himself on the highway, ejected from his home by his wife's rage and her instruction not to come back until the body is safely "lost forever" in the wilds of West Virginia.

Les thinks, Damn, is West Virginia far enough? Is anywhere far enough?

He worries about being destitute after spending his money on heroin the previous night. He doesn't want to drive far with an empty wallet. He stops at his bank at Seven Corners and withdraws three hundred dollars at the ATM. Don't want to be on camera too far from home ... don't want to use a credit card too far from home.

Through the chaos of the intersection, he joins US 50 headed west. He thinks of the body in his trunk. He pounds the steering wheel in frustration. He slams on his brakes in the sudden realization that a light has turned red. Damn, damn, damn, keep your eyes on the road. This is not a dream. It's real. We killed a man. She says I did it. It's a lie! She thought of it! We did it ... all for a dream ... a dream of wealth ... a dream I sold to her ... a dream to justify my curiosity ... a dream to make her respect me ... maybe not even a dream of reality ... all because I'm an ordinary man married to a woman with the body of a goddess ... a woman beyond my imagination. How the hell did I get here?

He comes out of a daze, sitting at a stoplight west of Chantilly. He knows he's probably gone through many stoplights, even stopped at some, but he can't remember. Why'd I come this way? I worried that

Interstate 66 would have too many state police cruisers. I didn't think much, that's why. I wanted to run ... to run away. But I can't. The damn body is in the trunk. I should have checked my lights before I left ... getting stopped for a burned-out light would be the ultimate stupidity. Getting stopped for anything would be a disaster.

He looks at the car standing next to him in the four-lane at a stop light. As he does, the woman in the passenger seat turns to look at him. He snaps his head back to study the stoplight, feeling like the woman is inside his head, reading his every thought. The light changes, and he steps on the accelerator to get away from her. That's stupid ... just drawing attention. I don't need attention. Keep your head straight. Shit, it hasn't been straight since I found Godfrey in the lab yesterday morning.

He eases off the accelerator and lets the woman in the car pass him. He's relieved as she leaves him behind. The car behind him honks. I'm going too slow. Get back to the speed limit. Get your mind back where it belongs.

As he goes through Middleburg, he thinks, Cathy would like this place. It would fit her dreams.

Before he gets to Winchester, he stops at a lumber supply store. He hopes they sell shovels. He hopes they don't have security cameras. He pulls his baseball cap low and goes in. He doesn't see a camera. But what do I know?

He buys a shovel and some gloves. Back at his car, he puts the shovel in the back seat. He tilts it at an angle to get it in.

As Les drives into Winchester, he ponders his purchases. What do I do with a shovel in Parkfairfax? Hell, no one has a shovel in Parkfairfax. There's no place to store it. Maybe I'll buy some flowers on the way home plant them next to the front steps ... lean the shovel against the back of the house. Or maybe drive to the river and throw the shovel in. Isn't that what people do with weapons?

He stops in Winchester and studies his map. He decides to continue west on US 50. He doesn't want to drive forever in West Virginia. He just wants to get into the mountains and into the woods.

The area west of Capon Bridge seems a possibility. He drives on. As he crosses the Capon Bridge, he looks over the rail at Lost River. The name seems appropriate. Maybe I'll dump the shovel there on the way back ... save a trip to the Potomac ... save planting flowers.

Past the town, as the US 50 turns south, he turns off to his right, finds some dirt roads that look lightly used, and follows one along the side of the mountains. After driving a half-mile, he stops and sits for half an hour. No one passes him. He gets out and opens the trunk. He quickly gets Godfrey's body to the ground and begins dragging him. He wants to be out of sight as soon as possible. After pulling the body a hundred or so feet into the woods, he finds an outcropping of shale covered with vines and hides the body. He is well away from the road. Les guesses he could leave the body there forever, and no one would find it. There are no trails nearby. He can't even see his car.

But he worries animals will get to the body, and bones will be dragged. He also feels a tug of conscience, picturing the body being torn apart by foxes and bobcats.

As he starts to return to his car to get the shovel, Les hears a vehicle. Thank God I'm still in the woods. What if the car stops and the driver checks on me? At least I'm not standing next to the body. I'll just tell him I stopped to take a leak. What if he asks where I'm going? I'll just tell him I'm exploring, trying to find where the road goes ... just an innocent guy out for a scenic drive.

He stands out of sight. The vehicle goes by—a pickup. He exhales and realizes he's been holding his breath. When he's sure the truck is gone, he hurries to his car, quickly removes the shovel and gloves, locks the car, and heads back to the woods.

He finds he is walking mostly on shale with periodic breaks for patches of soil. He wonders how deep the soil is. He fears it's just a dusting in gaps in the shale. Only where there are patches of vegetation does he find extensive amounts of soil, perhaps deep enough for a grave but filled with roots.

Finally, he finds a patch of moss and ferns next to a small creek. He begins digging, throwing the ferns into the creek to hopefully wash away. He quickly tires. Laboratory work hasn't kept him in shape.

When he has dug down two feet, he hits shale. He's discouraged that he can't dig further and have more earth to cover the body, but he is relieved he doesn't have to dig anymore. He lays the shovel down and goes back to get the body. Godfrey's not light. It takes an effort to drag the body to the grave, flattening the grass and breaking small bushes and briars as he goes. Les looks back. It's obvious where he's been—a path right to the grave. He decides there is nothing that can be done.

He goes through Godfrey's pockets and takes out a cell phone, a handkerchief, a wallet, keys, and some loose change. He throws the change into the grave along with the cash from the wallet. He doesn't want to steal. He stuffs the rest in his pockets. He decides to throw it into the woods elsewhere.

He rolls the body into the grave and begins covering it with soil. When finished, he smooths out the surface so that there is no lump in the ground. He returns chunks of moss to the top of the grave but has no idea if they would live. He also plants a few ferns. He tries to shovel some water from the creek onto the ferns. He wishes he had a bucket but thinks, That would be one more thing to throw into the river.

He stands back and looks at what he has done. He shakes his head. The damn grave is noticeable. I hope mother nature will hide it soon. Let it rain.

He sighs sadly. There was just a foot or so of soil over the body. He prays that it will be enough. He wonders how deep animals will dig.

He carries the shovel back to his car, knocks as much dirt off it as he can, and puts it and his gloves back in the car.

He turns the car around, drives a quarter mile, and stops. He takes Godfrey's cell phone, wallet, and keys from his packet. He leaves the handkerchief. It's a damn white flag. I'll throw it in a dumpster someplace later.

He removes the SIM card and battery from the phone, goes to the woods, and throws the items into the brush, distributing things over a hundred feet or so.

Back in the car, he sits, breathing hard. He begins to realize he's thirsty and hungry ... mostly thirsty. Damn, get going ... get back on 50 ... get rid of the shovel ... get out of West Virginia ... way out ... get back to Winchester. Then you can get a drink. At some place that doesn't have security cameras.

Chapter Twenty

In the days after his return from West Virginia, Cathy treats Les with irritation and scorn. She says she can't tolerate his suffering and self-pity. She tells him repeatedly that he has done what had to be done—to put it out of his mind, to get on with life. She no longer uses her sexuality to bend him to her desires. She insists his behavior is intolerable. She is damned if she's going to abide it.

But for Les, the murder will not go away. After all, it was he who had to go to his boss on the Monday morning after the murder and report that Godfrey hadn't shown up for work, to report that he had phoned Godfrey's house twice only to get the answering machine. It was he who was interviewed by the police detectives Tuesday morning, expressing his shock and ignorance. It was he who had to provide the police the names of Godfrey's friends and associates, to provide what he knew of Godfrey's interests outside the lab, to name Godfrey's watering holes, to provide information on where Godfrey has gone on vacations, etc. It's he who answered the calls from Godfrey's parents, imploring him for answers.

It was he who insisted he had no relationship with Godfrey outside the lab—that he didn't know about the man's personal life, didn't know his friends, and didn't know where he went in his private time. It's Les who lied over and over and continues to do so.

It was he who had to respond when the police detectives came back again together with a big guy starting to get a little heavy with age named Metzinger and a pretty black woman named Givens. They'd talked to a friend of Godfrey's named Devlin, who said Godfrey told him that his lab partner (presumed to be Warin) had been acting strangely, doing secretive work at all hours of the night.

They'd immediately put Les on the defensive as he explained

that it was work that wasn't part of his job—just something that caught his interest, something that as a scientist, he wished to learn about, something he was doing on his own out of curiosity. It was an interest that they would understand only if they too were scientists.

They had looked at him as if they didn't believe him. He told Cathy so. She told him to stay cool. There was nothing to worry about. The detectives don't come back. He wonders why. There's no way to find out. He'll always be curious.

Throughout the investigation, Cathy scoffs at his suffering. She gives him instructions on what to say and criticizes him when he once told her the answers he had supplied to questions from his boss, his coworkers, and the authorities. To her, he did little right. She tells him and continues to say they are covered, they are safe, and no one will find out what they did. She says to get on with it.

Cathy's goal is the future. She demands to know when he will resign from his job and proceed with their plans.

Les insists he can't quit while Godfrey's death is fresh in everyone's minds.

She remonstrates that it is the perfect time because he can say he's depressed over Godfrey having vanished.

Finally, Les gives in and resigns while following Cathy's instructions on feigning depression. He had once joked about taking a job as a mattress salesman, but that's what he does. He becomes a salesman at Mattress World in a small commercial strip on Route 123 in Vienna, Virginia. As the newcomer, he works the late-day shift. He gets home around 9:30 p.m. on the days he works.

Cathy doesn't seem to mind the work hours. Sometimes she seems pleased about it. She leaves most days at nine in the morning for her job. Sometimes she comes home after he does. He frets about that. She tells him that the functions she manages keep her late and that occasionally, after a long day of work, she visits a while with her coworkers and friends. She says it's all part of the job. She tells him he's always known that. She often smells of alcohol. When he notes it, she laughs and says she's been with friends and coworkers at a bar winding down from a demanding event. Les remembers her knowing of a heroin dealer and of her casual comments about blow jobs. He constantly wonders about who she has been with and what she has been doing. His thoughts are aggravated by the intermittency of their sexual encounters and the seeming indifference of his once aggressive wife.

He diverts his thoughts and uses his free time to produce more Blue. Over the years, as Mallet Pharmaceuticals upgrades its equipment, he buys surplus items that enabled him to establish a laboratory in the apartment's second bedroom. Cathy isn't happy about it. She worries about the chemicals, explosions, and poisonous gases, but she reluctantly accepts it as a necessity in their evolution towards wealth.

The problem with the lab is that the equipment he has acquired is meant to produce small quantities of medicinal materials for use in experiments. Les feels he needs large quantities of Blue, commercial-sized quantities for the future. He keeps his lab going steadily, storing the ground Blue in pint mason jars.

When he resigned from Mallet Pharmaceutical and began producing his own Blue, he bought two-dozen pint jars. He still has four jars left unfilled as he approaches six months of selling mattresses.

Sometime during the endless life of selling mattresses, Les looked up to see Cathy standing in the doorway of his lab. "Damn, Les, this is getting old. Are you getting anywhere?"

Les holds up a jar of Blue.

Cathy looks appalled. "God, Les, don't tell me that's it."

"No, I've got a dozen or so more jars."

"That's it? A dozen jars?"

"No, I've more. Maybe fifteen."

"Gee, Golly, whoopee. That's four-month's work."

"Hey, I've only got this small lab-sized equipment. We'll use industrial-sized equipment when we get going on production."

"Yeah, who's we?"

"After I sell the stuff, and the patent, the buyer, the producer, will set it up."

Cathy's pessimism is growing. "And you're going to sell it? Les, you're no damn salesman."

"Blue will sell itself."

"Yeah, it's going to grow legs and a mouth."

Les sighs in frustration. "Cathy, be real … be patient. You said you would be. This is a process. It takes time. I've always told you that."

"Yeah, but I thought the 'process' would get somewhere. Hell, a few jars of blue stuff. This whole thing doesn't seem real." She waves her hand at the room. "You've bought all this crap and spend your life in here, and all you've got is a few jars of the stuff. You're fiddling our lives away."

"Be patient, Cathy. It takes time."

"Damn, our lives are roaring by, Les."

She slams the lab door and stomps off.

Les throws up his hands. "Ah, shit, Cathy."

Chapter Twenty-One

As Les hears Cathy slams the front door, he picks up a pint jar of Blue, jiggling it loosely in his hand. He feels like throwing it against the wall. He restrains himself and gently sets the jar down. Damn, damn, damn, what am I supposed to do?

He has felt Cathy's equivocation over the past few weeks—her rapidly decreasing patience. Les tells himself that he hasn't promised immediate gratification. He's been honest, up-front with Cathy. She's said she can wait.

But she isn't, and it's my damned fault. I told her I'd make millions … told her the pot at the end of the rainbow was real … told her she just needed faith and patience … maybe tried to make myself live up to being her husband. I never understood her marrying me. Never thought I deserved her. Did I need to buy her love? What the hell was I doing?

He looks around his laboratory. I'm trying to make a fortune with a couple of thousand dollars of salvaged equipment. Who do I think I am…Steve Wozniak? Heck, I don't even have a garage. Just give me time, Cathy. I know I can do it. Blue can do it.

Chapter Twenty-Two

Cathy is still furious when she arrives at her office. She shuffles the papers on her desk. Finally, she focuses enough to see that the Foldbergs, whom she had left Peggy Sanchez working with the previous day, haven't signed up for the wedding reception they had been considering.

She storms into Sanchez's office. The girl says the people said they would think about it and get back to her. Cathy rages at her. "I had them set up. All you had to do was finalize the menu and some details. How did you blow it?"

She screams at the girl who cowered behind her desk for several minutes. Sanchez is routinely intimidated by Cathy, who now leaves her trembling.

Cathy thunders out of the office area, as if looking for someone to fight. A passing housekeeper cowers at the site of her. She paces the hallway.

Finally, she goes into the conference areas. They're empty this morning. God, this place looks drab … beige on beige … institutional as hell.

She glares at the potted plants set at regular intervals around the walls. She wishes for inspiration. She's able to sell the work of florists to women's functions, to wedding receptions, but the men just want the potted plants—fake palms, not even real ones.

She goes into the back room with its hallway leading to the kitchen. She looks at the folded tables. Gosh, they're battered. Thank heavens for the table clothes … for the in-house laundry. She thinks about the stainless-steel serving pans, the plastic cornucopia, and the fake greens she uses on the buffets. God, I need a budget for natural plants, for real flowers. She knows Sturges will never allow it. She's supposed to make money.

She heads for the kitchen storage area to check the condition of the serving pieces. She knows she must get her needs into the budget that's coming up shortly.

Billy Covington comes out of the kitchen area. He smiles at her. She smiles back. As he passes, she spontaneously reaches out and slaps the flat of her hand against the front of his hip. She doesn't know why she did it, but it's done. She feels him turning back to her.

She starts to turn to meet him, but she feels his hands on her arms, and she's pushed against the wall. One of Billy's hands goes around to her diaphragm, and she feels herself held tight.

Her skirt is flipped up onto her back, and her panties are pulled down on one side and gradually worked to her knees. She feels him fumbling, trying to do his pants with one hand. After an awkward moment, he enters her. Both hands are now holding her around her waist.

Nothing's said. He breathes hard. She realizes she's not breathing at all. She finally lets out her breath. She realizes her arms are up against the wall. She's looking at the wall paint. She realizes it's pealing.

He groans. One hand moves to her breast, and then she is released. She turns to him while pulling her skirt down. He's struggling with his pants. He didn't even unbuckle, just pulled his pants down.

She realizes her panties have fallen to the floor. She kicks them off, reaches down, picks them up, and holds them in a ball in front of his face. "You raped me."

"I didn't hear you scream. I didn't feel you fight. In fact, you stuck your butt out."

"I didn't ask for it."

"You didn't? What was with the hand?"

"Just a friendly swat."

"Friendly, huh? Almost over my fly."

"Almost, huh? If I'd been aiming, you would have known it. I'd have buckled you over."

"Yeah, tough girl, huh? You know you parade yourself all the time."

Cathy grins. "I am what I am. If you noticed, that's on you."

"Yeah, and on every other poor bastard in the building."

"You think I plan it? Plan to get roughed up."

"I think it's what you do naturally."

She stuffs her panties into his pants' pocket. "Next time, let's not do it rough and not in a public hallway."

Cathy goes back to her office. She sticks her head in Sanchez's office. "Sorry, I was in a bad mood." She immediately leaves a perplexed Sanchez, Why the hell did I do that? I should never apologize to Peggy. I'm her boss, for God's sake. Where's my damn mind?

Frowning, she sits at her desk and thinks about Covington. Not exactly bodice-ripping … skirt on my back … panties around my knees … face against a cold wall. Not exactly the romance I contemplated. Did I really stick my butt out? Damn you, Leslie Warin. I'm taking out my frustration with you through acts of insanity. Damn you and your dreams in blue.

Chapter Twenty-Three

Cathy broods about the Covington rape, as she calls it, over the next several days.

She tries to avoid him, but he comes to lunch. He smiles at her. There's a smugness about it. She hates it. She begins to hate him. Why the hell did I make a comment about the next time? What the hell was going through my mind?

Cathy knows he's going to follow up on it. It's just a matter of time. Maybe I should take the lead … play to his ego … put him in his place. She follows Covington out of the lunchroom. "I've been waiting to hear from you."

He stops. "Yeah, about what?"

"You're really being coy, Billy? You haven't kept thoughts of me in your head? I stuck out my butt for nothing. I feel like a failure."

Covington chuckles. "Oh, I remember."

"Yeah, have you got my panties in your desk drawer to check out from time to time?"

"You kidding? I got rid of them. Someone might find them."

"Gosh, I'm disappointed. Thought you might keep them among the souvenirs of your conquests."

"I don't have conquests, Cathy. I'm married."

"So things are fine at home. You never think of me. You're getting along just fine."

"What's all the shit, Cathy? Come out with it."

Cathy looks him in the face. She reaches up and runs her fingers down his cheek. "I had my face against a wall last time, Billy. I want to look at you the next time, to watch your eyes. Room 466 tomorrow night at six. I have a charity banquet at seven thirty. Should be enough time."

"Room 466 is one of the rooms getting new carpeting in two days."

"You're the maintenance guy."

"6:00 p.m."

"Yeah, 6:00 p.m."

***

Billy finds Cathy sitting in the room's club chair.

"You're dressed. You going to do a Sophia Loren for me."

"Who the hell's Sophia Loren."

"She did a bedroom striptease in a movie."

"No, no striptease. You'll have to strip me … show your virility … treat me like your slave."

She stands up, walks to him, holds her arms out, and says, "I'm ready."

He moves slowly at first but gains interest and, in the end, is into it.

***

The next morning, Billy drops a brown paper bag on Peggy Sanchez's desk. "Give this to Cathy when she gets in."

Sanchez looks perplexed. "Okay."

When Cathy arrives, she takes the bag to her boss. "Billy Covington asked me to give you this."

Cathy takes the bag. "What's this?"

"I don't know. He just said to give it to you."

Sanchez seems to wait for Cathy to open the bag. She looks at her and gives a nod. "Thank you, Peggy."

"Sure."

When Sanchez is gone, Cathy opens the bag. It is the camera—the camera she has hidden in room 466. She sits down, deflated.

She doesn't have the goods on Billy Covington. He has the goods on her.

As she has blindly directed, he will treat her as his slave whenever he wants to.

Chapter Twenty-Four

Life has not been good. Cathy has stayed in a lousy mood. Les doesn't know what's going on at work. He's not in a much better mood. Selling mattresses will never replace his career in the lab.

Production of Blue continues at a slow pace. He thinks of the frustration scientists must have felt in the 1940s as they tried to make the first atomic bomb using centrifuges to separate out the Uranium 235.

Six months of selling mattresses are more than any human should have to stand. Despite his small stock of Blue, he has to get on with it. Cathy is demanding it. It doesn't mean the stars are aligning. It simply means it's time.

He hires a patent lawyer and patents Blue. He feels exposed, but the step has to be taken.

Simultaneously, he buys a quart of Sherwin Williams alkyd paint base, fills a baby jar half full, and begins adding Blue. A spoonful isn't enough. He hates adding more but does so. He paints the mixture on a piece of sheetrock. It glows some. He adds another spoonful. He makes records of what he is doing. Finally, he thinks he has it right. The paint glows in the daylight. In the dark, it is almost a beacon.

His baby jar of paint is gone. He feels as if he has given away a stock of gold.

He mixes some more in one of the unused pint jars. He follows the formula he had written down. He holds the jar up to look at it and thinks, This is the beginning. This is going to make me famous … make Cathy happy. It's our future.

Chapter Twenty-Five

The damned tease ... strutted around here for months.

I never meant to have sex with Cathy ... certainly not in the hallway from the kitchen. It's such a public place. We might have been caught.

It's not that I never thought about it. Hell, every man in the building must think about it. I never would have done it if she hadn't slapped me with her hand. At the time, I didn't know how much of a lead-on it was. I thought I was being spontaneous. I didn't realize I was being set up. Now I know.

Well, the tart is going to pay for it.

When she wanted to go to an unoccupied hotel room, there was no way I could help but be suspicious. I'm not the maintenance guy for nothing. I know every nook and cranny of the hotel. I checked the room before we went there. It was easy to find the camera. It was almost funny the way she played to it.

I can't say I didn't enjoy it. After fifteen years of marriage, things have gotten a little routine. The way she performed was really exciting, although I knew Cathy was faking some of it...still, I'm sure she wasn't faking it all.

I wonder what she planned to do with the recording. She had to think she was setting me up for something. I can't believe she was planning overt blackmail. Was she trying to get back at me for what happened in the hallway...for what she called my raping her? Hell, if anyone was raped, it was me. Was she going to tell my wife? It's hard to imagine. I don't know what good that would do her.

Maybe she was going to hold it over me. Just keep it until she can use it. Keep me on a string.

Well, I showed her. She's the one on the string. And I'm getting free sex whenever I want it … free sex with the best-looking woman I've ever known.

She tries to be passive, so I need to remind her. Then she perks up. I think she even gets into it. Beauty on a string. Sex on a string … on a rubber band. Whenever I want it.

What could be better than that?

Chapter Twenty-Six

It has taken three letters and four phone calls to get the appointment.

Les hasn't been to Richmond before and follows Interstate 95 until he realizes he is passing the city. He bails out and finds himself downtown. He stops and studies a state map. Christ, he thinks, I'm acting like someone from the twentieth century using maps. Now I have to wander around this city and get to the western part—at least west of where I am.

He finally finds the Virginia Department of Transportation. After asking questions in the lobby, he reaches the office of the head of the Location and Design Division, Winston Overmeyer, and is led into a conference room. Overmeyer introduces himself and another man Dave Driscoll. "Dave is our chief engineer. We were interested in your letters because we must address traffic control and safety in designing highways, roads, etc. Highway markings and signage are integral to what we do. Please tell us more about your proposals."

Les picks up a large artist's portfolio and withdraws four boards painted with Blue. He places them on the table face down, goes to the windows, closes the blinds, and then turns out the lights. "The room is not as dark as I would like, but it will give you some idea."

He turns the boards over one at a time. The first shows a four-inch-wide stripe of blue on a white background. The second shows an I 95 against a dark green background. The third shows a HANDICAPPED PARKING against a white background. The fourth is a STOP against a red background.

Overmeyer looks at the signs and asks, "Does it just glow? You don't need headlights shining on it, ultraviolet light, or something?"

Les shakes his head. "No, it just glows. It's a lot brighter in the dark."

"That's interesting."

Driscoll asks, "Does it come in yellow, red, or white?"

Les's hopes begin to dissipate. "No, just blue."

Driscoll nods. "I'll be back in a minute."

He leaves the room, is gone two minutes, and returns. He holds a piece of gray chalk and proceeds to color the board next to the blue stripe.

Next, he studies the board. "You know, I don't know how much this paint costs. If it were cheap, there might be uses for it. The reflective white paint we have now is expensive as hell, but I don't see this blue contrasting enough with gray asphalt or the green highway sign's background in daylight. Stop signs might work, although there may again be some daytime problems. Overhauling all the existing signs would have to be a significant advantage. Even working by attrition, there would have to be a real step up. Right now, I don't see it. Even for the handicapped signs, I think you would have to outline your blue lettering with black to make it work in daylight. Is it cheap? Could we use it as a second line on the edge of roads or something like that?"

Les feels defeated. "I don't know how much it costs."

"You don't. How do you expect to sell it?"

"I had hoped that by convincing you it had potential, I could get paint companies involved, get them to gear up to produce it."

"So you wanted us to indorse it, order a lot, price unknown, and serve as a basis for some unknown company agreeing to produce it?"

"Yeah, I'd hoped."

Overmeyer shakes his head. "I'm sorry. You get this stuff produced, establish a price, and come back to see us. Then we'll put some time and effort into trying this out in various uses, seeing if it has potential, doing some pricing analyses, and such. Then we might consider it. Better yet, make it in white or yellow."

For Les, the drive home is difficult. He's learned a lesson he already suspected: It's hard to sell a product that only exists in a half-filled pint jar—a product that at the moment is almost priceless.

Chapter Twenty-Seven

Les gets back from Richmond in the late afternoon.

Cathy doesn't get home until almost eight in the evening, carrying a bag of Wendy's hamburgers. She plops the bag down on the dining table. "So have you got a million-dollar contract?"

"God, Cathy, where have you been?"

"At a bar with friends."

"Damn, Cathy, you do that nearly every night."

"Not at a bar with friends. You know my job keeps me late. Besides, most nights, you come home late too."

"Not tonight. You know I went to Richmond."

"Yeah, did you bring home a million-dollar contract?"

Les reluctantly feels chastened. "No, the transportation guys said it wouldn't work. The color didn't contrast enough with the asphalt roads."

"They wouldn't even try it out?"

"I only have a half-pint of the stuff."

"Half a pint. Shit! How did you expect to sell that? Damn, Les, you have to get your act together. Even I know you can't sell something if you don't have something to sell."

"Well, I had a sample."

"A sample … enough to paint a two-foot-long stripe. Shit, Les, be real. You must have more than an idea. You need something to sell."

"Yeah, okay, how am I going to do that?"

"Damn it, Les. That's not my job. You're the one who promised me millions if I would just suffer through six months of your selling mattresses. Now, get your goddamn act together and get us the money. I've been patient enough."

She takes the hamburgers and fries out of a Wendy's bag and flings a burger across the table to Les. "Get yourself a drink, eat up, and get your mind working. Time is marching on."

***

Les heads to the lab he has set up in the second bedroom. It doesn't have a comfortable chair, just a desk chair and a stool. He sits in his desk chair and turns on the computer.

He searches for venture capital companies. There are lists of them. Some of the companies they invest in are shown. They are focused on broadband, media, information technology, cyber security, consumerization, software-enabled businesses, and the like. Shit, where do luminescent lines and signs fit it?

Not knowing what else to do, he starts making a list of venture capital companies in the Washington area, trying to guess which aren't narrowly focused on computer-related technology, the ones in pharmaceutical and manufacturing.

As it approaches eleven o'clock, he leaves the lab and decides to go to the living room to watch the evening news on television.

Cathy has long since gone to bed, closing their bedroom door. He looks at the door as he leaves the lab. Damn, it's becoming routine. Cathy gets home many nights before I get home from the mattress store, and I find her in bed, with the door closed. I have to sneak in, change in the bathroom, and slip into bed. Is she sleeping or faking it? I don't know. I do know I can still smell the liquor on her. She gets home after I do other nights and slips into bed. When was the last time we made love? The weekend I didn't work. A month ago. God, this life is so screwed up. I need to quit the damned sales job and get back to a routine.

Les turns on the television in the living room as low as possible. The eleven o'clock news is already on. There's a shooting in DC.

So what's new? There's a protest in Lafayette Square. The weather will be hot, maybe a thunderstorm late in the day. Nontraceable guns are a growing problem in the District—ghost guns and computer-generated guns made on 3D printers. Les sits up, hastily alert. 3D printers to make plastic guns … and other things plastic! Why didn't I think of that?

Chapter Twenty-Eight

Cathy's frustration with Les grows by the day, by the hour, by the minute.

It constantly taxes her thoughts, leaving her having difficulty concentrating on her job. She'd like to get out of the office and go someplace, any place to just sit and be by herself. The trouble is she has an appointment—possibly a good sale.

The man called yesterday. When he arrives, Cathy meets him. She likes meeting with men. This man she especially likes. He's about thirty and very good-looking, although he has the small beginning of a second chin. She suspects he's carrying about ten pounds too much. Still, he has thick brown hair parted on the right and intense blue eyes under dark eyebrows.

He says he wants to put together a late-afternoon celebration. He wants it to be right after work ends so all employees can come.

The celebration is for a new product the company is introducing. There will be a press conference at the company, and then everyone will be invited to the hotel. He expects around two hundred people with the sales staff they have brought in from around the country, the local workers, and the press. He wants food, heavy hors d'oeuvres, and an open bar.

Cathy fills out the order forms. "May I have your name, telephone number, email, and such so that I can fill out the heading of this form."

"Oh, give it here, and I'll fill it out."

Cathy watches him as he takes the documents, pulls a gold pen out of his inside suitcoat pocket, and settles down to write with great confidence. When he has finished, he passes the documents back to her. She looks at the writing and looks back up. "Mallet Pharmaceuticals?"

The man looked pleased. "You even pronounce it correctly. Most people pronounce the 't' at the end. They don't know it's French. The family is French, at least its heritage."

Cathy smiles. "I can imagine. May I have your name so I know who to speak to if I need more information?"

"Etienne Mallet … Steve."

"Etienne is so nice. It's a shame to have to Americanize it."

The man smiles. "Great. So you may call me Etienne."

Cathy sees him glance at her left hand. She knows the ring is not there.

Cathy grins. "With your permission … thank you. So you're a member of the family."

"The family?"

"The family who owns the pharmaceutical company."

"Oh, yes."

"I'll have to check you out on the stock market. Which exchange?"

"None of them. The company is family owned."

"Oh, that must keep you all busy."

"Indeed, it does."

Cathy stands to shake Etienne's hand. "Well, it's a pleasure. We look forward to serving you. Is this a launch of a new product … a medicine perhaps? May I be excited too?"

He shakes her hand. "Indeed, you may. It's a lung cancer drug. It should be big … just approved by the FDA. The trials took forever."

Cathy walks him to the hotel entrance. "Please phone me if you have any questions or concerns."

The man turns to face her. "Did I get your name right? Cathy, right?"

"Cathy DuChant. Right."

"DuChant? Another French import. One of us."

"One for all."

"And all for one."

Why tell him that my DuChant ancestor came over at the end of the seventeenth century and all the rest of my ancestors are German?

He smiles at her. "I'll come back two days before the reception and celebration to finalize everything."

Cathy thinks, What to finalize? What the hell?

But she'll be pleased to see him again. More than pleased.

Chapter Twenty-Nine

"What the hell, Les? What is this stuff?" Cathy is gaping at the boxes sitting in their living room. The coffee table has been moved up tight to the sofa to make room for them.

"Just some stuff I needed," Les replies dismissively.

"Yeah, was it free? We're living off my salary with you only contributing a few bucks, and it looks like you're loading up."

"Just some stuff I need for the laboratory."

"Hell, the laboratory's full of crap already." Cathy's annoyance is growing. "What the hell did this cost?"

"A few thousand."

"A few?"

"Seven."

"Jesus, Les. That's more than you make in two months. Are you out of your mind?"

"That's about the minimum I could get away with. I could have spent more."

"Yeah and sink us into debt."

"Look," Les replies, "you've been giving me hell about not having a product to sell, saying I need more than an idea and a few jars of Blue. Okay, I hear you. I'm going to make a product."

"What? You're setting up a factory."

"Just going to make some demonstration items."

"Like what?"

"Plastic ducks."

"You're kidding me. You're going to make us millions with plastic ducks? How many ducks do you have to sell to make a million?"

"I don't know. It's just a starting point. I wanted to make hula hoops, but they were too big."

***

Les works on making bathtub toys. Fortunately, the software is already available for many things he wants to make. Not only does he make ducks, but he also makes hollow rings, boats, and blocks. He only makes two of each. He doesn't want to waste his stock of Blue, although he continues to manufacture more of that as fast as he can. He wants to buy a bigger centrifuge but knows the cost would really set Cathy off.

One night, he makes an extra duck. While Cathy was soaking in the bathtub, he enters the bathroom, throws the duck into the tub, and quickly turns out the lights.

"What the fuck, Les? Get out of here. A bath is private."

"Well, you should use bubbles if you want privacy."

"Yeah, very funny. And what's with throwing things at me? You think I want to play with a glowing plastic duck. Do I look like a three-year-old?"

Les flipped the light back on and looked at Cathy. "Well, you've got a point there. You certainly don't look like a three-year-old. I'm seeing things I've missed lately."

"Damn, Les, our hours don't jive."

"It seems like it's more than that. Our lives lately don't jive."

"Well, make the money, and I'll quit my job. Then our lives will jive better." She threw the duck back at him.

He caught it with a grin and held it up. "The beginning of our first million. Three-year-olds and ducks."

"Damn, Les. The next thing you'll be making are glowing blue dildos."

Les looks momentarily bewildered. "Gosh, that's something my mind hasn't thought of. I wonder if I might have the software to do that, somewhere between the ducks and boats."

She throws her wet washcloth at him as he quickly closes the door.

Chapter Thirty

Cathy wonders if there's some hope. Les was more chipper last night than she'd seen him in a while. She knew her bare body had always brought him to life, but last night seemed more than that. Plastic ducks … is that our future?

She feels a little spice has been added to her life. In addition, Etienne is coming today. Damn, she thinks, I'm calling clients by their first names.

They're customers, but she likes to think of them as clients. Besides, he told me to call him Etienne.

She opens the manila folder marked Mallet Pharmaceuticals Reception/Celebration and riffles through the papers. She shakes her head. Not a thing has changed since the man was last in this office. So why's he coming?

She checks her left hand. There's no ring. Wouldn't be a good day to forget. I need to check his hand. I forgot to last time he was here. Maybe he takes it off too. You never know.

She takes off her suit jacket and hangs it up. Before she returns to her seat, she tucks her shirtwaist tightly into her skirt. She sits and practices sitting erectly. She feels she's ready when Mallet arrives.

"Good afternoon, Cathy. You're looking alert today."

God, Cathy thinks, that's what I get for sitting up straight. "Good afternoon to you too, Etienne. I think we're ready for your celebration. Is there anything in particular that you wanted to check on?"

"No, I'm sure you have everything in hand, Cathy."

"I think so."

She hesitates, waiting for Mallet to take the lead. "So, Etienne, what can I do for you?"

The man looks around hesitantly. "I came by the conference rooms on my way in. It looks like you haven't got much going on tonight."

"No, it's kind of quiet. The weekend is scheduled, though. It will be busy. You got your reservation just in time."

"That's a relief. I'm glad to know we're settled."

"You're all set. We're looking forward to serving you."

"Er, and what do you do when things are quiet?"

"Like tonight?"

"Yeah, like tonight."

"Sometimes I go home. Sometimes I go to a bar or dinner with friends."

"Well, tonight, would you like to make a new friend."

Cathy smiled and looked under her eyelashes at Pollard. "Is that an invitation, Etienne?"

"It is."

Cathy chuckled. "For a drink or dinner?"

"For the works."

"Sounds intriguing. I'd be delighted."

* * *

Cathy gets home a little after two thirty in the morning. She goes through her usual routine in the bathroom, not pretending the night is any different from the many nights she arrives home late. She hopes Les won't realize what time it is but doesn't really worry about it. If he says anything, she'll just go through the usual routine of saying the hotel function she was working on ran late. She believes that it will work if she is no later than three. After all, who's Les going to check with? He doesn't know anyone she works with.

Etienne complained when she slipped out of his bed and started getting dressed. He told her she could just go to work from his apartment, that there was no need to go home. She wasn't about to tell him she was married, that her husband would hassle her, that he would worry. She didn't want him to know she was married.

Etienne's apartment seems sterile, almost unlived in. She had asked him about it.

He had thrown open his closet door to show her the clothes hanging there, to convince her he really did live there.

Nonetheless, when she looked in the kitchen cabinets and refrigerator, there was little food. He said he was a bachelor and ate out.

He said he often worked late, that he really spent little time in the apartment, that he had a cleaning woman who kept the place immaculate, and that she came Fridays and had just been there that day.

Still, the apartment seems too neat, almost unused. She can't help but wonder if it is an apartment where he lives or if it is an apartment he only keeps for his women.

Still, if it is, it appears he hasn't kept any women there any time in the recent past. It makes her wonder, Was I too easy?

Chapter Thirty-One

Cathy stands outside the hotel waiting for Etienne to pick her up in his gray S-Class Mercedes. It will be her third date with the man. She wonders where they will go. So far, he has taken her to restaurants in Northern Virginia and the District where she has never been before— places Les wouldn't even imagine, places she and Les wouldn't ever have been able to afford, safe places that are not likely to be graced by anyone she or Les know.

Tonight, he has promised her a surprise. For Cathy, any of Etienne's restaurants would be a surprise, a new and exciting place outside the realm of her restricted life. She wonders if the night will feature something else than an elegant dining experience followed by an adjournment to the apartment—the apartment, as he calls it, as she does now.

Although they've gone to the apartment on both dates immediately after dinner, he has never pushed her. They've always sat and had drinks, listened to music, and sometimes danced. She thinks of the size of the apartment. It is huge, with plenty of room to dance, to twirl, and to dip a fantasy world, a fulfillment of her imagination. And the bed is bigger than a king. She didn't know they made them that big. Lord, she thinks, we could have done with a quarter of the bed ... hell, we did.

"A penny for your thoughts."

Cathy whirls toward the voice and lets out a small gasp.

It's Billy Covington walking casually up to her with a warm smile. However, there's no warmth in his voice as he almost hisses. "Has the Cat got a new boyfriend, a fancy guy with a big car? I saw him pick you up the other night ... may be a good catch for you. Had your hook out, Cathy? You getting ready to reel him in? Well, you just remember, woman, I come first. When I want you, I get you. When I say jump, you tell mister big you've got more important things to do." He strides past her but turns back with a smile and a wave before he proceeds.

Cathy stares ruefully after him. Bastard! Are you going to ruin my life? Snap your fingers and control me ... make me jump out of my pants and run to you whenever you want? I'll be damned.

She's suddenly aware of movement and turns to the drive. Etienne is coming around the car, looking mystified. "You look like you're in another world. Are you okay?"

"Oh, Etienne, hi. I didn't see you drive up."

He opens the car door. "I'm parked right beside you."

"Oh, yeah, I'm sorry. My mind was elsewhere."

Etienne smiles affectionately as he opens the passenger side door. "Yeah, obviously. Now come back to me. I don't want a date with a zombie."

"I'm sorry. I'm back with you now." She seats herself and leans back comfortably in the car's leather seat.

Etienne closes her door and rushes around to the driver's seat while smiling.

She smiles back. "Now I'm all yours."

He laughs. "I couldn't ask for anything more."

As they drive off, she draws in her breath quietly. What the hell am I going to do?

She looks at Etienne—his dark hair, his blue eyes, the straightness of his nose, and his full lips. Well, tonight's not the time to think about it. "Hey, what's the big surprise?"

"Don't you want to wait and find out?"

She punched his shoulder. "Heck, no. I want to know ... to get excited. Tell me."

He chuckled. "Is knowing or not knowing going to turn you on?"

"Making me mad is not going to."

"Okay, then I'd better tell you. We're going to the Kennedy Center to see 'In the Heights.'"

Cathy doesn't know what 'In the Heights' is. "That's wonderful. I've always wanted to see it."

"Well, we're lucky it's back. After the success of 'Hamilton,' it's got renewed interest."

Cathy has heard of 'Hamilton.' Although she doesn't know much about it, she's beginning to feel more comfortable. She decides to turn to a subject she knows more about. "What time will that get us to the apartment?"

Etienne looks at her. "Anxious, huh? Ready to finish off a big night." He grins. "All in good time, girl. All in good time."

Cathy is discomfited. She doesn't want to sound that anxious. She doesn't want to sound like sex is the only thing important to her. She just doesn't know what "In the Heights" is. When he discussed it, she didn't know what to do. He must think I'm shallow as hell. Well, that's better than thinking I'm stupid.

Chapter Thirty-Two

Cathy sits in her office, wondering what Etienne will do next to spice up their dates. A musical at the Kennedy Center had been a first for her. She had seen some local theaters in Indiana, but it had been nothing like a show at the Kennedy Center. She's beginning to feel she's led a sheltered life or at least a middle-class, midwestern life, with little exposure to the world. Gosh, she thinks. I can't let him know how little I know of the world, how unsophisticated I am. I thought my looks were all I needed. Till now, they're all I've ever needed. I've always so easily made men make fools of themselves. Heck, I thought all men were fools. Etienne's in a league I've never known … a league I want … a league to aspire to. I hardly knew it existed, though I imagined it. Now it's within reach. Just don't make a fool of yourself, Cathy. It would be easy. Watch yourself.

There's a knock on the door frame. Cathy snaps out of her reverie.

Billy Covington leans his shoulder against the door frame, a lascivious grin on his face. "Hey, beautiful. Good to see you looking so refreshed today. Mr. Mercedes must be treating you well."

Shit, Cathy thinks. Where the hell is Peggy Sanchez? She's left me by myself. "What?" she snaps.

Covington holds up his hand, palm out, as if in self-defense. "Whoa, baby, I'm just here for a friendly chat."

"You don't even know what that means. What do you want?"

"Hey, be nice. You know what I want … what I always want. I have needs, Cathy. Needs only your beauty can satisfy."

"Bullshit, Billy. Get off at home. Leave me alone."

"Home's not the same. Doesn't feel illicit. I like feeling illicit. It gives me a charge."

"Like a little half-grown boy whacking off behind the barn."

"Shit, Cat. I'm not half-grown anymore. I've moved on to the real thing."

Cathy sighs in resignation. "When?"

"Damn, Cathy, you make it sound commercial."

"It's called extortion."

"Hey, that's what you had planned."

"You don't know what I had planned."

Billy barks a laugh. "Don't shit me, Cathy the Cat. You just got what you deserved."

"I've got a boyfriend. We've got to stop this."

"Yeah, well, that just means I don't want seconds. Five-thirty, gal, before your boyfriend gets here. Room 557."

"You're a slime, Billy."

"Yeah, but a sweet and cuddly one."

"Anyway, he's not coming tonight."

Billy laughs. "Good. You can concentrate on me."

Sanchez enters in through the outer office and approaches Billy from behind. "Hi, Billy. You need anything I can help with?"

Billy gives her a benign smile. "Not today, sweetheart. Maybe some other time."

Cathy glares as he turns and leaves.

Sanchez catches the look and hurries back to her desk.

***

Cathy lies on the bed and waits for Billy's breathing to settle down. She knows that sometimes he falls asleep after he finishes with her.

Tonight, he doesn't seem inclined. He crosses his arms under his head. "That was good, babe. You had your mind on it. A little fast, but good. Almost like you have some place to go. You got some place to go, Cat?"

"No, Billy, I've got no date tonight, like I told you."

"Good, you can cuddle up to me a while."

"You know I don't do that, Billy."

"Even if I ask, pretty please."

Cathy starts to get up.

"Shit," Billy protests. "You're not listening to me."

"I have to go to the bathroom. I'll come back."

"Okay."

Damn women, thinks Billy. He rolls over on this side, with his back to the bathroom.

Cathy grabs her purse, turns on the bathroom light, and closes the door while saying, "Sorry about the light."

"Just hurry your ass."

The toilet is flushed a few minutes later, the bathroom door opens, and the light turns out. Billy waits and feels Cathy climb back in bed and push herself against him. He sighs. "You feel good."

She swings her arm across him. "Yeah, Babe." She plunges a syringe into his stomach.

He tries to reach down. "What the shit?"

He swings his arm around violently and tries to hit her, but she's already hurtling out of bed. She had never crawled under the sheet and had been ready. His hand barely hits her rear as she races across the room.

Billy throws off the sheet with a roar, catching his foot in it as he staggers out of bed, stumbles, and heads toward her. "You bitch. What did you do?"

Cathy points the empty syringe at him in self-defense.

It's not necessary. Billy falls to his knees and then flat on his face, with his head against Cathy's right foot.

She jerks her foot away. "Just a prick, Billy." She scoops up her clothes from the floor. "A prick for a prick."

She heads for the bathroom to dress, closing the door as if Billy could watch her. Thank God I saved that stuff from the night Les and I killed what's-his-face.

Chapter Thirty-Three

Cathy drives home in a daze. She remembers the lights from the other cars—the red lights, the green lights. She thinks she has stopped when she's supposed to, but she's not sure. She convinces herself she had no choice but to kill Billy.

Fortunately, it's the weekend. The workers rehabbing the floor won't be back until Monday. Room 732 isn't due for a makeover for two more weeks anyway.

It isn't as if there was blood. That's the best part of fentanyl. It's like poison unless the murdered sod falls over and breaks something. Billy Covington didn't. He just fell to his knees and then lay himself out neatly at her feet. I just had to shuffle to the side to get to the door. The killing's nothing … easy. It's getting rid of the body that's the problem. That will take work. Billy should be okay till Monday. I wonder when bodies start smelling. I'll have to get rid of him on Monday. I have the weekend to think about it … a wedding reception Saturday afternoon … Saturday night with Etienne … not going to miss that … anniversary celebration Sunday afternoon … Sunday evening to myself to get the plan together … piece of cake … the plan's already in my mind.

With these thoughts on her mind, Cathy pulls into the parking space in front of her apartment. She draws a deep breath and frowns. Something's wrong. Her parking spot is dark.

Why the hell didn't Les leave the porch light on for me? Then she senses a glow and looks at the front porch at the front door. It's glowing blue. Blue … he's painted that damn stuff on the door. Shit, it really does glow.

She gets out of her car, walks to the porch, up the steps, stands, and studies the door. Carefully, she sticks out a finger and touches the door. The paint's still tacky.

She inserts her key in the lock, turns the doorknob, pushes the door open, and feels resistance where the new paint is sticking to the door frame.

Les is sitting on the sofa. A bottle of beet sits on the coffee table. His hands are crossed behind his head. He looks pleased with himself. "Hi, beautiful. You like the door?"

"Why the devil didn't you leave the door open until the paint dried?"

"Well, hello to you too."

"It's going to be a mess. Paint on the door frame and puckered paint all around the edge of the door."

"Hell, I'll fix that tomorrow. A little sandpaper and a touch-up."

"Does it glow in the daylight too?"

"A little bit."

Cathy looked around the apartment. "How come the phone is blinking?"

"It's got messages on it."

"Why don't you listen to them?"

"Memory's full … and besides, I've listened to them. Left them for you to hear. You'll have fun."

Cathy is appalled. "Fun?"

"Yeah. Most of our neighbors are pissed. The door's an eyesore … detracting from the neighborhood … just awful. But the language is more colorful. The calls are still coming in, but I can't record them all. Jean Capelli admits her son thinks it's cool. Lester Green's was the first call. I made the mistake of answering. He said he'd be over in the morning to repaint the door. I told him my paint costs a fortune, and I hoped he could afford to pay the restitution."

Cathy is growing angry. "Damn, Les. You sound like you're enjoying this. We have to get along with the neighbors. And what's the neighborhood association and Parkfairfax management going to do?"

"Maybe try to throw us out. It would be great publicity."

It's the last straw. "Publicity, hell. It's downright embarrassing."

Les is sanguine. "Hell, babe, it's the start of making millions."

"Shit, as if I didn't have enough worries. This is it, Les. I'm getting out of here." Cathy storms off into the bedroom.

Les quickly follows. "What do you mean you're getting out of here?"

Cathy throws open her closet door and starts pulling out her clothes and throwing them on the bed. "Just what I said. You've promised a fortune for months, and all we have to show for it is a blue door that's pissing off the world." She is thinking about Etienne. She's thinking about her rich boyfriend. Hell, I can manipulate him too. It might as well be a rich one rather than a dreamer. She whirls on Les. "Get my suitcases out of the storage bin."

"What? No, you can't leave. You're my wife."

"Damn it, Les. You don't own me. Wives aren't owned. I'm tired of your dreams … of your fiddling our lives away in that back bedroom. You made promises … promises you damn well can't keep."

Les stammers, "C-c-cathy, you've got to be patient. I just need time."

Cathy storms out of the bedroom door. "Time's fucking up. I'll get the suitcase myself."

After she leaves, Les sits on the bed's edge and blows a long breath. He shakes his head and breathes deeply again. Damn, I knew it was coming someday. From the day we married, I knew it. I had no business marrying a beautiful woman … just stupid of me. I knew eventually I wouldn't meet her expectations. Hell, it's probably better this way. I'll make money, and she'll be sorry. Then I'll marry someone else hopefully not someone who will marry me for my money, but even then, I'll be in charge. No more a simpering wimp. Damn it, Cathy, the hell with you. I never needed beauty in the first place … it's nothing but trouble. It's resolved!

Les leaves the bedroom. He walks through the apartment, out into a hallway, and finally to the storage bin where Cathy is moving boxes aside and cursing. He squeezes in past her. "Hey, let me get them."

Cathy's startled. "What?"

"Let me get the suitcases."

Cathy exits the bin and stands back while Les takes out the suitcases, sets them on the hallway floor, locks up the bin, picks up the suitcases, and heads back to the apartment. Without looking back, he directs, "You get things packed, and I'll take them out to the car."

Les sits in the club chair in the corner of the bedroom and watches Cathy pack. "Where are you going to go?"

With growing resentment at Les's apparent indifference, Cathy responds, "What do you care?"

Les shrugs his shoulders. "Just making conversation."

Cathy is slightly intimidated. She looks at Les. "I'm really leaving. You know that, don't you?"

"You said you were."

"Yeah, I am."

"Okay."

Cathy is suddenly uncertain. "Don't forget about your lab partner."

"Godfrey?"

"Yeah, Godfrey."

"It's hard to forget."

"I've got the syringe."

"Yeah, I'm not surprised. I know where you got it."

"I didn't blow him."

"Doesn't matter."

"I want my car."

"Okay."

"And the furniture."

"You'll have to move it."

"I'll get a lawyer. Have him contact you."

"Why don't you get a no-fault guy?"

"Do they advertise that way?"

"Yeah. We'll split the cost."

Cathy snaps the suitcase closed. "Okay, I'm ready."

Les picks up the suitcases off the bed and hurries off through the apartment.

Cathy rushes to follow him. "There's no hurry."

"Yes, there is."

Chapter Thirty-Four

Les lies in the big king-sized bed, alone, on the left side where he always sleeps. He slides closer to the center and throws his leg over into territory he hasn't occupied except in moments of passion.

What the hell just happened? A door. A blue door. Was that the last straw?

He tries to shake his head in disbelief, but the pillow constrains him.

Hell, I've known it since day 1. Why would a beautiful woman choose me? Sometimes it made me believe I was something I knew I wasn't—a virile, handsome man that women drooled over. I knew better. This bed … this damned bed had been the world of a man's dreams.

I knew it was always a dream. What beautiful woman would live in a two-bedroom apartment when she could have a mansion? Hell, the only thing that held her here was the dream I provided of the mansion. Things take time. Damn, they take time.

It takes patience, Cathy. I know it will come. But not fast enough … I know not fast enough.

I felt your impatience building. Felt it in your complaints. Felt it in your ignoring me in this bed. Felt it in the hours you spent away from me. I knew it wasn't the job. You went to bars instead of coming home.

Damn, I should have been patient. I asked it of you, but I didn't have it myself. The damn blue door. I had to show the world my Blue. Well, hell. Be gone. I'll keep my millions. You'll be sorry.

Chapter Thirty-Five

Cathy spends the night in the hotel room next to where Billy Covington's body lies. She'll be there for the weekend.

It seems macabre, but she feels like it gives her some control over what is happening in her life. She isn't sure she has control. It's unnerving. She has always been in control. Now she has left Les, but she isn't sure if she has Etienne. She has work to do.

She was amazed it was so simple. There was no preamble. It just happened … came out of the blue.

Ha ha, she thinks. Out of the blue. Out of the goddamn blue. A blue dream. An unfulfilled blue dream … a dream that dragged on and on, going nowhere. Then he goes and slams me in the face with a blue door.

A door glowing out of the dark as I came home from killing a man … when I came home solving the problem of a dead man … slaps me in the face with a reminder that I'm wandering aimlessly.

So I get angry. What the hell did he expect? Angry enough to say, "Let's split," and the son of a bitch says, "Sure." It doesn't even bother him. It doesn't bother him that he's giving up a beautiful woman. What man does that? What's he, queer or something? He never acted like he was. What the hell's with him?

Well, fuck him. I don't need him. I can get another man. I can get all the men I want. The bastards drool all the time. I just need to snap my fingers. I'll get back to the dead man in the morning … get rid of him. Then I'll move on. Etienne, you're first up. You're a good catch. Hell knows I'm a good catch.

Do it, gal. The world's yours. You've always known it.

Chapter Thirty-Six

Les wakes up Saturday morning. He throws the covers over to the far side of the bed as if trying to hide its vacancy, its emptiness. Leave it that way.

He makes his way to the bathroom, stands at the sink, and realizes Cathy's electric toothbrush is gone. He opens the medicine cabinet. It's empty. She always made him use a drawer. He stares at it for a moment. Then he takes his shaving creams from his drawer and puts in in the cabinet. Mine now.

After he finishes in the bathroom, he puts on a robe. There's no need to get dressed. He's not going anywhere.

He goes to the kitchen and takes a frying pan from the drawer under the stove, causing the pans stored there to clang. He thinks he hears an echo but isn't sure. It just feels that way. I've never felt this way before. I've been here by myself before and never heard an echo. Maybe it's because she's not here … perhaps because she's not coming back … probably because she's gone.

He sets up the coffee pot, turns it on, and thinks, I should have made only half a pot. I'll have to throw it out.

He fries bacon. Then he cracks two eggs into the grease. Hell, she never liked eggs anyway. Ate cereal. Now I can make anything I please … do whatever the hell I want to do.

He pours a cup of coffee and takes it and his breakfast to the table. He sets it on his table mat and looks across the table at her mat. Hell, I don't need that anymore.

He picks it up and takes it to the linen drawer. He pulls the drawer open a couple of inches, changes his mind, and closes it. He takes the table mat to the trash bin and stuffs it into the trash can.

He returns to the table and sits down with a sense of satisfaction, as if he had accomplished something important—he'd cut the tie.

He sprinkles an abundance of salt and pepper on his eggs … *Anything I want to do* … and begins to eat.

***

Later, Les sits on the living room sofa with his coffee. His dishes are in the kitchen sink. He'll wash them later. He'll wash them when he gets around to it.

He turns on the television, on the TODAY show. He doesn't turn up the sound. He's not really interested. He never watches morning television, but what else is there to do?

He hears a knock at the door. His mind suddenly emerges from his doldrums. It's not the knocker. It's a small knock—a knock by a hand.

Lord, I hope the paint's dry.

He rushes to the door, opens it, and vaguely sees a young boy standing on the stoop while he quickly looks at the door to see if it's damaged. It's not. He turns back to the boy and recognizes him as living across the parking lot. Les has seen him, and an older brother headed for school in the morning.

"Did you get any paint on your hand?"

"Uh, no, sir."

"Good, good. What can I do for you?"

The boy's eyes glance away, glance at the door. "It's about the paint."

Les's mind becomes wary. "Oh, what about it?"

"My dad wants to know where he can buy some."

Les relaxes. "He does, huh? Does he want to paint your door?"

The boy looks hesitant. "No, my mother wouldn't let us do that."

"Your mother doesn't like it."

"No."

Les knows he is giving the boy a hard time, knowing that the conversation has become innocuous. "Yeah, what did she say about it?"

The boy is turning red at the feeling of intimidation and uncertainty. "She says it's a-a-atrocious." He's surprised when Les chuckles. He quickly speaks, "But I like it."

Les continues, "And your dad?"

"He thinks it would be wonderful."

"For your door?"

"No, no, sir. For my soap box derby car."

Les laughs. "Yeah, I can see that. It would be."

"Yes, and my dad wants to buy some."

Les sighs. "I'm sorry. I really am, but it's not for sale."

"It's not? Well, where can we get it?"

"You can't. I make it in my back room." Les points over his shoulder with his thumb.

"Could you give us some?"

Les looks down and studies the boy. "What's your name?"

"Ben. Ben Easley."

Les twists his mouth in thought. "Well, Ben Easley. Do you do endorsements?"

Ben looks perplexed. "Endorsements?"

"Yeah, like the NASCAR guys' advertisements all over their cars and clothing."

"Oh, yeah. I don't think the soap box derby allows that."

"Do they allow you to name your car?"

"Yeah, I think so."

"So you could name your car?"

Ben looks uncertain. "I guess."

"So how about 'Blue' in big letters? Like that's the name of the car, with Les Warin's' in small letters right above it?"

"Uh, I don't know. I'll ask Dad."

Les nods. "Yeah, you do that. If I give you some paint, will you at least talk up where you got it from?"

The boy looks relieved. "Yeah, we'll do that."

"Okay, you wait right here on the stoop."

Les hurries to his laboratory room and picks up a pint of paint.

He brings it to the front door and holds the jar out to the boy. "Careful. Be very careful with it. It's worth a fortune. Drop the jar, and there's no more. Prime the car in another blue first, so this will cover. It's all you get. Okay?"

Ben takes the paint, looking nervous. "It's really valuable?"

"Like liquid diamonds."

"Gosh, yes, I'll be careful."

Les watches nervously as Ben crosses the parking lot. When the boy is back in his apartment, Les breathes a sigh of relief. I hope too. The soap box derby is a good place to advertise. One thing for sure, the car will stand out.

He returns to his living room and picks up his coffee and the morning newspaper. I guess you advertise wherever you can.

The coffee is cold. He goes to the kitchen and puts the mug in the microwave for thirty seconds. He sits at the table to read the paper while listening to the sound of the microwave, waiting for it to bing. Before it does, the telephone rings.

He vacillates, wondering if he has time to grab the coffee before he answers the phone. The microwave still shows ten seconds. That makes the decision. He picks up the phone from the counter. "Les Warin. May I help you?"

A woman's voice responds, "Yes, hi. This is Mary Murphy. I'm a reporter with the Washington Post ... work on the Metro

Section."

A chill of trepidation runs through Les. He has felt this way ever since the murder whenever he is faced with anything that gives a whiff of authority or establishment. He gives out a tentative "Yes."

"Yeah, Mr. Warin. Are you the one with the blue door?" Les mentally prepares to be defensive. "Yes ... yes, I am."

"You've caused quite a stir in the neighborhood."

"Well, yeah. Some of my neighbors ... a few ... don't seem to care for it. They think it stands out too much ... isn't appropriate."

"Yeah, well, it's just blue, isn't it? Not like it's pink or orange. It must be some unusual blue to upset people. Is that what it is ... some unusual blue?"

"Yeah, you might say that."

"I know colors are hard to describe over the phone, like dark blue, sky blue, ocean blue, and so forth. How would you describe this blue?"

"Glowing."

"Glowing—like real shiny? Some kind of enamel?"

"No. The door glows. Puts out blue light."

"Like when you shine ultraviolet light on something?"

"No, it glows ... all by itself."

"Really? May I come to see it."

"Sure ... that'd be fine. When do you want to come?"

"Uh ... tomorrow afternoon. Say two o'clock."

"Yeah, two o'clock. Two's fine."

"I'll put on my sunglasses."

"Yeah ... sunglasses ... that's funny. See you at two."

Chapter Thirty-Seven

Cathy isn't in a terrible hurry Monday morning. She wants the hotel staff to be at work before she appears. She hadn't bothered to hang her clothes in the hotel closet when she arrived after leaving Les.

After all, she wasn't staying—at least not in that room. Now, she thinks it was a mistake.

She takes her clothes from one of her suitcases and shakes them out. She wants a dress. The suits she regularly wears to work are set aside. None of them have skirts that are short enough. She believes that executives don't wear short skirts. Today is different. She wants men to be nervous and rattled. She knows short skirts do that, especially to the men she'll see today.

As she exits the elevator into the lobby, Jennifer immediately notices her from behind the registration desk. The girl gapes at Cathy as she approaches the desk. She knows it's the dress. Jennifer has never seen her dressed like that before.

"Good morning, Jennifer. Is Mr. Wigram in? I'm going back to see him."

Jennifer looks perplexed. Cathy has never asked before about who was in or not when she's gone back to the executive offices. She just goes, "Yeah, he came in about half an hour ago. I haven't seen him since."

Cathy nods, as if satisfied. She's pleased with Jennifer's reaction to the dress. She rounds the desk as another reception staff member Skeets comes out of the room behind the desk. Skeets sees her as she turns into the hallway leading to the executive offices. She looks at Jennifer and raises her eyebrows. Cathy catches the look as she vanishes.

Wigram's door is closed. She opens it and walks in.

Wigram looks up. "What the hell. Don't you know how to knock?"

Cathy grins. "Weren't doing anything requiring privacy, were you?"

"Damn, Cathy. Is that supposed to be funny?"

"Nothing's funny between you and me, Stanley. As always, we need to work together."

Wigram grimaces. "You mean, do something for you?"

Cathy realizes that Wigram is so concerned that he hardly notices her dress. "I just need a little help."

"What? I quit my job so you can move up?"

Cathy makes a face as if she's shocked by the statement. "Aw, Stanley. I'd never do anything to hurt you. I just need a little favor."

She walks around the desk and stands next to Wigram. She reaches out and strokes his hair. He flinches and tries to move his head away. Cathy smiles. "Just a little favor."

Wigram seems to sag into himself as he leans away from Cathy in his chair. "Yeah, and you'll release a CD if I don't do it."

"Yes, Stanley, that's good for you to remember."

Wigram gets out of his chair and moves around the desk, as if trying to escape. "If you're saying that, the favor's not little."

Cathy stands behind the desk. "Hey, you can't run away, Stanley. You've got no choice."

Wigram sighs. "Okay, what the hell is it?"

"All in good time, Stanley. We need to find Eddie Chisholm. Have a little pow-wow."

Wigram hesitates and then seems to realize there's no use. "He's working on the ice machine on the third floor."

Cathy raises her eyebrows in surprise. "You know where he is? The mechanical maintenance man? I'm amazed. You're more into this hotel than I knew."

Wigram puckers his mouth in annoyance. "That damn Billy Covington didn't show up this morning. I had to do this job."

Cathy smiles benignly. "Oh, shoot, Stanley. For a moment there, I was impressed. Let's go find Eddie."

They go out past the registration desk and head for the elevator.

Skeets and Jennifer watch them.

Skeets speaks out of the side of her mouth. "Cat leading the mouse."

Jennifer glares after the two. "More like a panther. A black one."

Wigram stands stock still in the elevator, while Cathy handles the controls. She casts a glance at him. "Relax, Stanley. With Eddie's help, you'll do this just fine, and nobody will know."

When they exit the elevator on the third floor, Cathy looks at Wigram. "Which way?" Wigram points down the hallway but doesn't move to lead.

Cathy hunches her shoulders in resignation and heads down the hallway.

Chisholm has the machine pulled away from the wall. A bag of tools is sitting on its top. He's on his knees behind the cooler.

Cathy moves around the machine to be near him. "Eddie."

Eddie looks up and sees legs. He looks further up. "What the shit, Cat?"

He catches a glimpse of Wigram and looks back at Cathy as he gets to his feet. "Er, Ms. DuChant?"

Cathy smiles. "Cat's all right, Eddie. We're among friends."

She turns to Wigram. "I need a little favor, and Mr. Wigram, er Stanley, is going to help. Grab your tools and follow me. We're going to the fifth floor."

"But I have to finish the ice machine."

"Later. Stanley will help you push it back against the wall." Wigram looks surprised. "What? Oh, okay."

Eddie looks uncertain, and then with Wigram at one end and him at the other, they push the machine back. It's easy. After all, Eddie had pulled it out by himself.

Eddie grabs his bag of tools and briefly looks at Cathy, who nods as she leads them back to the elevator.

On the fifth floor, Cathy heads to room 557 with the men trailing behind her.

Eddie says aloud, addressing no one in particular, "I thought the contractor was working this floor."

Cathy answers, "They haven't gotten to this wing yet."

Wigram wonders, "So what are we doing here?"

Cathy chuckles. "Patience, guys."

At room 557, Cathy inserts the passkey into the door mechanism. She turns the handle, hesitantly looks at the men, and then opens the door. She leads them in.

Chisholm stops two steps into the room. "Shit!"

Wigram, trailing behind, almost bumps into Chisholm. "What?" Then he sees. "Oh, shit."

Cathy looks at them blandly. "He lured me up here Friday night and tried to rape me."

Wigram, his mind in shock, gasps. "It's Billy Covington."

Cathy shakes her head as if she's talking to idiots. "Yeah, Billy Covington. Thinks he's a real stud … can do anything to women he wants to."

Wigram stammers, "B-but he's dead in the hotel. It's going to be a scandal."

Cathy puckers her mouth in mild frustration. "No, it's not. You're going to take care of it … you and Eddie."

"Whoa, lady," Eddie protests. "What the hell have I got to do with this? I'm leaving now."

As he heads for the door, Cathy blocks his way. She pulls a syringe in a clear plastic bag from her purse. "You recognize this, Eddie? It's what I used to defend myself against Billy. It has your fingerprints on it along with Billy's blood. Maybe you killed him, Eddie. I wonder."

Eddie glares at Cathy. "You bitch. I had nothing to do with it."

He tries to grab the syringe, but Cathy pulls it away from him. "Easy, Eddie. I've got another just like it."

"Damn, I tried to help you out."

"And you did. Drugs and murder. Killed your boss. Doesn't look good, Eddie."

"You said he tried to rape you?"

"That he did, but I'd hate to be involved in a messy investigation. It wouldn't be good for my image."

"Image shit. We've got a dead man."

Cathy smiles at Eddie and then at Wigram. "No, you and Stanley have a dead man. You're going to take care of him."

Wigram looks appalled. "Get rid of him? What are you talking about?"

"Hotel image, Stanley. Your personal image. Your job. Yeah, with Eddie's skills and friends and your help, Billy Covington is going to vanish."

She returns the syringe to her purse and turns toward the door. "Good luck, guys. I know you won't let us down. I emphasize the 'us.'"

Chapter Thirty-Eight

The two men stand in silence.

Chisholm looks at Wigram. "What the hell does she have on you?"

"It's between her and me."

Chisholm nods. "Yeah, I'm sure. So what do we do next?"

Wigram looks nervously at Chisholm. "Do you really sell drugs?"

"Yeah, big deal. It's got nothing to do with what we're into now." He looked down at the body. "Good thing there's no blood. That'd be a real problem."

"Real problem? This isn't a problem?"

"Course it is, but we won't have to clean up. Even the bed's been stripped."

"You think she did that?"

"Absolutely."

"Why?"

"Hair, semen, whatever. She was raped, or she wasn't, but the bed was used. It has nothing to do with our problem."

"Shit, shit, shit. Do you know what to do?"

"Why should I?"

"You're a criminal."

"God, man. I sell narcotics. I don't kill people. I do my best to avoid that kind of shit. So what the hell are you? She's got something. Don't tell me you're lily-white."

"Well, it doesn't have anything to do with getting rid of a body."

Chisholm decides, "Okay, first time for everything. We need to move him. Get him out of the hotel. Dump him somewhere."

Wigram remonstrates in alarm, "Not in my Mercedes."

Chisholm responds in disgust, "Well, la de dah, you think you're going to get blood in your pretty upholstered trunk."

"Hair. Hair in the trunk … DNA in the trunk … fibers in the trunk."

"They won't find hair if they don't have any reason to look in your car."

Panic is growing in Wigram's mind. "Hell, the police are smart. They'll look."

"For God's sake. We'll get rid of the body, and they'll have no reason to look."

"What if we're caught moving the body to the car?"

Chisholm groans. "Then they'll really have no reason to check your car."

"Funny … really funny. Glad you can joke. If you're so smart, tell me what we're going to do."

"We're going to move the guy, put him in my van, and take him away. Then I'll power wash the hair and the DNA out … leave it and your Mercedes immaculate."

"And getting the body to your van?"

"You're going to get one of those room service rolling serving tables … one with a long tablecloth. Make sure there's a shelf underneath. I'll wait here."

Wigram leaves reluctantly.

Chisholm stands, afraid to sit … afraid to leave hairs and DNA.

He wonders what he's touched. Cathy opened the door. I think I just walked in … Damn, Wigram just went out. He touched the door and turned the knob. I need to wipe it down … No, shit, he's coming back. I'll need to wipe it down later.

He wants to pace, to walk back and forth in the few feet between him and the body. He doesn't want his shoe prints in the carpeting near the body.

He tests his shoe steps and tries to leave a pattern. It doesn't look like anything's there. Thank goodness for commercial carpeting … old commercial carpeting that's worn. That's about to be replaced.

After an eternity, Wigram returns. He taps on the door.

Chisholm puts on the door security chain. I'll have to wipe that too. He opens the door an inch, sees it's Wigram, removes the chain, and opens the door. Wigram wheels a cart in. His brow is covered with sweat.

"Jeez," Chisholm exclaims, "sweating like that is going to make anyone seeing you know that something's up."

Wigram is breathing as if he's just run a mile. "I wiped my brow. No one saw me."

"Nobody? That's great."

"Well, one of the sous chefs saw me getting the cart, but I had wiped my brow."

Concern blooms in Chisholm's face. "He just let you go and didn't say anything?"

"No, he was curious about what I was doing. I told him I needed to move some things a guest had requested. He didn't suspect a thing."

Chisholm isn't so sure. To him, Wigram looks as if he is going to melt into a puddle on the floor. He grabs the cart and moves it near the body, folding back the tablecloth as he goes. "Let's get a move on … put this body on the cart … get him out of here."

He positions the cart next to Covington's feet and looks at Wigram. "I'll pick up his legs, and you push the cart under them."

Once that is done, Chisholm walks around the cart and tells Wigram, "I'll grab him by the feet and pull him through the cart. You hold it so it doesn't roll."

He struggles to pull the body. Wigram grunts to hold the cart, bracing himself and rebracing himself.

Covington's body slides through until his wallet in his back pocket catches on the edge of the shelf. Chisholm walks around the cart, and the two men study the situation.

Chisholm nods to himself. "I'll pick up his ass by his pockets, and you push the cart under him." They do so.

Chisholm stands back and realizes the body's arms are sticking out. He lifts the arms one at a time and tries to stick Covington's hands into the front of his pants, but it's too tight. He unbuttons the dead man's shirt and sticks the arms inside. He tells Wigram to brace the cart. He then sits the body up, but the head bangs against the top shelf. Chisholm braces his body against Covington's back, bends the man's head forward, and shoves. The body seems to wedge in place.

He switches places with Wigram and tries to fold the body's legs up, knees against the chest, but when he does, the man's upper body becomes unjammed and flops back onto the floor.

Chisholm stands up and stretches in frustration. Wigram looks at him desperately. Chisholm walks to the club chair in the corner, leans around it, and using a folding pocketknife, cuts off the cord to the floor lamp. He returns to the cart looking at Wigram. "Brace the damn thing again."

With the cart braced, Chisholm raises the body, wraps the cord around the man's neck, and roughly shoves the head under the table again. He then ties the body to the cart's vertical posts. "There, damn it, stay in place." The body has become his challenge—an uncooperative enemy.

He walks around and shoves his legs tightly. He goes to the closet, takes out the clothes iron, and cuts off the cord. He uses it to tie the body's calves in place. He then stands back to look at his work.

Wigram looks at him as if imploring Chisholm to announce success. Chisholm does and folds down the tablecloth. He then walks to the door and, with his handkerchief, opens the door. As he leans out to check the hallway, Wigram asks, "How do you know your handkerchief is clean … clean of DNA snot?"

Chisholm studies his handkerchief. "I guess I don't." He goes into the bathroom and tears off toilet paper and wads it up as he returns to wiping the door handle hardware.

Finally satisfied, he grabs hold of the cart. "Let's go. Grab the other end, and we'll head for the freight elevator."

Wigram hesitates. "What if we bump into someone?"

"If we do, we'll improvise. All the workers are in the other wings anyway."

Out in the hallway, Chisholm closes the door and wipes it down again. "Let's roll."

At the elevator, they push the down button. The elevator is on another floor. They don't know where, but they hear it moving. The two men shift their feet nervously. It seems like the elevator is taking forever.

The elevator finally arrives, and the door opens. They push the cart forward, and it bumps over the threshold. As it does, Covington's arm falls out from under the tablecloth and drags on the floor. In a panic, Wigram jumps forward and pushes the arm back.

"Shove it in good," Chisholm directs.

"Yeah, well, you didn't do so well the first time."

"Stuck it in his shirt. What else am I supposed to do?"

Wigram struggles to shove the hand under Covington's belt, but it's too tight. He mutters to himself as he pushes the hand as far over as it will go. "Damn, damn, damn."

"You got it?" Chisholm half begs. "We'll have to be careful … no bumps."

"Yeah, easier said than done."

The door has closed, and Chisholm pushes the down button. "When the door opens, be casual … no bumps going out of the elevator or onto the loading dock. Just ease it along."

"Shit, we might have to lift a little. He's heavy as hell."

"You can do it. I've been impressed. You really braced the cart up there."

"I work out."

Chisholm nods in satisfaction. "Not as much a desk jockey as I thought."

The door opens. No one is there. They ease the cart out and move to the loading dock. Dom Scampini, the electrician, is sitting on the edge of the dock, smoking.

Chisholm tries to be calm as he eases the cart onto the dock. "Hey, Dom. You smoking anything good?"

Scampini looks up. "Hell, Eddie, just a cigarette." He seems to be startled when he sees Wigram.

"What's with you making the boss work?"

"He wants the cart repaired. Need to take it home to do it."

Wigram sees a bulge in the tablecloth on the side away from Scampini. He pushes it back with his foot and thinks, Same damn elbow, as he addresses the electrician, "Scampini, didn't I give you a job to do on the ovens in the kitchen this morning? You finished?"

Scampini scrambles to his feet. "Almost finished, Mr. Wigram." As he leaves the loading dock, he continues talking defensively, "Be finished a half an hour or so."

"Get on it. The chef's going to need it soon."

"Yes, sir. I'm on it."

With Scampini gone, Chisholm smiles at Wigram in admiration. "Advantage of being a boss. Well done. I'll go get my van."

"What," Wigram protests, "you're going to leave me alone with the cart?"

As Chisholm runs down the concrete steps next to the loading dock, he shouts, "Hey, you've done well so far."

"What if you don't come back?"

Chisholm laughs. "You'll think of something."

"Damn it, hurry."

Wigram looks around, afraid someone is watching. He stands in the doorway to the loading dock, as if he can block anyone from coming out and finding the cart. He turns his face away from the parking lot when a car drives by, hoping they won't recognize him.

Finally, Chisholm returns. He backs toward the dock, stopping a couple of yards short. He gets out, goes to the rear of the van, and opens the two doors wide. He stands back and looks at the van and then at the dock. "Van's at least three feet too low. We're going to have to lift the cart down. Push it over to the edge of the dock and then come down here. We'll have to each take a side."

Wigram scrambles down the steps and comes around to the van. "He's heavy as hell. We'll have to be careful not to dump him out."

"Don't worry. He's tied in good."

"Wired in."

"Yeah, wired in."

They lift, grunting and groaning, and get the cart into the van. The arm falls out again. They both look around in a panic to see if anyone is watching and then shove the arm back.

Chisholm slams the rear door closed, climbs in a side door, and ties the cart in place with a rope he has in the van.

Wigram slaps the side of the van with his palm. "Looks like you're set. Drive safely."

"Hey, hey, you're not going anywhere. I'm going to need help. Get in the passenger seat."

"Ah, hell, Chisholm, you don't need me. People are going to ask questions if I vanish."

"Hey. You're a damn boss. If people ask questions, just blow them off. You're not getting away that easily. Get in the seat, or I'll sic Cathy the Cat on you. You understand?"

"Yeah, okay."

The men climb in the van, and Chisholm drives away.

Wigram asks, "Where are we going?"

"My house to get some shovels and a pickaxe."

"We're going to bury him?"

"If we can't figure out what else to do."

"Where's your house?"

"Close your eyes. I don't want you to know."

"The address is in your file."

"Not the real one."

Chapter Thirty-Nine

Sunday afternoon, there's a knock on the door. Les glances at his watch. It's two-o-five in the afternoon. He goes to the door, half expecting a neighbor to be standing there, ready to unload with her thoughts. A small woman is standing on the stoop with a leather document case held across her chest.

Lord, is it filled with petitions? Has it gotten that far? He then pulls the door open wide and holds it so that it doesn't block the woman. "May I help you?"

She looks him in the eye. "Mary Murphy from The Post. I phoned you on Saturday."

Les smiles and nods. "About the door?"

"Yes."

Les apologizes, "Sorry, I forgot." He motions his hand toward the door. "Well, there it is."

Murphy squares herself in front of the door. "Yes. I see it. Kind of bright."

"You should see it in the dark. It makes a statement." Murphy looks back at Les and smirks. "I bet."

Les motions for the woman to come in. As she passes, he gets a slight whiff of perfume. His senses react. He leads her to the living room. She seats herself in a wing chair while Les studies her. Do women realize they're being studied? "Drink of water? I was just pouring mine."

"Yes, please," she responds as she opens the folder in her lap. Nothing like Cathy's long legs … freckles … red hair. Does every woman have to be compared to Cathy? Is that what life's done to me? "Ice cubes?"

"Yes, please."

"Coming up."

Les goes to the kitchen and pours the water and ice from the refrigerator door. He returns to the living room and hands Murphy her glass. He notes that she has taken out a pen and paper. He looks around, considering where to sit. The sofa's too low. Too submissive. The other wing chair is too far away.

He picks up a chair from the dining room table and sets it next to Murphy. He sees her slightly lean away. I'm in her space. He slides the chair forward and turns it toward her. "What would you like to know?" Murphy seems to settle, to become comfortable in her work. "Tell me about yourself. Then we'll talk about the door."

"Well, I'm from Indiana. I have a bachelor's degree in chemistry from Purdue. I work in a mattress store. Someday I hope to get back to chemistry."

Murphy looks confounded. "You have a degree in chemistry and work in a mattress store? That's kind of brief. There must be more of a story than that."

"No, not really. I have to pay the bills."

Murphy looks around at the apartment, and Les knows she's thinking, Selling mattresses can't pay for this.

Les responds quickly. "My wife has a job too."

"Oh, you're married."

"Just separated, sad to say."

"Oh, I'm sorry."

Les gives a slight guffaw. "Probably for the best."

Murphy is in a hurry to change the subject. "Okay, the blue paint, where do you buy it?"

"I don't. I make it."

"Make it? You have a factory somewhere?"

"No, I make it in the bedroom."

Murphy is thrown. "You make it here in the apartment?"

Les is becoming slightly reluctant to talk further. He suddenly thinks that it might not be good for his neighbors to know. "It's not dangerous ... not like making meth or something. It's not flammable ... not explosive ... doesn't give off fumes. It's probably not a good idea to put that in the paper."

"Oh, but that makes the story."

"I'd really appreciate you're not doing it."

Murphy doesn't respond. "What else do you make?"

"Uh, I'm trying to make a plastic doped with Blue."

"With Blue?"

"Yeah, I call the material that glows, Blue, with a capital."

"And what are you going to do with the plastic?"

"Hopefully, sell its use for making things." Les tries not to get excited. Suddenly, he has a vision of the future. "Like plastic soldiers, hula hoops, Star Wars sabers, frisbees, anything you can make out of plastic."

Murphy suddenly looks interested. "Car bumpers?"

"Why not?"

Murphy grins. "Sounds like fun. I'll be interested in what happens. Let's get back to the product you have now. You've painted a door. Have you done anything else?"

Les feels silly, but he has nothing else. "The boy across the way is painting his soap box derby racer with it."

"Hey, that's fun. I'll have to go talk to the boy. It should make a good story."

"Yeah, you need to do that. Tell the world that painting things Blue is the future."

Murphy folds up her pad of paper and puts it into her folder. "Yeah, I can imagine all kinds of things."

"You can?"

"Can't you?"

Chapter Forty

Cathy returns to her office, leaving the two men standing in the room looking lost. She hopes they wake up and take care of things. If they don't, *Chisholm will have to make many excuses, and I can hear Wigram stuttering like crazy.*

She chuckles to herself as she starts going over the schedule for the banquet rooms. She's thankful that she had the weekend events set up before meeting with Billy Covington. She had told her assistant that she was taking the weekend off and that, as her assistant, she was in charge. As of this morning, Cathy has heard no complaints and doesn't find any on her desk. She assumes everything went well.

Today, she sees there's a corporate celebration in one of the banquet rooms. Someone got promoted. She concludes she needs to check out what is happening. There's a pay-as-you-go bar and hors d'oeuvres laid out on tables. There are no pretty little things passing trays—no big deal.

The phone rings. She picks it up.

"Hi, babe. It's Etienne."

"Let me close the door."

She does and returns to the phone. "Hey, Etienne. Sorry, big ears in the outer office. Where've you been? I've missed you."

It flashes through her mind that she hasn't missed him. She's been too busy. *God, where's my mind been? I need Etienne now that Les is gone.* Then she catches herself as she almost snickers. *Well, the idiot Les is not gone, gone. I could reel him back in at a moment's notice.*

"Missed you too, babe. Been traveling."

"Yeah, you didn't tell me."

"Kind of spur of the moment. Trouble in Minneapolis."

"Minneapolis? What's in Minneapolis?"

"Our other plant is out there."

"Oh, yeah. We're switching it to making the Pfizer booster for the new Covid strains … the mutants."

"Oh, shit, I had hoped we were through with that."

"Not so. It's ended up like flu. We're going to have to give new shots every year. Pfizer doesn't want to limit themselves, so they're licensing us. It'll boost our profits and let them go back to some of the other work they do."

"So you're involved."

"Just looking over things. We've got some smart guys out there."

"So you're back, and everything's under control?"

"Yeah, things are great. Did you really miss me?"

"Every minute."

"Good. I need to see you. Are you available tonight?"

"I've got a party at five, but it will be over by 7:30. How about then?"

"Pick you up at the front door."

"I'll be out on the sidewalk. Let's hold down the show."

"Anything my beauty wants."

She makes a kissing noise over the phone. "Till then." She hangs up the phone. What is he going to think when I show up with two suitcases?

Chapter Forty-One

The cute little reporter came through. There's an article in the Metro Section of The Washington Post along with a picture of the soap box derby racing car being painted. It's hard to tell that the paint glows, but it doesn't look ordinary. Les can't really describe it, but it is different.

He cuts it out and puts it on the refrigerator, held up by a magnet that says Pleasure Hotels. He thinks, I've got to throw that out and get something different. That's the past.

He settles in a wing chair with the rest of the newspaper and a cup of coffee. As he sips his coffee, he hears a creak from the front door. Oh, oh, did I fail to latch the screen door? Is it swinging in the wind?

He sets down the paper and the coffee and goes to the door. He opens it and reflexively steps back as he finds a man there, staring at the door. He's chubby, with flushed cheeks, wearing an ugly brown suit and a brimmed hat that looks too small.

"I'm just looking at the door," he says as if that's normal. "It does glow."

Les nods and starts to say, "You should see it in the dark," but decides that's getting old. "Yes, it does," he agrees.

"The paper says you made it."

"That's right."

"That you make it in the back room."

"She wasn't supposed to say that."

"Oh, why's that."

"Some of my neighbors might not like that."

The man seems to think. "Oh, yeah, I can see that. May I see where you make it?"

"Uh, and you are?"

"Oh, sorry." He sticks out his hand to shake. "Bryn Sebold. Almost forgot how to shake hands since Covid."

Les glances at the hand and says, "Les Warin." He shakes the hand reluctantly. After all, the man might be interested in Blue. "Saw it in the paper, did you?"

"Yeah, is the soap box car here."

"No, it's where it's being built."

"Oh, shame. I would love to have seen it."

"Sorry, but may I help you?"

"Yes, yes, no doubt. Could I see where you make it?"

"Uh, what's your interest, Mr. Sebold?"

The man seems to momentarily have to think. "Interest? Yes, yes. I'm from Mosaic Art Supplies. We make craft paints ... gold, silver, and the like ... colors too. Sell it in little bottles for craftwork. Sell it in Michaels and such. We might be interested in your paint."

"You would have to make it."

"Yeah, we do that. Make or mix. It's what we do. Buy some ready-made and repackage it, but we make it too."

"So you have a plant?"

"A plant ... right ... warehouse and plant."

"Okay, let me show you. Come in."

Sebold suddenly becomes aware that he's on a stoop. As he enters the apartment, he looks around. "Nice place you got here, Mr. Warin. Hard to believe it's a paint factory."

Les leads Sebold down the back hallway to his lab. "Not really a factory ... Just a laboratory."

He opens the bedroom door and leads Sebold in, but the man stops at the door. "No, I see. It's not a factory."

Les points to his array of pint jars. "That's what I've made."

"Yeah, how much do you make a day?"

"A couple of ounces."

Sebold's mouth hangs open. "A couple of ounces?"

"Right. How much are you going to need."

"Uh, maybe a couple of thousand gallons a year."

Les acts nonplussed. "Well, that would take some scaling." Sebold looks uncertain. "Yeah, like what?"

"Well, some big 1500-degree Fahrenheit furnaces and several large mixers, chemical storage tanks, and some large centrifuges."

Sebold blanches. "Sounds like a significant capital investment."

"Well, you could start small. See how it does in a limited sales territory."

"I guess."

"I could help set you up."

"Yeah … we would need a contract … need to hold down the initial investment."

Les Smirks. "Are you saying you don't want to pay me much, Mr. Sebold? Just want to use my patent for a few bucks."

Sebold sighs. "We'd have to work something out."

"Well, Mr. Sebold. I might be amenable to a conversation."

Chapter Forty-Two

Cathy steels herself as she rolls her suitcases out of her office and down the hallway. The wheels rattled, sounding to her like a locomotive. At least it's on carpeting, she thinks as she rolls it across the lobby, with all the staff gaping at her. The sound grows a magnitude louder as she exits the front doors onto cement while the doorman and the parking staff try to look casual. She strains not to paddle her foot as she waits for Etienne and struggles to look like it's just a typical day.

When Etienne arrives, he rolls down the passenger window and leans over quizzically. Cathy leans down to the window and urgently says, "Open the damn trunk."

Motivated by Cathy's voice, Etienne punches the button to open the trunk, jumps out of the car, and rushes around to help her with the suitcases. "What the hell is this?"

"I'll tell you in the car."

She slams the trunk lid, quickly moves to the side of the car, and gets in the passenger seat. "Everyone's gaping at me."

Etienne puts the car in gear. "Well, you're acting kind of funny … real tense."

"Well, I rolled two suitcases out of there, looking like I've been living there."

"Have you?"

Defensively, Cathy snaps, "Of course not."

"Okay, take it easy. So what's with the suitcases?"

Cathy thinks quickly. "I moved out of my apartment. The super was making moves on me. I was getting nervous."

God, she thinks, thank you for 'sexual harassment.' It can cover a world of female sins.

"Gosh, do I need to go down there and do something about it?" Cathy replies with mild disgust, "What are you going to do, go to the apartment in your suit and tie and beat the hairy thing up?"

"Ur, no, but I could talk to the management ... maybe the police."

"Oh, hell no. More trouble than it's worth. Comes with being a woman."

Etienne chuckles. "Comes with being a good-looking woman."

Cathy smiles. "Thank you, Etienne."

"For what?"

"For thinking I'm good-looking."

Etienne laughs. "For saying the obvious. So what are you going to do?"

"Find another apartment."

"Tonight?"

Cathy shakes her head. "Not likely."

"So what are you going to do?"

Cathy sighs. "Maybe go back to the hotel."

"No, you can't do that. You can stay at my place tonight."

"Oh, Etienne, thank you, but I don't want to put you out."

"Hell, you've spent time there before. You've even got some clothes there. Just stay until you can get resettled."

"Oh, thank you, Etienne. You're so sweet." She leaned over and kissed him and rubbed her leg against his. God, Etienne. Why'd you take so long to ask?

<u>Chapter Forty-Three</u>

Les was gone for almost two months—back to Lafayette, Indiana, where Mosaic made or bottled their craft paints. He had gone home at least to the state of a single man. At least he would be single soon. The divorce was in the works.

In Indiana, he had helped the company set up the equipment to make Blue. The furnace was easy; they already existed. He wished they were larger, but he set up and bank of them—six in all. Centrifuges were a similar task. He obtained ten of them. The ceramic crucibles were more difficult to find. The ceramic companies that made the laboratory crucibles he had used to make Blue were companies that specialized in lab equipment. They didn't know how to scale to larger vessels, nor did they want to. It took some searching. He finally found a company in China willing to try, but only if they were allowed to make Blue. Although Les was uncomfortable signing an agreement, he eventually did so for $50,000. That, added to the $25,000 he was making from Mosaic, allowed him to pay for a motel room in Lafayette and his apartment in Parkfairfax and have a little money left over.

While he had waited for the crucibles, he had worried. He had heard so much about Chinese companies skimping on or substituting materials. He feared he would get an inferior product—a product that didn't match the crucibles he used in the lab, something with a different chemical makeup. He didn't know if that mattered. He didn't know if a metal crucible would work just as well as a ceramic one. All he knew was that he could not afford to try again. His budget wouldn't allow for it.

When the crucibles arrived, they worked. He didn't have the budget to analyze the crucibles to see if they matched the lab crucible. He never found out if the crucible material really mattered. He had thought, Don't rock the boat. The stuff works.

When he returns home to Alexandria, the mail is piled high inside the door. He separates the bills and the overdue notices and stacks them on the dining room table to work on tomorrow. He finds a letter from a lawyer and opens it. He reads his divorce papers. He scans the invoice and finds it has been paid—$390 plus postage. Gosh, Cathy must have paid it. Small change to get rid of me. She must have been in a hurry.

He opens a letter from a company in San Francisco—Dunhill Products Inc. Inside, he finds a letter, stationery with Dunhill Product Inc. across the top, and Oriental characters right below the words. It's signed by Jimmy Chai. Sounds Chinese, but who knows?

He reads the text. The man is inviting him to meet in New York City at NY NOW. He gives a date, an aisle, and a booth number. He wants to talk to Les about a product he wants to manufacture.

The date is in two days. Why doesn't the guy come to me? Shit, am I so important that I can ask a question like that? What the hell is NY NOW?

Les goes to his computer and turns it on. It seems to take forever. It's been turned off for a long time. Finally, he's logged in. He Googles NY NOW. It used to be the New York International Gift Show. It's at the Javits Center. Now the aisle and booth make sense. He thinks, I thought the Javits Center was being used for Covid. Maybe that's all cleared out.

He leaves the computer and picks up his telephone to check his messages. The machine is full. Among the messages, he finds three from Cathy from a strange telephone number. He phones her at her old work telephone number. Somebody named Peggy Sanchez answers, "Cathy Warin? I'm sorry, I don't know that name. You don't mean Cathy DuChant, do you?"

Les starts, "DuChant? Yeah, yeah, is she there?"

"No, she quit two weeks ago. She got married and didn't want to work anymore."

"Married?"

"Yeah. Said she was moving on with life."

"So she's gone."

"Yeah, that's what I said."

"Okay. Thank you," he says and thinks, Damn ... divorced three weeks ago and married two weeks ago. It didn't take long to forget about me.

Les copies down the phone number Cathy had called from and then dials it.

Cathy answers, "Mrs. Mallet. May I help you?"

"Mallet! Mallet, as in pharmaceutical?"

"Les? Les, is that you?"

"What the shit, Cathy? Did you marry a Mallet?"

"Yeah, Les. How'd you know?"

"I called the hotel."

"Yeah, I'm not there anymore."

"Yeah. You're rich now ... don't need to work ... married a Mallet kid."

"The only kid."

"God, you are rich ... going to inherit the whole company."

"He's not dead, Les."

"Only a matter of time. Only took you one week after the divorce to get married. You make time fly."

"Les, don't be mean. You always promised me millions, and you got nowhere."

"I've got a contract ... Hell, two contracts."

"How many millions?"

"Seventy-five thousand."

"Seventy-five? You're teasing me." Cathy almost gags as she laughs. "Damn, Cathy. I told you I would make money. It's just the beginning."

Cathy fights to hold back her laughter. "Okay, Les. It's only the beginning. All these years and seventy-five thousand. I made that much at the hotel in less than a year."

"And now you're rolling in money."

"Kind of … just got back from a nice honeymoon in Paris. Did we have a honeymoon, Les? I don't remember."

"You know we didn't. We were just starting out."

"Still, I don't remember ever having a honeymoon … or even a nice trip."

"Fuck you, Cathy."

"Ah, be nice, Les. I just wanted to tell you that you can keep the furniture. I won't be needing it."

"Yeah, I guess you have a mansion full of it … maybe two or three mansions."

Cathy chuckles. "Only one now, Les. Who knows about the future? I think I'll learn to ski. May need a place in Colorado or Wyoming. Who knows?"

"Live it up, Cathy. Spend the guy's money. Live your dream. I guess that's what you wanted."

Before Cathy can retort, Les hangs up.

Chapter Forty-Four

Les spends the night in a large hotel across from Penn Station. New York is fully in motion again. In the lobby, he has seen only a few masks. Long lines have been queued in front of the registration counter. Since there's no furniture in the lobby, people are sitting with their luggage on the floor. Six feet of separation is obviously a thing of the past. Foreign languages have been part of the cacophony. As he gets on the elevator, he feels he is escaping.

He eats at McDonald's in the next block and goes to a Broadway musical, thinking he has to do it if he is in New York. He thinks that when he gets back to Virginia, someone will surely ask what he has done in the Big Apple, and he needs to have an answer. Still, he enjoys the show.

Today, he takes a cab to the Javits Center. It's driven by a guy who is obviously a Middle Eastern, probably Muslim. He seems nice enough, but somehow Les doesn't feel comfortable. After hearing all the foreign voices the night before, he shouldn't be surprised. Northern Virginia isn't much different. I'm not in Indiana anymore.

He hurries toward the Javits Center, squeezing between buses lined up in front. Men are shouting everywhere among people streaming off the buses, stopping to get their bearings and then heading for one of the multitudes of doors.

He follows, entering a bustling atrium to the glass and steel frame building. To his left is a labyrinth of coat racks filled with coats, and the floor is covered with suitcases. To his right, across the back wall, are tables with white clothes. Numerous women behind them are servicing the people lined up before them. Signs over the tables, propped on metal frames, identify who the women are servicing—guests, vendors, etc. At kiosks centered in the vast foyer, people fill out forms before heading to the tables.

He hopes that he doesn't have to do that. He gets in the queue for guests, as he had been told to do. When he reaches the woman, he gives his name. She asks for identification. He shows her his driver's license. She looks at it and studies his face. Finally, she nods and begins fingering through a box of badges. Finally, she hands him one and admonishes, "You can't buy anything."

Les looks her in the eye and tries to look superior. "I wouldn't think of it." He thinks, Who the hell does she think I am, some kind of shoplifter?

He looks at what she has given him—a plastic holder and a piece of heavy paper, perforated and a badge covering a third of it with words describing the show on the other two-thirds.

He tears off the badge, inserts it in the plastic holder, and pins it onto his lapel. Always wondered what lapels were good for.

He follows a stream of humanity through a doorway, from one level of noise to another, carefully protecting his shins from the carts people drag behind them.

He enters a vast room. There are stairs up to a higher level, but that's not where he's going. His aisle is directly in front of him, backing against a central wall in the building. He enters it, marveling at booths full of games, stuffed toys, plastic this and plastic that, and even some children's books. Balloons are everywhere. Hawkers are behind tables of wares or in the aisle, corralling people.

He finds his numbered booth and sees a Chinese man behind a table of plastic soldiers, London Bridges, Eifel Towers, and Statues of Liberty. Another Chinese man is to the side dealing with a woman. He was scribbling on a long piece of paper. God, is she ordering this stuff?

He turns back and studies the merchandise. Red soldiers, blue soldiers, in addition to the olive drab. I've never seen a red soldier. I guess you have to tell the sides apart.

The man tears off a large sheet of paper and hands it to the woman while shaking her hand and nodding. "Thank you. Thank you."

He turns to Les. "May I help you?"

Les inquires with uncertainty, "Mr. Wang? I'm Les Warin."

The man nods while smiling broadly, with a gold tooth glittering in the lights of the center. "Ah, yes, Mr. Warin, the blue man." He reaches out and shakes Les's hand heartily. "Charlie Huang. So good you come, Mr. Warin." He spreads his hand toward his merchandise. "You see, maybe, glowing blue Statue Liberty, soldiers. Maybe you make red, green?"

"No. Sorry. Make only blue." Oh, goodness, I'm talking like him.

"Only blue … okay … that still good. I make blue Statue Liberty."

"You and I make deal?"

"Yeah, deal. That would be good."

"Yes. I go back to San Francisco. Have lawyer make contract. Send to you. You sign … come to Changzhou … teach us to make."

"Changzhou? Where's Changzhou?"

"Ah, Changzhou. You know Shanghai?"

"Yeah."

"Changzhou near Shanghai."

"Okay. You pay me … buy my airplane ticket?"

"Yes, yes. Pay you … maybe half a million."

Les is suddenly excited but wants to be sure. "Dollars?" Mr. Huang's smile grows broader. "Yes, half-million dollar."

Les tells Mr. Huang he thought they could work something out. I wonder how long it takes to get a passport.

Chapter Forty-Five

Les stares at the computer screen at the statement from his bank account. $501,067.27. God, is that real? Feels like I'm living in the Cayman Islands or something.

The money transfer has come in from Changzhou Industries. A money transfer ... Never had one of those before. Never had more than twelve thousand in the bank ... not since I worked for Mallet. Should I get another account? How much does the FDIC insure ... a quarter-million? I think? Shoot, Cathy should have waited. Nah, she would have just said I promised millions. She married her millions. The hell with her.

It's not millions, but Les feels good. He still wonders if he could have asked for more. Heck, if I know. Wang offered a half million, and I took it and ran. Maybe I need a lawyer, an agent, or something ... somebody who knows what Blue is worth. Is there anyone like that? How do you find them? Too late now. Now I have to go to China. God, is that safe? Would they think I'm industrial? Hell, I didn't write the contract. It's on them ... on Charlie Huang and his whole company. I'll get in and get out. Send them the plans, wait until they're set up, wing over and check them out, and bail.

He pictures the Javits Center in a couple of years. He imagines the toy aisle with Charlie Huang's booth glowing. I could make the whole aisle glow ... maybe the whole damn Javits Center. Christ, did I sign some kind of exclusive contract? Boy, I'm stupid. Bet I gave an exclusive for toys and souvenirs. Wonder if it covered frisbees and hula hoops ... refrigerator magnets ... whatever? Damn, damn, damn! I'd better get someone to read the contract.

While thinking, Les sinks lower and lower in his chair, forgetting the coffee he's holding in his hand until he feels his leg burning and a wet spot on his trousers expanding. He quickly moves his other hand to the cup to steady it with two hands. He leans back and sighs. What a goddamn klutz. A klutz in every way. I have no idea what I'm doing.

He hurries to the kitchen and grabs a paper towel. The quicker picker upper. He dabs the wet spot on his trousers and then rubs. The site is still damp and is now covered with white fuzz. He throws the towel in the trash in disgust.

As he turns to leave the kitchen, there's a knock at the front door. Les looks down at his trousers and makes a "shh" noise. He crosses the living room and opens the door a crack, holding it to shield his pants.

A man is standing on the stoop on the front edge. Just admiring Les is caught off guard, and he's suddenly uncomfortable holding the door only partially open.

He looks around the door's edge and grins at the door. "You like it, huh?"

The man twists and holds his hand out toward a man with a camera hanging around his neck, standing on the sidewalk. "You mind if we take a picture of it?"

"Have at it. I'll close the door so that you can get the full view. Need to answer the telephone, and I'll be right back."

Les closes the door and runs to the bedroom, unbuckling his belt and pulling down his fly zipper while he kicks off his slippers. He finds some jeans in the laundry basket, slips them on, and runs back across the living room, pulling up the zipper. No damn time for a belt or putting my slippers back on … just casual … enjoying my morning coffee.

He opens the door and hears a click. The cameraman is on the sidewalk, standing on a step ladder with his camera pointed at the door.

The man who knocked is standing by the ladder. "Hey, that's great. The door and the inventor together. We'll save that."

"An abomination. Horrible, horrible, horrible." It's Lolo Sturgill standing by the parking lot. She's a neighbor—one of those who hates the door.

Les knows her name is Lois. Why the hell would she permit herself to be called Lolo? She thinks she's a Latin singer or something?

The man who knocked turns to her and grins. "The future, lady … the future. Blue doors across the nation, across the world." Lolo turns and walks away. "Oh, god!"

The knocker turns back to Les. "Close the door a couple of minutes. We'll finish with the pictures, and I'll come in."

Les closes the door and stands with his back to it. What the hell!

Does the guy make doors? What if he wants a contract to make doors? What do I charge?

He rushes to the kitchen, reloads the coffee maker, and starts it. He returns to the living room but doesn't sit. He expects a knock at the door any second.

There's no knock. The door bursts open. The knocker enters. "Appreciate your patience, Mr. Warin."

"You know my name?"

"Hell, you were in the paper. Yeah, we know your name."

"We?"

The man sticks out his hand to shake Les's. "Merlin Paints and Industrial Sealants Incorporated. Name's Rusty Tanner."

Les hesitates. It's a reaction left over from the pandemic. He finally shakes. "Coffee?"

"Yeah … spoon of sugar. That'd be nice."

Les scoops sugar into a mug and fills it. He hands it to the man. "So, Mr. Tanner, your interest is in doors?"

Tanner almost gags. "What I said to the woman out there. Heck, doors are just a drop in the bucket … bucket? You get it? No pun intended. My company makes paint. We picture blue doors, blue window sashes, whole blue houses, blue roofs, whole town streets of blue facades, and blue signs. Can't you picture it? architects eating it up? A blue world ... all glowing with your blue paint. We'll blind the satellites."

"And can you make it ... make enough to do all you say?"

"You give us the formula and the process, and we will make it."

"I already have a contract with Mosaics."

"Mosaics? Hell, they're just a niche company ... no competition there. We'll buy them out if they give us a hard time."

Les tries to sound cunning. "And you'll pay me for this."

"Course. It's what we do."

"Have a seat, Mr. Tanner, and let's talk."

"Sure, sure."

They sit.

Les takes a sip of his coffee. It's cold. He tries not to make a face. "What do you propose?"

"Off the top of my head, I'm not quite ready. I'll have to check with senior management. What would you propose, Mr. Warin? Give me something to take back to headquarters."

To his horror, Les realizes that the ball is back in his court. He wings it. "Maybe five million."

Tanner gulps or pretends to. "Well, I'll take that back. Would you consider a cut of the sales price ... a commission per bucket?"

"Per gallon?"

Tanner smiles. "Per gallon ... yes, of course."

"You'll make a proposal."

"Certainly. Should we send it to your attorney as well as to you?"

"No, just to me."

Les thinks he sees a slightly quizzical, wraithlike look flicker in Tanner's eyes. "We'll do that." Tanner then rises, takes his mug to the kitchen, returns, and sticks out his hand. "It's been a pleasure, Mr. Warin."

Les shakes the hand, thinking, That's twice in one day … in one hour.

Tanner leaves, and Les closes the door behind the man.

Holding the knob, Les leans his forehead against the door and thinks, Lord, I need help. I need a lawyer. I need one badly.

Chapter Forty-Six

Les is flying high.

He had signed a contract with Merlin Paint and Industrial Sealants Incorporated for $500,000 plus five cents for every gallon of Blue-based paint sold. That required a lawyer. The man had been hard to find. Les had been bounced from attorney to attorney until he found one on K Street in Washington who claimed he could do what was needed. Les had had difficulty reconciling the attorney's fees with his own past life and the life he was entering. There was a time when it had taken six months to earn an equivalent amount of money. Finally, he had concluded he was flying at a new altitude. With a million dollars in the bank, a new visa in a pouch tied around his waist, and a new suitcase and briefcase, he flies to China. It is the first time he has ever left the eastern half of the United States. He lands at Pudong International Airport, a vast modern building on the China Sea east of Shanghai. He follows the passengers from his plane to get out of the building, hoping they are headed for baggage. He recognizes few signs. A Chivas Regal advertising sign and Starbucks shop make him feel that maybe he hasn't left completely the world he knows. The Chinese people swirling along with him or blocking his path are varied. Some are well dressed in suits. Many men are wearing black pants and white shirts. It seems to be a uniform. Many women wear baggier versions of the black pants. He also sees short skirts and jeans. What Les's father had called sneakers are prevalent. He almost stumbles over some men squatting by their suitcases along the side of the aisle. He wonders how they hold the position for more than a few minutes but don't move. In the baggage area, a man in the black pants and white shirt uniform is holding a sign with "Warin" on it. Les feels he has been rescued from an imaginary, distant world. He hurries to shake the man's hand with a great deal of smiling and happiness.

"Choi," the man says, pointing at himself.

"Choi," Les repeats, pointing at the man, and then says, "Warin," pointing at himself.

The man nods enthusiastically, grinning broadly, and then points at the luggage carousel. They soon have the luggage and go out the door where Choi gesticulates to tell Les to wait.

After an uncertain twenty minutes, as Les's blood pressure has climbed, a small white car pulls to the curb. Choi jumps out and puts Les's suitcase in the trunk. He then opens the back door of the car. Les shakes his head and points to the passenger seat. Reluctantly, Choi allows Les to take the seat and thus begins a long drive. When it is over, Les guesses they have driven at least a hundred miles. In the early going, Les sees the towering buildings of the Shanghai skyline in the distance and is saddened to not be able to really visit. Among the buildings, he sees a pointed tower that looks like two large balls crammed down on its spike. He concludes that he isn't into architecture.

They pass miles of low buildings. Downtime streets are crowded with signs hanging out from the front of buildings, people swarming, and cars inching by. In the country, he sees compounds, often with inverted u-shaped buildings within. Human beings are everywhere. Les sees children squatting and defecating along the streets and men urinating against buildings. He tries not to think about it.

They pull off the main highway and are suddenly in another world, wandering through narrow streets. Finally, they arrive at a building on a street of buildings larger than the houses they had been passing. Choi stops the car next to it, and Les gawks at the wide river behind the building covered with small boats. Many are parked on the edge of the river, and others are moving about busily.

There suddenly is a tap on the passenger window, and the door is opened. Charlie Huang greets him, introduces his brother Billy, and then points at the building. "Factory. Make Blue here."

Les nods and follows the Huang brothers. Fifteen or so men and a couple of women wearing black pants (a couple khaki) and white shirts are standing in the building gaping at Les. He wonders if they have ever seen a Caucasian man before.

Against one wall of the building, there are shelves, mostly empty, but some with what looks like shards of pottery. At the far end of the room are four large pieces of equipment that Les recognizes as centrifuges. He looks at Charlie. "The centrifuges look nice. Where did you get them?" Charlie grins. "From country you call Iran. They make good ones."

Les catches his breath. "We, er, I can't trade with them." Billy joins in, grinning. "We can."

Les looks around, consternated. "Where are the shaker tables?" Charlie points at some boards that appear to have handles along the edges. "Men shake."

Charlie stares at the boards in disbelief. "All day?"

"Men switch off."

Les shakes his head and inquires apprehensively, "And the furnaces?" He has been looking at some brick chimney structures with openings at the bases.

Billy and Charlie point where Les was looking. "Kiln from China factory."

Les is horror-struck. "How do you maintain temperature?" Charlie nods as if it were a reasonable question. "Men stand at each and measure temperature. Keep control."

"Have you tried it?"

"We wait for you."

***

Two days later, they had separated the first batch of Blue.

The next day at another pottery factory, Les signs another contract for the decoration of Chinese pottery and fine China with Blue.

He is on a roll. He asks what the name of the river is.

"Yangtze."

He finally decides he's seen enough. He'll skip visiting the building with the spiked balls and go home.

Chapter Forty-Seven

During his last night in China, Les stays at the Ramada Plaza at the Pudong Airport. He doesn't know one Shanghai hotel from another, but he feels that he recognizes the name.

He is relieved to be back in a place where he doesn't feel like he was staying in the middle of nowhere or a million miles from somewhere, depending on how you look at it. He is glad to breathe the filtered air, free from the coal-fired stoves easing a constant level of haze into the air. It has been a fantastic experience. He wonders if the process would work and thinks, So much for fine-tuned science.

He leaves his room to explore the hotel and soon finds himself standing at the entrance to the bar room. Oh, why the hell not? They've been a hectic few day.

He studies the bar where people of all nationalities are crammed shoulder to shoulder, speaking a million languages. He shudders at the thought of crowding in with strangers. He walks to the side of the bar. He sees a man sitting alone, with a drink seemingly held down to the table with one hand while he reads a paperback book with the other. The guy looks lonely … Doesn't have anything better to do but read a book in a bar. Wonder if he speaks English. What the hell, I'll ask him.

"Pardon me, may I join you at this table?"

The man looks startled and quickly looks around.

Les tries to read the man's thoughts. "Yeah, other tables are available, but I'd prefer not to sit and drink alone. And I'm not gay. Never been good at pickup lines anyway."

The man nods and motions to the other chair.

As Les moves to sit, he reaches across the table to shake the man's hand. "Les Warin." As they shake, the man locks on Les's eyes.

"American?"

"Guilty."

The man closes the paperback book. "Name's Berty Brin-Holland. English. Maybe we can communicate."

"Berty?"

The man smiles soberly. "As I said, I'm English."

"You don't have a strong accent."

"I've been living in the States for a bit, I have."

"Oh, where's that?"

"Washington."

"You're kidding. I live in Alexandria."

"Okay. While we're pinning it down, I live in Arlington, a high rise on the other side of the river."

"So you're just visiting China."

"Attending a conference, I was"

"Oh, what kind of conference?"

"Banking."

"You're a banker?"

"Not exactly. I work for the World Bank. Shuffle a lot of papers."

"Heck, it sounds important to me."

"Pays the bills. Let's me travel ... see the world."

"Must be exciting."

"Sometimes. What brings you to China, Mr. Warin?" "Les."

Berty nods. "Les it is. And I'm Berty. Born with it and live with it."

Les smiles. "Yes, well, I'm Leslie, and I don't live with it. But to answer your question, I'm in China fulfilling the requirements of a contract."

"Oh, who did you have to murder?"

"Not that kind of contract … much more mundane. I sold a patent right to a Chinese toy company so that they could use it to make plastic toy soldiers and souvenirs."

"A new kind of plastic?"

"No, the Chinese are experts on plastic. This is a color, a dye. They were setting up a factory to make it, and I was there to help and observe."

"Sounds fascinating."

"Certainly interesting. Quite an experience."

"And this was in Shanghai?"

"No, a little town named Changzhou, though it's hard to tell where one town ends and the next begins."

"Yeah, like any metro area, except this one's bigger than LA. Anyway, I never heard of it."

"It's on the Yangtze."

"Yes, 10 percent of the world probably lives on the Yangtze."

"From what I saw, I believe you."

"Aye, it's pretty near true."

Berty seems to think for a moment and then becomes inquisitive. "So what do they do with this dye?"

"They're going to mix it in the plastic … make toys that glow."

"Do they pay you for that?"

"Half a million dollars."

"Shit, that's brilliant."

"Does that mean it's good?"

"Yes. Bloody, yes. I hope you're stashing the money someplace."

"Should I be?"

"Mate, you're going to pay taxes. If you're getting it from China, hide it."

"Well, it's in an account I set up in Macau. That's where the toymaker has accounts. We transferred the money."

"That's good and not so good. Macau's no longer belongs to China. You should probably move your money out of there to the Caymans or somewhere."

"How do I do that?"

"Hey, I can help you. Give me a call when we get back to DC." Berty pulls his wallet from his back pocket, extracts a card from it, and passes it to Les. "You can find me there. How about your card?"

"I don't have any."

"Damn, some businessman you are."

He gave Les another of his cards. "Write your name and phone number on the back."

Les wonders if he should tell Berty about the other half million he had gotten for using the dye on pottery.

Berty is signaling for more drinks.

Nah, thinks Les, if I tell him that, there's no telling what I'll tell him next. Les cups his fingers around the new glass that Berty has bought, tapping two fingers against it. Should I pay taxes? Hell, I've never avoided them before. If Berty can help me move a half million, I ought to be able to move the other half million. I've got the money from Mosaic and Merlin. Hell, that will hold me while I decide.

***

The phone in the hotel rings at four thirty the next morning. Les fumbles for it, picks up the handpiece, and hears a mechanical voice telling him what time it is.

He squeezes his eyes shut and throws his hands hard against his forehead. Damn, damn, damn. It's time to get up to make my flight. He rolls on his side. Maybe I can sleep another half hour … skip breakfast.

He rolls back, face up, and presses his fist even harder against his head. Damn it, I've got to get up … get some tomato juice. Maybe they serve breakfast in the bar … get some vodka in juice … then add coffee.

Les is suddenly relieved that he had set up the wake-up call before going to the bar. God, sometimes my wisdom amazes me.

Les thinks about the evening. He vaguely remembers Bert guiding him to his room, telling him Les is his new best mate. He had helped Les get the door lock card in the slot, saying two hands were better than one. Les knows they had missed the key slot several times.

He wonders if Berty had gotten to his own room. Maybe the man is still walking the hallways. Perhaps he's back in the bar. Oh, no, I shouldn't have left him going off on his own, although he did seem to act like he knew where he was going.

Damn, the man could talk. They'd talked and talked and talked as they got drunker and drunker. God, what did I say? Hope I didn't tell him things I shouldn't have. Oh, goodness, what if I did? I shouldn't ever drink that much. Just needed to celebrate a million dollars, even if Berty only thought it was a half million. Hell, having a best mate might be a mistake.

***

At the United departure gate, Les finds Berty slumped in a seat, seemingly asleep. Les sits down beside him.

Berty opens an eye. "Don't say anything. Just get me on the damn plane."

Chapter Forty-Eight

Les sleeps most of three days after returning from China.

On the fourth day, there's a knock at the door. Les cringes as he slowly gets up from his club chair. He opens the door and finds Berty looking at the outside of the door, as if he has been scrutinizing it from inches away. "God, mate, is this the Blue? It really glows. A beam in the morning mist."

"Berty, what the hell?"

"It's Saturday, in case you don't know. Thought I'd make a visit to millionaire's row. Not much I can say for it. You need to move up. This is no place for any mate of mine to live."

"Well, the money has come pretty fast … fast and chaotic. And you won't let me get at the money in Macau." Les backs from the door. "You going to come in?"

Berty is rubbing his thumb over a spot in the door. "You've got a bad spot in the paint … a bit of crazing."

Les moves to the door and studies it. "Must have brushed it wrong. Come on in."

Berty enters the living room. "Blimey, even the furniture is tired."

"Does that mean shabby and worn out?"

"Didn't want to say that."

Berty brushes off a club chair with his handkerchief and sits. "Mate, you need a complete upgrade. From what you said in Shanghai, the Macau money I'm here to take care of is only part of the loot you've derived from your enterprising clients. I assume the remainder is residing peacefully in some bank account, easily accessed through government technology. You might as well acknowledge it to the world and pay the associated taxes. Having done that, you need to move on, establish a cache appropriate for a man of means."

"In other words, you want me to move, physically and monetarily."

"Expeditiously, mate ... as in the next few days."

"And replace the furniture too?"

"With my help, yes, but the apartment comes first ... even before you have those engraved business cards ordered ... After all, the address must have something important to say."

"Lord, how did you remember what was said in Shanghai?"

"There's a layer of my brain that's pervious to all in its environment."

"Yeah? Well, I'm impressed, but it's even better than you know. I just got an email from Merlin Paints saying Ford Motors has contracted with the company to buy paint to create a special Blue edition of the Mustang. I get ten cents a gallon. How many gallons do you think it takes to paint a Mustang?"

Berty laughs. "Do they pay you in dimes? You'll need more storage. The new place is going to have to be large."

"With a secret elevator so I can sneak in my lab equipment."

"Hey, can't you give that up now?"

"I don't know. It's part of my veneer. I won't feel the same without it." Berty gets up from his chair and clamps Les on the shoulder. "Have I gotten you worked up, mate? So excited you can't even offer me a cup of coffee."

"Gosh, I'm sorry. You come in like a tempest ... bigger than in a teapot. Don't you want tea? I can make it."

"No, coffee, please. I've been on this side of the pond too long."

"I'll have it for you in a minute."

"Brilliant. Connecticut Avenue is next."

Chapter Forty-Nine

Cathy has moved on. She seldom thinks about Les—only occasionally at how disappointed she had been in him, how she had wasted years of her life with him, and how she had wasted years of her beauty.

She seldom thinks about the hotel—how the job had been so much beneath her and how it had been more of a waste of her time.

She thinks even less about Billy Covington. He had abused her. He wasn't worth thinking about. Therefore, she didn't. He was just a blip in the timeline of her life. She never thinks of it as murder.

What she does think about is her position in her new life. She enjoys enormously being wealthy and reveling in all its benefits. She enjoys being waited on. She enjoys buying the clothing without a thought of cost. She enjoys the banquets, the fundraisers, and the whole whirl of activities in the new society in which she lives. Most of all, she enjoys being admired not just by hotel guests or the man in the street but by men of wealth and power.

The only thing that is not good is her relationship with her mother-in-law, Suzanne Mallet. Her father-in-law, Richard Mallet, is seldom seen. When she is with him, she might as well not be. Cathy knows he has dismissed her as unimportant, a wisp of smoke he'd like the wind to carry away.

Suzanne is different. Her hatred of Cathy is palpable. In society, she ignores Cathy, even turning her back on the younger woman in social situations, pointedly excluding Cathy whenever she can.

Cathy knows she's viewed as an interloper, a gold digger, an inferior. She knows Suzanne despises her beauty, hates that she is so middle-class, and hates that she worked in a hotel.

Cathy realizes that Suzanne wanted to find Etienne's wife, organize a grand wedding, and put on a display for society. But she had talked Etienne into a marriage in city hall, and he had only given his parents an hour's notice. Cathy accepts that she deserves to be hated. She also knows that her husband feels ashamed for having wilted before her wants and demands. As a result, she knows her marriage will always experience a certain vacuum, an uncertainty as to its reality.

***

When the phone rings, Cathy's alone, working on her nails, fixing a hangnail the manicurist has messed up, and thinking she's going to get someone new. She picks up the phone, being careful not to damage her nails.

"Hello."

"Cathy?"

"Les?"

"Hi, Cathy, how are you?"

Cathy thinks, God, such a lack of imagination. Same-o, same-o. "I'm well, thank you."

"Living the good life, I would suspect."

"Is that sarcasm, Les? Yes, it's not bad."

"Sarcasm? Oh, hell no. Just wishing things are going well for you."

Okay, play nice. "What can I do for you, Les?"

"Right, I'm fine, Cathy. Thanks for asking."

"Now, you are being sarcastic."

"Right, I am."

"So why'd you call? You didn't miss my voice."

"Your voice? No. Maybe, sometimes your body, but not your voice."

"Cut the shit, Les. What's this about?"

"The furniture."

"The furniture? What about it?"

"Do you want it?"

"Want it? The furniture in the apartment? Hell, no, I don't want it. What would I do with it?"

"Hell, I don't know. Just wanted to check before I throw it out."

"You're going to throw it out?"

"If you don't want it, yes. It's pretty shot."

"It was shot before I moved out."

"So you don't want it."

"God, no."

"That's all I wanted to know. The divorce papers said you had a claim on it."

"Well, I don't want it."

"All my best, Cathy."

Cathy starts to say goodbye, but the dial tone has come on.

She holds the phone and considers the voice she had just heard.

What the heck was that all about? Who'd want that old furniture? She hadn't thought about it since moving in with Etienne. She guessed she had assumed Les would use it forever. Now he's getting rid of it—all of it at once. What the hell does that mean? He doesn't need it anymore. Why would that be? Christ, what would that mean? Did someone pay him for Blue? Interesting. I'll have to learn more.

Chapter Fifty

Les hangs up the phone. He shivers with a sense of trepidation. He had recorded the phone call. Now he is off the hook. It was the only requirement for the divorce that remained. Still, he wonders if it would have ever been an issue. After all, Cathy had moved beyond any need for the old furniture. He doubted if she had ever thought about it.

Nonetheless, he wants to be clear of Cathy. But, by contacting her, he wonders if he would reignite something in their relationship. He would have preferred not to have contacted her at all.

While he has the phone in his hand, he dials a junk removal company. They advertise they work to midnight, but that isn't necessary. They say they'll be by later in the afternoon.

He leans back in his club chair. He pats the arm. "You've done good, old girl. You got me through the rough times." He gets up. Time to move the lab.

Les has decided to move it himself. He wants to be inconspicuous. He's afraid his new neighbors might think he is setting up a meth lab, making pipe bombs or whatever they worry about these days.

He's gathered a lot of cardboard boxes the equipment can be packed in. Only the furnace doesn't fit. He hopes people wouldn't know what it is. He'll have to take it in on a hand truck. He figures he'll cover it in a packing blanket so the controls and door will be hidden.

He and Berty had shopped for a new car the day before—an SUV. Berty hadn't been sure about it. He complained it was too pedestrian for a man of means, but Les had argued that he still had to move the lab and needed the space. Now, it's parked in front of the old apartment, loaded with boxes, and ready for Les to get on with his move.

The phone rings as Les stands in the doorway to the lab room, deciding what to do first. He returns to the living room and picks up the phone. "Les Warin."

"Good morning, Mr. Warin. Can you be here at three tomorrow afternoon?"

"Is that you JoJo?"

"Please. Joseph L. DeSilvo, Esquire."

"Right, you've moved up in the world since you became my attorney, slash agent, getting the big commissions."

"I've got you rolling, Les."

"Glad you can take credit for it."

"Well, before you put me down, let me tell you I've got a big one."

"At three o'clock tomorrow. Can't you do it earlier?"

"She doesn't wake up till midday."

"Who's that?"

"Della B."

"B's the last name."

"Nah, the letter B."

"Some entertainer or something?"

"You been living under a rock, Les? Yeah, she's a singer. Hip hop, I think. Not the station I listen to, but she's big."

"Somebody named Delores Broomwicz, who's shortened her name?"

"Don't know her real name, but yeah, probably a shortened name. It's the thing. Adele, Beyonce, etc., etc."

"What does she want?"

"She wants to be blue."

"Blue? Like what?"

"Like blue lips, fingernails, toenails, eyeliner, the works. As long as it glows."

"A cosmetic line?"

"You got it."

"I don't make cosmetics."

"We'll find someone who does."

"I've never put Blue on people."

"Yeah, what are mice for?"

"Damn, JoJo. It might kill them."

"Not your problem, boss. Just be here at three, or better yet, ten of."

Chapter Fifty-One

Les parks a block from DeSilvo's office.

It annoys him that the office building doesn't have its own garage. After all, it has a grand marble lobby with a beautiful receptionist behind a marble reception desk, elevators with actual wood paneling, and elegant carpeting on all floors. Besides that, DeSilvo is inexpensive. He can't use the word cheap. That's a word that can't be used with regard to the building, not to most buildings of K Street.

Les exits the elevator on the eighth floor and heads for DeSilvo's office suite. He hesitates his step when he sees a large black man in suit standing outside the attorney's entrance door.

Maybe "large" isn't the correct word. "Huge" is more like it.

Les approaches the door with foreboding.

The man steps in front of the door and faces Les. "May I ask your name and business."

At least for a thug, he's articulate. "I have an appointment with Mr. DeSilvo."

"Yeah, are you the blue man?"

Les gulps. "Yes, you might say that."

"Turn around."

"What?"

"Turn around."

Les draws in his breath and turns around. He feels large hands reach around and pat his chest. Then they run across his waist, around his back, and finally down his legs. Jesus, who does this guy think I am?

The man takes Les's shoulders and gently turns him toward the door. "You're clean."

Les gives the man an incredulous look. "My god, you think I might have a gun? I don't even own a gun."

The man gives Les an equally incredulous look and turns away from him.

Les opens the door, enters the suite, and is met by DeSilvo's secretary sitting behind her desk.

"You get a good frisking, Mr. Warin?"

"I think the term is 'pat-down.'"

"Yeah, we haven't had anything like this since JoJo had a mafia soldier as a client a couple of years ago."

"For real?"

"Yeah, for real."

"What do I call you today? Nancy D."

"Ha, no. The same old Nancy Dunning. But watch it. They might hear you."

"Where are they?"

"Conference room down the hallway."

She points toward the hallway, although it's the only hallway they have."

"Thank you." Les heads down the hallway. At the entrance to the conference room, he knocks on the door frame and finds four pairs of eyes looking up at him. DeSilvo is on the far side of the table. Les does a bit of a double take. In DeSilvo's usual place at the head of the table sits a black woman—pretty? handsome? No, maybe exotic. She's not light-skinned like many black entertainers. She hasn't got the narrow celebrity nose or the thin lips, but she is a presence. She emits power beneath a vast Afro. Clearly, she belongs at the head of the table.

DeSilvo stands. "Hey, Les, welcome. Let me introduce you." He turns toward the woman and extends a hand. "Les Warin, this is Della B. You know, My Crazy Love." With that, DeSilvo sings a few words and makes some dance moves with his arms. "My crazy love is steaming hot and moist." Then he stops and looks slightly abashed. "Della's why we're here today … to build on her ideas … ideas she'll turn into reality through her appearances. Tell us about it, Della B."

Della B stretches her ample chest. Les hasn't noticed before when she is sitting slightly slumped. He looks quickly back up to her face as she speaks, addressing Les, "I bought myself one of those blue Mustangs, actually, two. One for Los Angeles and one for Connecticut. The other day, I was sitting in the LA Mustang thinking, wouldn't this blue look good on me … give me a hell of a presence on stage … People could see it from the back row … lipstick, eyeliner, eye shadow, paste-on eyebrows, the works. I found out who your agent was … He's advertising it on the internet … and gave him a call. He had a good idea … make jewelry too … drop earrings and broaches. Make it all as the Della B Bleu Glo Cosmetic and Jewelry lines. And why not a fabric line too … dresses, slacks, blouses, bolero tops, etc. Can't you see girls at their senior proms whirling in glowing blue. I just thought of that … should have brought in a clothing designer today. But we'll start with what we have. Let me introduce Vincent Raby of Vincent Cosmetics and Georgina Makoff, a ceramist. Georgina makes lovely ceramic jewelry. We've already started talking before you got here. Vincent and Georgina are both in … ready to go to work."

During the speech, Les stands with his mouth open. Now, he hurries to shake Raby's and Makoff's hands, thinking, I've never heard the word ceramist before. He guesses it's self-explanatory.

Makoff speaks up, "This is exciting for me. I can think of all kinds of jewelry piercings noses, eyebrows, tongues, belly buttons, nipples … the whole thing."

Les gulps. "Nipple piercings?"

Makoff nods. "Babe, if it can be pierced, it gets pierced."

Della B gives a belly laugh. "Go at it, girls. Not guaranteeing I'll wear them. Sure as hell I'm not going to do endorsements of nipple piercings on TV, though it would really be something to see."

DeSilvo has sat back down. He looks at Les. "Sit down, Les. I guess this has come on fast. You're still standing."

Les pulls out a chair and sits. "Yes, it has. What's next?"

DeSilvo smiles. "You in on it, Les?"

"Sure. As long as it's tested."

Raby interjects, "Hey, don't expect this to be instant. As Les says, we'll have to do some testing." He looks at Les. "Has this material ever been used on people, applied to the skin, or ingested?"

Les shakes his head. "No."

"That's what I thought. In my business, there's liability associated with cosmetics. We need to do some testing."

DeSilvo nods. "Yeah, yeah. We understand that, but it needs to be done quickly. Della B needs it. She didn't come up with the idea for nothing."

Della B agrees, "This needs to happen. How long will it take to get lines out?"

Raby looks uncomfortable. "Well, we've got to be safe." He turns to Della B. "And you don't want to be associated with something with health issues."

Della B agrees, "Shit, no. How long is it going to take?"

"I don't know. I need to talk to my chemists. We'll do it as fast as we can."

Makoff interrupts, "We can do the jewelry right away. Get it on the market in a couple of weeks."

DeSilvo chuckles. "Tits glowing in two weeks—a major breakthrough."

Les shakes his head. "Don't know how you'd advertise it."

Makoff laughs. "I can assure you I know the ways."

"Women really do it."

"Men too. It's an equal opportunity world." Les frowns. "Damn."

DeSilvo concludes. "It's enterprise, Les. It's making money."

"So, as I asked, what's next?"

"I meet with Vincent, Georgina, and/or their representatives to negotiate a contract and then send it to you for comments and/or approval."

"And/or what about Della B?"

Della B breaks in, "That's got nothing to do with you. I'll work it out with Vincent and Georgina. They're the ones making the stuff."

"They'll pay you for the endorsement?"

"Hey, that's between them and me."

Les turns to DeSilvo. "Will you look into a clothing line?"

DeSilvo grins. "Absolutely. Maybe Della B will give me a little help. Maybe give more three endorsements."

Della B exclaims, "I'm with you … know exactly what to do."

Les frowns in thought. "And wallpaper, plastic boats, swimming rafts, bikinis, swimming pools, gym equipment, appliances … "

DeSilvo laughs happily. "Toilets, bathtubs, toilet paper, paper plates, napkins, greeting cards—hell, anything you can think of."

Les joins the laughter. "Do it."

Chapter Fifty-Two

Three months later, Cathy is sitting under the dryer at Antoine's Salon reading a copy of Glamour, scanning the new products. Her eye catches a swath of blue and realizes it is supposed to represent a swipe of lipstick. She scans the associated blurb: "New cosmetic scheduled for spring release, a product of Vincent Cosmetics, endorsed by Della B Della B's Bleu Glo: Lipstick that glows; Company talking about a complete line of products."

She looks at the blue stroke of the page. It doesn't glow, but the product isn't out yet. Uh-oh, could this be Blue? Les Warin's Blue? Has the SOB actually produced something? Who the hell is Della B?

She pulls her head out from under the dryer, ruffles her hair with her hands, and concludes it's dry enough. She heads for the chair where her hairdresser is waiting. As she sits, she asks, "Emil, who the heck is Della B?"

"The singer?"

"I guess."

"Lady, you're not hip."

"Damn, Emil, I thought hip was out of another age."

Emil scurries across the room to the magazine rack and returns with a well-used copy of People. He hands it to Cathy. "Maybe I should have said up to date, or whatever."

Cathy starts to open the magazine, but Emil's hand reaches out and stops her. "No, no ... the cover."

Cathy looks at the cover—a black woman, full body shot, and white slacks.

Cathy's mind reals. God, her legs are longer than mine. And her breasts, Lord, way beyond decent … ugly … lewd … way beyond what's reasonable for beauty … God, I'd never. She shakes her head. Les Warin and this woman … what the hell … how could that happen?

Emil is talking as he approaches her with a comb. "Something, huh?"

Cathy nods. "Yeah, something."

"What's your interest?"

"Uh, saw her name in the magazine I was reading."

"Yeah, she's pretty much everywhere."

Emil hands her a card with her next appointment written on it. She glances at the card: Antoine's Salon.

Cathy chuckles. She knows his real name is Tony aka Anthony Castiglia. She wonders what Emil's real name is. It's all about image. Is Les Warin creating an image? Shit, it's going to be something … famous? … infamous? … tarnished? Who knows?

In her mind, as she leaves the salon, she pictures opening a copy of People to its middle section and seeing a two-page spread of Les Warin applying a glowing blue lipstick to the lips of Della B, in all her glory while wearing a low-cut gown.

With these thoughts going through her mind, Cathy turns the corner into the salon's parking lot and is slow to register what she sees. Parked behind her Mercedes, blocking its exit, is a Mustang—a bright blue Mustang, a glowing blue Mustang.

She looks through the open passenger window. There are keys and a note on the seat. She doesn't need to read the note. "That fucking bastard!"

PART TWO

The Dream Is Stolen

Chapter Fifty-Three

Cathy hadn't thought about Les in a while. Yet she knew right away where the car had come from. I gave that man some of the best years of my life, and he produced nothing. Now he's throwing it in my face. Well, fuck him.

Still, she thinks the car is kind of cute—a convertible, glowing blue with a white top. She can see herself driving it. But how the hell do I explain it to Etienne. It's not as if I have enough money in my bank account to buy a car. Besides, he's already given me a Mercedes. It'd be hard to claim that I need a new ride. And besides, I couldn't park it in the underground garage … we're already using our two spaces. Maybe I could park it out on the street. Nah, it's too conspicuous. Someone would see me getting into it, and they might ask Etienne about it. Tell Etienne it's a gift from my ex-husband? Shit, that would be a laugh. He doesn't even know I have an ex-husband.

Cathy gets in the car, looks at the keys lying on the set, and pushes the ignition button. She feels the car start and then almost nothing. The dashboard says it's running. Damn, it must be electric.

She puts it in drive and exits the parking lot. CARMAX, here I come. Wonder how much you'll discount it for ten miles? What'll I do with the money? I'll open my own bank account. It'll be nice to have money that Etienne doesn't know about. For special purchases, I won't have to use his credit card. Thanks, Les. At least I got a little out of you.

But, now that I know you're making money, I'm going to get more. But how do I do it? How do I tell Etienne that Les discovered Blue while working in a Mallet Lab? How the hell would I explain how I know that? And how do I explain I haven't said anything before? How do I explain that his virgin wife had a life before?

She takes a detour before going to CARMAX. She drives to downtown Alexandria. She parks on Queen Street in front of the public library, the Kate Waller Barrett Public Library. Her mind tries to picture Kate Waller Barrett—an elderly, gray-headed woman, hair in a bun on top of her head, rimless glasses. Cathy shakes the image from her mind. For all I know, she was a babe. Why the hell can't a librarian be good-looking?

She gets out of the car, having trouble getting out of the low seat in her high heels. She crosses the street, enters the library, and looks around. When was the last time I was in a library? College? Yeah, senior year at Illinois State. I don't need them. If I want to read a book, I buy it.

She goes to the desk and asks where she can find the computers. In the computer room, people are waiting. She stands behind a man who is just sitting down at a machine. As he logs on, she reads over his shoulder.

She smiles in satisfaction. Mr. Seagraves, you're my man. You just became an expert on personal and secret discoveries at the laboratories of Mallet Pharmaceuticals.

Chapter Fifty-Four

"Mate, are you daft?"

Berty sits at the kitchen counter in Les's new apartment off Connecticut Avenue, drinking a beer. His face is red. "You just got on a roll. You're about to make the world blue. All you need to do is sign the contracts and bank the money. And you go and do this."

"It was too much of a temptation."

"Bollocks. You've screwed up. You don't mess with an ex-wife, especially one who's married a fortune. I didn't know you'd been married. I didn't know there was an ex out there who could drain your money."

"She doesn't need my money."

"Hell, no one has enough money. The more you have, the more you want. And an ex-wife … there's no one more vicious, more brutal. You don't try to stick it to them. Shove it in their faces. They don't take it well, especially after you've made promises. The damn woman's going to want her share."

"She hasn't got a share. She bailed out. She didn't have faith."

"She hasn't got the money either. She's going to want it. She'll claim you owe it to her. She'll say she stuck with you, shared your bed, did for you, and you didn't do what you said."

"You think she's going to sue me?"

"Maybe, but I doubt it. It might be too messy. Ex-wives can connive. What's she got on you?"

"What … er … nothing."

"You don't sound sure."

Thoughts of Godfrey whirl through Les's mind. No, she wouldn't do that. She's too complicit. Besides, she doesn't know where he's buried.

"Hey, mate, where's your mind? You've got a problem here. With ex-wives, you say yes ma'am, no ma'am, thank you ma'am. Otherwise, they'll stuff their years of loyalty and sacrifice down your gullet."

"I don't think she will. She married a fortune … is living the high life. She won't want to screw it up."

"Well, I'm telling you, mate, I'd watch my back. I would."

With that, Berty slides off his stool, goes to the refrigerator, and gets another beer. As he does so, he glances down the hallway that leads to the bedrooms. "Why do you have a door leaning against the wall in the hallway?"

"Get me another beer too."

Berty returns to his stool carrying two beers. "And the door?"

"It's the one from the apartment in Alexandria."

"Aye, I can tell that by the color."

"I switched the door out and replaced it."

"Yeah, you had to do that, or it wouldn't be in your hallway."

"Right."

"I'm observant that way."

"Right, I'm going to study it when I get time."

"Study it?"

"The crazing you noticed."

"Yeah … bad brushwork."

"Maybe."

"Maybe? What are you talking about?"

"Maybe the paint is changing."

"Changing?"

"To glow, it has to change … give off energy."

"Like it's radioactive."

"Not quite the same, not nuclear, but something like that."

"What does it change into?"

"That's the question."

Chapter Fifty-Five

Les has put off thinking about the door, but Berty has jolted his mind back to thinking about it. Unfortunately, he only has a rather rudimentary microscope and none of the sophisticated equipment he had had at Mallet Pharmaceuticals. Still, he wishes to study the material in the door as best he can,

He carefully scrapes the paint into a Petri dish. He then scrapes the paint from another part of the door. He visually compares the two dishes. The Blue from the defective part of the door appears to glow less brightly.

He then scrapes away some of the wood from under the paint that appears to have lost its texture, much like Les would have expected from wood that has suffered dry rot. The softened wood is as blue as the paint but much duller. He wonders if the wood is blue because it has absorbed the paint or if the paint has chemically reacted with the wood. To Les, the latter seems possible because it appears the polymers, the cellulose, and other polymers in the wood have had their chains broken, thus producing the apparent deterioration of the wood.

He contemplates the last thought. Could the molecules of Blue interact with other organic materials when it undergoes their transformation? He knows Blue can undergo transformations by itself without interacting with other materials because he has observed it in his pint jars.

Gosh, he thinks, if it interacts with other organic compounds, there could be major problems. Paints have latex and acrylics, eye shadow has preservatives, lipstick has wax and oils ... even plastics are organic polymers. His mind pictures plastic soldiers disintegrating into blue powder. If Blue interacts with organic materials, he hopes it's not all organics, but he doesn't know.

From his past studies, he knows that Blue by itself has a half-life in excess of twenty years, which seems reasonable for most modern products. He asks himself, Is the half-life shorter for interactions with other organic compounds? Is that why the door is already showing signs of deterioration? And what does all this mean to me? I need to know. I need to experiment. I need to lay out a plan.

***

Over the next few days, Les sets up a series of experiments he can do without sophisticated lab equipment.

He spreads Petri dishes over his dining room table. Into each, he pours or places common organic materials—alcohols, benzene, oils, waxes, plastics, wood, stalks, sugars, organic cloth to include nylon, wool, cotton, metals, marble, granite, quartz, plexiglass, glass, latex rubber, etc. He spreads a layer of Blue over each.

As an investment, Les purchases a light meter and a Styrofoam box. On the bottom of the box, he cuts out a hole so that the box can fit over a Petri dish. On the inside of the top of the box, he fastens the light detector that came with the meter. He runs its wire out a notch on the edge of the top, which fits over a similar notch in the box. With this device, he measures the light being generated by Blue. He knows that the amount of it in each Petri dish is different. He is not interested in comparing dishes. He is only interested in following each dish over time to see how the light changes.

In a log, he writes down Day 1, and under that, he writes the measurement on the meter of each Petri dish.

It will take time, but if there are changes, he might see them. He knows from the wood in his door that there might have been a significant change in a little over a year. If he observes his experiments carefully, what will he see?

Then he thinks about skin, and he buys a rat.

Chapter Fifty-Six

Cathy lounges in the living room of her apartment, reading Janet Evanovich's Fortune and Glory. She can't imagine being someone like the book's character, Stephanie Plum. I'm too beautiful, too sophisticated. Still, Stephanie seems to have fun. I guess some people think that's what life's about. Heck, I have almost as many escapades as Stephanie. I just can't write about them.

Cathy had gotten the book out at the library when she went there to work on the computer. She had to open an account to do it. She shoved the library card behind her credit cards. She wasn't sure why. She will never use it and will never go back to the library. She will send the book back with the maid.

Etienne comes out of the den holding a sheet of paper. "Hey, listen to this."

Cathy feigns innocence. "Oh, what ya got there?"

"A strange email. Anonymous."

Cathy looks alarmed. "Something threatening?"

"No, no, not at all. It's someone who wants to give me a heads-up."

"Yeah, about what?"

"It says there's a man I should know about. His name is Leslie Warin, and he's marketing a dye he discovered named Blue, with a capital B." Cathy wants to make it sound important. "Yeah, I've heard of him. They put the dye in paint. Use it on Ford Mustangs. Makes the cars glow."

"Oh, is that what that is? I've seen a couple of them."

"They're putting it in other things too … toys and the like, even some eyeglass frames coming from China. I hear it's the next big thing."

"No kidding?"

"Yeah, it's in all the magazines."

"I haven't seen it in The Wall Street Journal or Forbes."

"Well, I expect Forbes is behind People by a few weeks."

"You read about it in People?"

Cathy tries not to be too excited. "Yeah, Della B is working with a cosmetic company to get it out in all kinds of makeup products."

"Della B?"

"The singer."

"Oh, what does she sing?"

"Hip hop."

"Oh." Etienne's mind turns back to the email. "Anyway, it says the guy worked in our lab. It says he discovered this Blue there."

"You don't say. That means Mallet should own the patent. If it was discovered in your lab, it's yours."

"Yeah, but we don't make paint and cosmetics."

"So what, you can license other people to do it. I bet that's what this guy Warin is doing. Heck, Etienne, this guy is raking in money that should be yours."

"Yeah, I need to talk to Dad about this."

"Make sure you tell him how I pointed out the importance of this both to him and your mother." Etienne smirks. "You're taking credit?"

"Points for you and me both. It won't hurt."

Etienne turns and walks back into the den. Cathy hears him picking up his phone.

She opens her book back up while she thinks, Okay, Mr. Warin, you don't see it coming, but you're about to be screwed.

Chapter Fifty-Seven

Les is having a morning of relaxation, reading the newspaper more carefully than usual and working on his third mug of coffee when the phone rings.

He walks to the kitchen, sets his coffee on the counter, and picks up the phone. "Les Warin," a serious woman's voice inquires. "Mr. Leslie Warin?"

For no apparent reason, Les feels a sense of disquiet. "Yes, speaking, may I help you?"

"Yes, let me transfer you to Mr. Bourdeaux."

There's a moment of clicking on the phone. Then a deep man's voice comes on. "Mr. Warin?"

"Yes?"

"This is Andrew Bourdeaux."

"Yes, may I help you?"

"Yes, I think you can. I represent the firm of Tibbets, Bourdeaux, and Fincham."

Les gulps. "Is that a law firm?"

"Yes."

"And you're one of the partners?"

"Yes."

"So this must be important?"

"Yes, for both of us, Mr. Warin."

Les doesn't want to talk anymore.

The man's voice continues, "Are you there, Mr. Warin?"

"Yes."

Are you the same Les Warin who graduated with a degree in chemistry from Purdue University and, following graduation, worked for Mallet Pharmaceuticals?"

Les hesitates. "Yes, I did."

"And are you the Les Warin who patented a blue dye called Blue 322?"

Again, Les is silent.

"Mr. Warin?"

"Uh, maybe you should be speaking to my lawyer?"

"Your attorney, Mr. Warin?"

"Y-yes. My attorney."

"Yes, I can do that. What is your attorney's name?"

"Er, Joseph L. DeSilvo"

"Joe DeSilvo?"

Les can almost hear the sneer in Bourdeaux's voice. "Yes."
"Fine. I'll look forward to talking to Mr. DeSilvo."

Les is beginning to panic. "Are you going to phone him right now?"

Les hears a chuckle on the phone. "Would you like me to give you some time, Mr. Warin?"

"If you wouldn't mind."

"Of course, Mr. Warin. I'll wait until after lunch."

"Yeah, okay." Les is almost breathless. "Have a good day, Mr. Warin."

"Yes and—" Les realizes Bourdeaux has hung up.

Les hangs up the phone. "Damn, he's connected me with Blue and Mallet Pharmaceuticals," he barks aloud. This isn't good! It's not good at all! How the hell? Cathy! That damn Cathy!

He picks up his coffee mug and slams it on the counter. Stupefied, he finds himself holding the finger grip from the mug, as the rest of the mug rolls off the counter onto the floor, and coffee begins to run off the counter. For a moment, he stares at it as if it is happening in another world.

Then he turns and hurls the finger grip into the sink. He leans on the counter and breathes hard. He picks the phone back up and reaches to dial but then realizes he doesn't know DeSilvo's phone number.

He hangs the phone back up, goes to the living room, and picks up his cell phone. DeSilvo's number is listed there, and he touches his finger to it, far harder than the phone needs, as if it could tell the difference.

Desilvo's secretary answers, "This is the office of Joseph L. DeSilvo, Attorney at Law. How may I—"

"Nancy, get JoJo on the line."

"No Nancy D this morning, Mr. Warin?"

"This is serious, Nancy. Get JoJo on the damn line!"

"I'm sorry, Mr. Warin. He presently has a client in his office. May I have him return your call?"

"Nancy, this is a damn emergency. I need to talk to him before lunch. Do not let him get away! If you do, we may both be screwed."

Chapter Fifty-Eight

Les and Berty are sitting at the table by the window of a restaurant near Dupont Circle.

Les sighs. "It's a real mess, Berty."

"Blimey, I'm having trouble getting my arms around this. Can't DeSilvo sort this out?"

"DeSilvo's a mental wreck. His commissions are in the wind, just as is my money." Then Les's mind seems to wander as he looks out the window. "Do you guys really say blimey?"

"What? Yeah, sometimes when it seems appropriate."

"And now it does?"

Berty nods. "It seems proper."

Berty is staring at Les in amazement. "First, you tell me you were married when you committed that Mustang cock up … married to a beauty, no less … and now you think she screwed you. I mean, mate, this is all out of nowhere."

"I thought I was free. I thought the divorce settled things forever."

"Hey, you gave her the Mustang. What were you thinking?"

"I thought she'd be impressed."

Berty throws up his hands. "Mate, mate, you were sticking it to her. Now she's sticking it to you."

"Yeah, big time. She's going to take all my money and add it to her money pot. It probably won't even take much room in the pot, but it will put me out of my apartment. Who knows where I'll live?"

"What about the money in the Caymans? Isn't that safe?"

"Man, when the Chinese sell glowing soldiers and lamps in the States, her lawyers will know something is wrong."

"And Mallet's case is solid? You really were working for them when you discovered this stuff?"

"Yeah, kind of."

"Kind of?"

"Yeah, the stuff was a waste. I was about to throw it away."

"Do you have pictures of it in the trash?"

"No, of course not."

"You carried it out of the place?"

"Well, yeah. But no one saw me. No one knows it."

"Except this beautiful ex-wife of yours."

Les sighs deeply and twists a crick out of his neck. "Her word against mine."

"And a big-name law firm against JoJo DeSilvo."

Les moans. "Yeah, yeah, JoJo," he groans. "Don't remind me."

"Don't need to. This Boudreaux guy will take care of that."

"Look, JoJo has his own money involved with this. He's bound to try."

"Yeah, he'll settle and bill you to assuage his feelings."

"You can't get blood from a beet."

"Turnip, Les. Turnip, and whoever said that ended up giving the real vegetable a pummeling."

"Christ, Berty, you're a big help."

"Wish I could sort it for you, mate, but things don't look good."

Chapter Fifty-Nine

As Les drives out of the underground garage for the last time, he wonders if the building management is busy deleting his PIN. His leaving the apartment is sad but necessary. He has been lucky. The management people have found a new tenant and have only charged him one month's rent for early lease termination.

Even that could have been a disaster because his bank accounts have been frozen due to his being sued by Mallet.

He's beginning to understand the plight of homeless people. He doesn't know what he'd do if it were not for the money in the Cayman Islands.

Still, he's concerned about spending too much of that money. He worries that Mallet will find out about that money and make him pay it back. He thinks, I'll worry about that later.

He drives across the Potomac River and follows Interstate 66 west. He's found a one-bedroom apartment off U.S. 50 in Fairfax. His old apartment had been too expensive to rent in his current world of uncertainty.

His furniture is piled in the tiny space. He can hardly open the door. Some will have to go. All his lab equipment is in a storage bin. It's hard for him to contemplate continuing to work on Blue or anything else.

Les worries that the suit will follow him all his life, keep him from ever getting a job as a chemist again. His future doesn't look bright.

He wonders if his mattress selling job is still available. He'll check tomorrow.

How long will a million dollars last?

Chapter Sixty

Cathy returns home from her Pilates studio and parks her Mercedes in the garage beneath her apartment. Each time she does, she's miffed. This damned, damp, and ugly place. Seems like they could have done better with these high-priced, luxury apartments. I'm tired of parking in this place. Etienne's parents live in a big house with a curved driveway in front and a three-car garage. Why the hell don't we? The SOB's just lazy ... doesn't want to deal with a house, with maintenance, with grounds, with gardens, with grass ... shit, most of all with grass. Why the hell does he worry about that? Does he think he's going to mow the damn place? That's what you hire people for.

Still fretting, she takes the elevator to the fifth floor. She gets out and approaches her apartment door, taking her keys from her pocketbook. Gee, we should at least have a private elevator with none of this access key stuff. If we're going to live in an apartment, it should at least be luxurious. It should fit our importance as Mallet heirs.

She enters the apartment and finds Etienne sitting in a club chair in the living room, an old-fashioned glass in his hand. Startled, she blurts, "What the hell? It's three in the afternoon. What are you doing here?" Etienne raises his glass in greeting. "Among other things, I live here. Further, I'm celebrating. Get yourself a drink, and we'll toast."

"Toast? Toast to what?"

"To our settlement with Les Warin ... a real triumph for me."

"For you?"

"Yes, I'm the one who figured out the guy had stolen from us."

"And I told you to pursue it."

Etienne raises his glass again. "And you know I appreciate your support. We're a team."

"Shit, Etienne, you lucked out with that anonymous email, and without me, you'd have just sat on it."

"Hey, what I did, I did. I made the whole thing work. Don't be a killjoy."

"Damn, Etienne. You never give me credit. And what do you mean by settlement? Didn't you take this guy Warin for all he's worth?"

"Hell, babe, we're a team. We get the credit together. And, yeah, settlement. Suing people costs money. Boudreaux is practically ten dollars a minute. And this Warin has almost nothing. We'd kill him in a suit. The poor guy knows it, and he just caved."

"Of course, he caved. He knew he'd lose."

"Not as I understand it. Boudreaux says our case is weak as hell."

"Weak? What the hell does that mean? You have an email saying he developed this Blue stuff at your lab."

"An anonymous email."

"Yeah, what else do you need?"

"Witnesses."

Oh, shit, Cathy thinks, I'm the only damned witness. I'd have to say I was married to the dolt.

"Aren't there records of what he did at the lab?"

"Sure, but none of the things he produced was a blue dye."

"Uh, what if it was a byproduct?"

"Well, that probably wouldn't have been listed in the reports."

"But it is possible?"

"Yeah, I guess. But the guy didn't patent the dye until long after he left Mallet."

"That doesn't prove anything. It just means he was smart enough to wait."

"Maybe, but conjecture doesn't help us."

"So, if he's not guilty, why did he settle?"

"Money."

"That's it … money?"

"He hasn't got much. He can't afford to fight us. We're too big."

"So what was the settlement?"

"We stripped him of his funds here in the States and bought the patent from him."

"Bought it? … For how much?"

"For almost a million dollars. We said we wouldn't bad-mouth him."

"A million dollars?"

"Yeah, kind of. It was his money."

"I don't understand."

"Seems he sold the right to use the dye to some Chinese companies that make toys and decorative pottery. They paid him a million dollars. We don't know where the money is, but we told him he could keep it if he signed over the patent. It was an easy thing to do since suing the Chinese isn't easy."

"You could have sued the U.S. distributors."

"I guess it seemed like a small price to pay for a settlement when we really had no case."

"Shit, so the guy has a million dollars?"

Etienne hunches his shoulders in a so-what gesture. "So why do you care? You act like you've got a grudge against the guy."

Cathy feels herself becoming defensive. "Hell, he stole from us." Etienne chuckles. "Allegedly, but we've got the patent. It might be us who stole it from the bastard through intimidation. But, hey, that's business."

Cathy goes to get herself a drink, but she's damned if she's going to toast the deal.

Chapter Sixty-One

Seventeen months have passed since the debacle of Les losing the patent to Mallet Pharmaceuticals. He'll always wonder if he had been right in ceding the victory to Mallet's lawyers, but he had been afraid of piddling away the money in the Cayman Islands and ending up with nothing.

As Berty had warned him, Les still paid a hefty bill to DeSilvo. It had been hard believing the hours the man had billed. It seemed like fiction, but how do you contest an attorney's fees? Every contract negotiation was covered, even though Mallet now controlled the contacts. It really hurt.

Les had worked selling mattresses for three months before finally finding a job at the National Institutes of Health in Bethesda, Maryland, where he was careful not to discuss his work history.

After finding the job, he moved to Laurel, Maryland, finding an apartment just off U.S. 1. It is in one of a half dozen brick buildings that had probably been built in the 1950s and were showing their age.

Still, he is now back in a two-bedroom apartment and has rescued his beloved laboratory equipment from storage.

Throughout the months, he had painfully watched as Blue became the nation's rage. He imagines the Sherwin-Williams logo of paint covering the world, only with a change of the paint color to glowing Blue. Not just doors were painted Blue, but there were initially Blue shutters as well and then whole houses. Metal roofs were painted Blue, and then Blue roofing shingles were developed. Panels were developed to become the siding on new skyscrapers in cities worldwide.

And not surprisingly, anything made of plastic now comes in

Blue: frames for eyeglasses, coolers for picnics, toys of all forms, swimming pools for back yards, cases for electronics to include laptops and cell phones, batons for directing traffic, trash cans to set by curbs, all kinds of packaging—if you can think of it, it's Blue.

And with sports, of course: Blue skis, Blue bicycles, Blue skateboards, Blue golf balls, Blue volleyballs, Blue fishing poles, Blue basketball nets, Blue tennis rackets, Blue hockey pucks, Blue feathers on arrows, Blue croquet wickets, and so on.

And advertising, as one can imagine: Blue billboards, Blue logos on trucks and anywhere a symbol is used, Blue ads in newspapers and magazines, Blue covers for books, Blue name signs on stores and buildings, hanging Blue signs for professional offices and pubs, fine print in Blue where it is needed, and thousands of T-shirts printed with Blue sayings and logos.

The fabric industry is not excluded. Everything that can be made, from clothing to draperies and boat sails, is made in Blue. Hollywood stars appear on Blue carpets in designer dresses and tuxedos of glowing Blue.

Airplane stabilizers are painted Blue. Marinas are full of Blue yachts. The sex industry makes Blue toys and condoms. The Times-Square New Year's ball is made of Blue glass. Jewelry is made of Blue glass and Blue ceramics. And last but not least, the cosmetic industry has gone wild. Della B's Bleu Glo cosmetics are the rage. If a cosmetic can be made, it is made Blue. Lips glow Blue. Eyes are circled in Blue. Hair is dyed Blue. There is even Blue rouge for cheeks.

If something can be made Blue, it is. And people are making money from it, but not Les.

He often feels cheated. Sometimes he borders on depression. Other times, he experiences a sense of alarm.

Les knows Blue has a half-life, although he doesn't completely understand the implications. To him, it's disconcerting.

Chapter Sixty-Two

It is almost time for Etienne to come home.

Cathy is lying on the sofa, a pillow propped behind her back. She's wearing a white silk negligee and a sheer cape over her shoulders. She thinks of Ingres' Odalisque and unconsciously pulls the cape tighter over her breasts. She wishes she had a one-armed chaise, but the sofa will have to do.

She stretches, breathes deeply, licks her lips, and tastes the lipstick. It's Blue—Della B's Bleu Glo— as are her eyeliner, mascara, and shadow. It's the first time she's used them. Hell, all the world is using them. Why shouldn't she? She wants to know Etienne's reaction. She's tried to be conservative. She hasn't applied eyebrows or used rouge. She hasn't dared to dye her hair. Still, when she looks in the mirror, she's startled.

She wants to look in the mirror now, but with her body carefully arranged, she is afraid to move. She hears the key in the door.

Etienne comes in and goes to the coat closet to hang up his coat, with his back to Cathy. He turns and comes into the room and stops in his tracks. "Jesus, Christ. What have you done? You look like a French harlot from the nineteenth century."

She feels the shock of his words. She sits up and defends herself. "It's the stuff you sell. You bought Vincent Cosmetics. You're paying Della B."

"Della B's a tart. She plays a role."

"Then half the women in America are tarts."

"Yeah, that might be true."

"You're comfortable with that?"

"Sure, it makes money."

"Then why can't I use the same stuff?"

"Because you're beautiful. You don't need that shit to make people look at you. I married you because of the way you look. I like it that way."

"But I wear cosmetics all the time … lipstick, shadow, eyeliner."

"Yeah, but it's subdued. It's been accepted for centuries."

"So it's Blue, your Blue, that makes a difference … makes a woman a tart?"

"Yeah, it's not natural."

"So red and black cosmetics are natural."

"No, but they're accepted. History has defined it that way."

"Well, maybe you're redefining history."

"God help us. The Lord didn't make blue women."

"Well, somebody did."

Etienne pours himself a bourbon from a decanter. "A poor wimp named Les Warin. He did it."

"And you're making money from it."

Etienne raises his glass. "And here's to a world of tarts."

"Well, I'm your wife. How does it look that I don't wear your products?"

Etienne considers this. He studies Cathy's face and sighs. "Well, maybe a little eyeliner when we go out at night … just at night."

Cathy gets up and wraps her arms tightly around herself. She heads for the bedroom. "You don't understand, Etienne. Women have fun with this stuff. It's fun to dress up. You should be glad."

"Okay, I'm glad, babe. I'm glad women are having fun. But you're beautiful. Don't screw it up."

Chapter Sixty-Three

Les can see some change in the light intensity. He doesn't see it in the Blue that is on metal or glass. Well, maybe a little. He sees the change in almost everything else.

And he sees changes in Rudy's skin. Rudy is his rat—the rat he bought and shaved. He has applied a suspension of Blue in water to the rat's skin daily for nearly a year and a half. The skin is now retaining the Blue coloring and has become rough. He can't tell if it's painful. He doesn't want to hurt Rudy, but he is becoming fitful and unsettled. Les is worried.

It appears that Blue, when applied to anything organic, is losing its brightness more quickly than it does in his pint jars. Practically, everything you can think of is organic. If it's not organic, it is coated with something organic. Automobiles are coated with organics, coat preservatives, or waxes. He wonders if Mustangs are losing their glow. More importantly, he wonders if the half-life of Blue in contact with organic materials is less than the twenty years he had determined for Blue by itself.

He hasn't got the equipment he needs. He funds a professor in the Department of Chemistry at the University of Maryland to do some research.

He needs to know if Blue is interacting with organic materials. Did it break down the cellulose, lignin, and/or other polymers in the wood of his door, or was it interacting with the resins in the door's paint or all the above? In that case, the instability of the Blue is being stabilized through a chemical reaction rather than the reconfiguration of the blue molecule itself.

If it is a chemical reaction, is it a slow reaction, and does it have a half-life? Coincidentally, does that mean there is a time over which destruction will occur and become noticeable?

And what does it do to skin? What's it doing to Rudy? What's it doing to a significant fraction of the citizens of the World? Is a fad doing serious damage to the human race? Do skin pigments affect what's happening? What's the long-term effect? Can you simply stop using it, or is the effect on the human body there for all time?

And how do you stop it? How do you cure it? What's the proper term for what needs to be done?

PART THREE

The Dream Is Reinvented

Chapter Sixty-Four

Almost a year has passed since Les has last seen Berty. They meet for lunch at what appears to be a college hangout near the University of Maryland campus.

Berty slips into the booth opposite Les and looks around. "Well, mate, I'm glad to see you, but this place has a dearth of ambiance."

"It's the mystique of American college life."

"The mystique of bottles of catsup on the tables."

"The American way of life."

"Right, so you Yanks can ruin your chips."

"With a shake of the wrist."

"For all the idiots of the world."

Les makes a defensive motion of his body and gives a look of grievance. "That bad, Berty? Seems like you've been here long enough to have absorbed our way of life."

"Right, I should be kind. I'm chuffed out of the world ... at least to see you, mate."

"Well, thank you for that. This place just seemed convenient, halfway between Laurel, where I live, and the aura of Connecticut Avenue ... and besides, I had to pick up some research results from the Chemistry Department at the University of Maryland."

"Oh, are you teaching now?"

"Heavens, no. I'm trying to understand Blue."

"Blazing hell, are you not knackered of that. Your making money from the stuff is a lost cause ... gone."

Les flicks his palms up in resignation. "Not the making of money … the stuff itself."

"Blame me, but I would have thought you would have had enough of that, which reminds me, did you see the story in the red tops?"

"Red tops?"

"The London tabloids. I get the Daily Star in the mail … need to keep up with the scandals."

"Are you telling me Blue has made the scandals?"

"Yes, well, indirectly. The Della B in the cosmetic world of Blue has turned out to be a real wanker. She's threatened to take her name off the product line. Seems that some porn star has called herself Delta B, or Delta B and her Bleu Delta, and is strutting herself around with her bush dyed Blue, along with anything else she can make Blue. Della B is raging and wants the woman banned, but there's no way the company that makes the stuff can do that. It's on the market."

"That's crazy. It's not as if this Delta B is a world-renown personality."

"She is now. Hell, the whole industry has stopped shaving. We'll never know how many women are walking around with Blue patches."

"Men, too?"

"Now, I wouldn't know, would I?"

"Of course not."

"So what are you sorting now?"

"I'm worried women are going to lose eyelids."

"Chuffing hell, I didn't hear what I just did, did I?"

"You did. These Blue cosmetics interact with the skin. If you don't wear it too long or clean it off thoroughly every day, you're probably all right. But if you're lazy about it, leave it on, it stays … latches onto the skin, breaks down the skin, maybe causes small ulcers."

"Gorblimey, didn't they test it?"

"For a few months, yes, but it's a slow process … takes time."

"Insidious?"

"Nasty work, but yes."

"Lucky you don't hold the patent to insidious."

Les raises his glass of soda. "To disaster, Berty. To potential disaster."

"Christ. You sound happy about it."

"It's our fortune, Berty. The fortune I missed."

"Are you daft, mate? What are you talking about?"

"Disaster brings opportunity, Berty. We're ahead of the game."

"We?"

"Berty, no one knows the disaster is coming. We have a chance to be ready … ready to make a killing."

"We again?"

"Right. I need a little capital."

"What about the Caymans?"

"It's being eaten up, a gulp at a time. A hundred thousand to DeSilvo, another hundred thousand to the Maryland research, and bits and pieces here and there. I need to keep a little."

"All right, mate, I intuit you have a plan."

"You intuit correctly. First, we figure out how to cure Blue."

"So Blue is a disease?"

"Somewhere between a disease and a creeping tattoo."

Berty sighs with impatience. "The point, Les?"

"The point is, if we find a cure and set up facilities to apply the cure, we'll have millions of patients. Whatever the means of curing Blue are, we can sell them to others to offer the cure, but we'll be there first with an endless queue of Bleu men and women."

"Men?"

"Haven't you seen them? Blue goatees, sideburns, and Blue streaks on top? The variations are infinite."

"And you have ideas about how to do this cure ... magic pills or something?"

"Lasers."

"Of course, why didn't I think of that? They work on pigmented skin, blast away tattoos, etc., etc. The magic cure. So you're going to blast Blue to pieces."

"No, we're going to tickle Blue, break the bonds, throw it back into its original state. Make it let go."

"Let go, like it's bitten something?"

"A metaphor, my friend."

"And you need some quid to do this?"

"I need to try different lasers on my door. I need to buy lasers."

"The door is still in your hallway?"

"It travels with me."

"And after the door."

"I'll try it on Rudy."

"I'll bite. Who's Rudy?"

"My rat."

"Of course." Berty nods as if he should have known. "And Rudy suffers from Blue?"

"A mild case now, but it's getting worse."

"Okay, let's assume you cure Rudy. What's next?"

"We build laser equipment that can precisely maneuver the laser beams over the human body to break the chemical bonds. Then we need to train operators and physicians, buy facilities for the work to be done, and buy hostiles to hold the patients."

"And staff and money handlers."

"Right."

Berty considers the scenarios. "You really don't think we should warn people."

"Hey, it's like the covid pandemic. People won't believe it until it hits home. Then the industry will bloom overnight. We'll only have a short window, but we'll make it big. We'll cure people and sell the equipment. Speculators won't be able to get the stuff fast enough."

"How are you going to keep people from knowing about this?"

"We won't. We'll depend on lethargy, self-interest, and denial. Same as with the masks during the pandemic. Those are human instincts. Wearing masks proved it.

"I'll do the initial laser work. The engineers developing the machines will think it's for pigment treatments. Only the investors will know at that stage, and it's in their interest to stay below the radar. People will wonder after we start developing facilities, but if we're early enough, they'll be slow to understand and believe. It's known as inertia."

Berty groans. "If it works, it's bloody brilliant." He looks down and sighs deeply. "And you want me to find the money?"

"Hedge funds. And you get a cut."

"Bloody hell."

Chapter Sixty-Five

"What the hell, Etienne, you've painted your car Blue!?"

"It's the company car ... an advertisement."

"Yes, but you drive it. It's your car."

They are in the basement garage under their apartment, standing beside Etienne's S-Class. They're headed for a fundraiser.

Etienne is annoyed. "Get in the damned car."

After Cathy is seated, he slams the door and stalks to the driver's side. "Live with it. The company's gone through hell about this car."

Cathy glares at him. "When I wore a little Bleu makeup, you gave me the devil ... called me a tart. So now am I riding in a tart car?"

"Don't be ridiculous. This is a car, not a woman. Besides, if I remember, I thought that maybe eyeshadow would be all right. Now you have Blue eyebrows, Blue streaks in your hair, and Blue fingernails."

"Just some subtle changes."

"Subtle, hell. You can be seen from across the room like a Blue floodlight."

"Damn, Etienne, no one will notice. When I get out of this glowing Blue barge in front of the hotel, the car will outpower me by a million lumens. Besides, I bet the doorman is wearing a Blue uniform, and that half the women in the ballroom will have Blue makeup and Blue dresses. I'll be lost in the crowd. 'Subtle' is relative, and I'm subtle." At least, I hope.

"And what do you mean the company went through hell?"

"Ford Motors sued the paint company over this car. Their Mustangs are supposed to have sole use of Blue paint. They say this car violates the agreement … That paint for cars other than Mustangs shouldn't be available on the market. The paint company said the only paint on the open market is for touching up Mustangs. We all had to agree that this car is a one-off and that the paint will only be sold at Ford dealerships."

"Sounds like you got off easy. Any money involved?"

"The paint company paid Ford two hundred grand, which Mallet reimbursed."

"So I'm cruising in a two-hundred-thousand-dollar vulgar Blue boat."

"Damn it, just smile when you get out."

Chapter Sixty-Six

Les finds that a Q-switched ruby laser works to perfection. He doesn't use the power that is needed for tattoo removal. He has no black or navy-blue inks to break up. The damage done by Blue is to the surface of the skin, to the epidermis, for the most part, and seems to inhibit the body's ability to shed skin. Blue apparently breaks the keratin filaments, much as it does to the polymers in wood, and disrupts the keratinization process, disrupting the skin's ability to shed dead cells. Because skin shedding is inhibited, cells build up, and the skin thickens and hardens.

In addition to thickening the skin, it leaves a layer of blue pigmentation beneath the outer skin surface. The laser loosens the Blue's connection to the keratin so that it can be removed with a micro-abrasive moisturizer.

Les has bought and worked with several lasers, configurations of lenses for focusing beams of light, and systems for varying laser intensities to reach this conclusion. His lab has expanded from the second bedroom of his apartment to the living room. He sits on a chair at a small table in the kitchen or on a corner chair in his bedroom.

Berty has been able to get him a little funding, but Les has, in frustration, taken more money out of his account in the Cayman Islands. He hates using the money but believes he is close to his objective. Sometimes he feels he has spent his life on the verge of economic success, but it has always remained just out of his reach. Now he senses he can touch it—touch it with his skin.

He just needs more money—more money than that remaining in the Cayman Islands—and lots more. He needs money to hire engineers to create machinery that will automatically search the human body for Blue that needs to be removed, follow the body's contours, and work without human intervention. He needs to buy a building to serve as a clinic where the machines can be installed. He needs to train technicians to work with the patients and doctors to oversee the "cures." He needs to be ready when the moment comes. He needs to buy motels for holding his patients.

Berty has set up a meeting with the managers of MacGregor Investments in New York City. In preparation, Les has shipped his door ahead. They find they can't carry a rat with them on Amtrak and rise early in the morning to drive Interstate 95. Les hates Interstate 95, but sometimes there's no other choice.

Five investment company managers are gathered in the conference room on the twenty-sixth floor of a New York office building. Several are admiring the view when a receptionist taps on the door, enters the conference room, and announces that Les and Berty have arrived. The managers nod and wave them in. As perplexed millionaires watch, Les and Berty carry in the door and set it against the wall. Les then goes back out the door and momentarily returns with a box covered in a shroud with a handle projecting through the shroud at the top. He places it in front of him at the end of the conference table.

Berty sits against the wall at the side of the room, while Les stands at the head of the table. The managers sit still in curiosity.

Les bites his lower lip in anticipation and looks up. "Gentlemen and lady, my name is Leslie Warin, and my associate is Bertram Brin-Holland. We're from a private firm in Maryland. If I may, I'd like to walk around and meet you. I believe we'll get to know each other better in the coming months."

With that bit of bravado, Les walks around the table counterclockwise, meeting firm partners: David Sturgis, Christopher Wray, Charles Sternglass, Tony D'Angelo, and Beverly Knowlton.

Then Les stands at the table's head, looking sternly at the assemblage. "First, let me thank you for having us here today. It may be just in time. The simple fact is that this country is about to experience a human calamity. It is a calamity from which fortunes can be made. It is a calamity from which you in this room can make fortunes."

He wonders if "fortune" is the right word to use. After all, these people have already made fortunes. Now it's time to pile on the money, but that sounds too gross to say.

"What I'm talking about is Blue. That's blue with a capital B. Blue is about to create a crisis. We're all familiar with Blue. Its presence has become pervasive. Unfortunately, for the citizens of the world, Blue was put on the market without adequate testing. Blue is not a stable material. It glows because it is not stable. When I say it's not stable, what do I mean? It means that Blue gradually interacts with any organic materials it comes into contact with, but it does it slowly, methodically, and insidiously. Presently, the effects are starting to show and are only slowly being recognized. The effects will become dramatically apparent in the next couple of years."

Les walks to his door. "You no doubt wonder why we've brought a door to this meeting, a rather battered door at that. Let me show you something." He takes a knife from his pocket, opens a blade, and scrapes a door panel with the edge of a blade. A cascade of paint and powdered wood falls to the elegant carpeting. Les picks some of the material up from the floor and blows it from his fingers in the direction of the managers.

"This was my apartment's door. It was one of the first items ever painted with Blue paint. In the upper left-hand corner, I recently repainted the door with Blue. See how the corner glows. Compare it with the rest of the door, which has lost some of its glow over time. That clearly is not the only deterioration. The paint and the wood themselves have deteriorated. The wood in this door has become a powder. Blue has interacted with the polymers, the cellulose, and others in this door to break their chains and turn the wood to powder and small bits of the polymer chains that have survived. Lady and gentlemen, imagine that this is not wood. Imagine that it is skin … the skin of a hundred million women in the United States, a billion women globally, and several million men."

Les walks to the conference table and pulls the shroud off the box, displaying a plexiglass box with holes in its sides. Rudy rises on his hind legs and scratches the side of the box, as if trying to get out. The managers around the table momentarily recoil, two grabbing the arms of their chairs, ready to bolt, as if the rat might escape and attack them.

Les continues, "Folks, this is Rudy. He's a laboratory rat. Believe me, he's more frightened than you are. Over the past few years, he has undergone a lot. Part of his back was shaved, and Blue was applied to it repeatedly. If you look at his back, a large section of the area I shaved is thick and cracked and covered with some fuzzy hair. In the middle of that is a half-inch square patch where hair is thriving. If you touch the skin under that patch, you will find the skin is soft and pliable. It is normal skin. Six weeks ago, that patch looked just as bad as the remaining area exposed to Blue. I treated that patch with a laser. I corrected the damage. I made the skin normal again. I will correct the rest of Rudy's back in the next few weeks. Rudy will be normal again. He deserves that. He has sacrificed a lot. He has sacrificed for humanity.

"This same damage is occurring now to the women of the world who have used Della B's Bleu Glo cosmetics. They are only slowly realizing it is happening. In the next few years, they will be horrified by what is happening. They will see their hair shattering and breaking off in patches, eventually down to the scalp. They will see their fingernails and toenails crack and flake off in chips. They will see their eyelids become thick and stop easily opening and closing. They will see their lips hardened, almost as if calloused."

Beverly Knowlton tries to hide her fingernails under the edge of the table.

Les looks meaningfully at her. "People will panic. They will be angry. They will demand punishment for the purveyors of these cosmetics. But, most of all, they will seek a cure. Don't worry, Ms. Knowlton. I have the cure!" He holds his hand out to the managers in the room, with his palm up as if making them an offer. "You can provide the cure! We can be ready to provide that cure! But we must start now! We must be ready."

Les goes on to tell his fascinated audience of the need to manufacture equipment, buy facilities, and train personnel.

Berty and Les ride home with eighty million dollars in their bank account. They have work to do. They have people to hire. They need to be ready. Beverly Knowlton wants to be first in line.

Why not? She's paying for it.

Chapter Sixty-Seven

It began four years after Blue paints were introduced and three years after Bleu Glo cosmetics came on the market.

A tennis racket broke at match point in Wimbledon. The player was left holding the handle as the racket's head careened past the chair umpire. It was caught by a ball boy as if it were a frisbee. He immediately dropped it and tried to shake the sting out of his hand. The players stood in dazed silence until the umpire told them to get a new racket and continue. The match went on for another forty minutes.

Two days later, a wading bowl leaked empty in Paterson, New Jersey, and a two-year-old girl was left crying.

The next day in Evanston, Illinois, the driver brought his Mustang back to the dealer and complained that the finish was becoming dull. The dealer agreed to have it repainted. In Dallas, Texas, the head came off a toy soldier the same day.

The next day, a basketball net was shredded halfway through a game in Portland, Oregon, and a volleyball deflated during a high school match in Erie, Pennsylvania. In Santa Fe, New Mexico, a dog stood confused when he caught a Frisbee and was left with part of it in his mouth and the rest on the ground.

A piece of a woman's skirt disintegrated as she exited a cab in New York City. In Manchester, England, a croquet wicket broke when hit by a ball. In Paris, a show was stopped when a dancer's pants split during the cancan.

After five weeks, Ford had thirty-seven complaints about the paint on Mustangs and issued a recall for over five thousand vehicles. They offered to repaint the cars in any color other than Blue, but the car owners wanted Blue. They told Ford to fix the problem.

Jane Olaffson, in her beauty salon in Fairmont, Minnesota, worried about the excess of blue hair she was sweeping from the floor during the day. In Alexandria, Virginia, Cathy Mallet was annoyed at having to redo her fingernails every couple of days because the polish kept cracking.

The singer Della B canceled her tour in Australia because her lips were stiffening, and she couldn't form the words to songs. The porn star, Delta B, canceled a film appearance because she was losing her hair. Stories of new horrors were heard and witnessed daily.

When Cathy Mallet viewed dozens of blue hairs in her hairbrush, she screamed at Etienne. Women were screaming everywhere.

Men, being berated, were hiding.

Chapter Sixty-Eight

For several months, Les watches the turmoil with satisfaction and panic. He worries his clinic isn't coming together quickly enough. He and his partners have bought an enormous building outside Martinsburg, West Virginia. It had been an automotive parts distribution center. Now it's a clinic built to cure human beings of the Bleu syndrome, as it has come to be known.

Finally, everything is ready. Les and Berty sit in their plush suite, much like the owner's boxes in major league stadiums and arenas. They look out over fifty twelve feet by twelve feet cubicles that handle four to five hundred clients daily. Les and Berty prefer to refer to them as clients rather than patients. They don't want to be subject to the regulations and regimens of medical facilities.

Their box is high up on the west wall of the building. Their view is through a window of one-way mirrored glass. They don't want to be seen by their clients. They just want to witness the commotion of clients and technicians in the aisles like bees buzzing in their hives.

The building has fifty outside doors so clients can enter private reception areas. Before entering the maze of patient rooms, they can, as they wish, don clothing that will maintain their anonymity.

Les and Berty have built two helipads on the roof of the building, each having an anonymous elevator entry nearby.

Around the building, they have installed defensive fencing. It looks like the U.S. Capitol after the January 6 riots of 2020. Les and Berty don't want to be "after the riots." They want to be ahead of the game, although they are uncertain what the "game" will be. The two men feel enormous satisfaction and trepidation.

The day before, they had visited the eight motels they had bought along U.S. Highway 11. The motels have been upgraded to provide the comfort Les and Berty believe their clients deserve. The motels are operating normally but no longer taking future reservations.

Both men believe they are ready—as ready as they will ever be.

They will begin with a news conference. The helipads will be used by their sponsors from MacGregor Investments to attend. Reporters will be invited from all over the world. Les and Berty don't expect many to attend. A former distribution center surrounded by black fencing topped with razor wire attracts local curiosity, but Martinsburg isn't on the national news radar.

When they discuss it, Les and Berty chuckle. The hayseed West Virginia reporters are about to have a national story.

***

Les and Berty have raised a sign on their building ahead of the news conference—BLEU REGRETS LLC. Below the name, in smaller letters surrounded by quotation marks, reads a slogan … "GET RID OF THE BLEUS—GO BLEULESS."

A rental company has set up a large tent in the parking lot. Inside the tent is a head table with chairs for MacGregor Investments' managers and Les and Berty. Microphones and speakers are set up. Some fifty folding chairs are carefully aligned in the space. At the center, Les and Berty have hired a firm to set up a camera to record the session in preparation for it to be put on YouTube following the meeting.

When the conference is scheduled to start, at 10:00 AM, the MacGregor managers, along with Les and Berty, are sitting at the head table. Beverly Knowlton has tried to clean her fingernails, but they are still tinged Blue and badly cracked. She tries to keep them under the table.

Les waits until five after ten. Only five reporters are seated in the vast sea of chairs. Four are local, two men and two women. One of the women has blue hair. The fifth reporter is from The

New York Times. Christopher Wray has cajoled her into flying down with him on his helicopter. She has a wisp of blue hair across her forehead and a dusting of Blue on her eyelids.

Finally, Les taps on his microphone. "Ladies and gentlemen, thank you for coming today. I know all of you are wondering why you are here, and many of you are curious about the purpose of the building behind this tent. I have watched you become impatient for the last five minutes, and I understand, but I'm confident you will find what I am about to say worth your time.

"As we are all aware, Bleu Glo cosmetics and the blue dye in other formats—paints, plastics, fabrics, and what have you—have become a pervasive part of our lives."

The Blue-haired reporter reaches up to feel her hair.

Les tries to ignore her and continues, "What no one has told you, what no one has told the American people and indeed the world … what they should know … is that things don't glow without some kind of internal change. Materials that glow without external stimulation are called luminescent. Why do they luminesce? They glow because they are undergoing a chemical reaction or are subject to some form of stress.

"In the case of Blue, the material is unstable. It corrects the instability by altering its molecular configuration or interacting with other organic materials. Both are slow processes. They occur over years. The reactions with organic materials occur at a slightly faster pace than the reconfiguration of the molecules. In science, we would say the two processes have different half-lives. Visually, it means that Blue gradually loses its ability to luminesce but at different rates, depending on which process occurs.

"I know you did not come here for a chemistry lesson, but a brief lesson is necessary. What is happening is that the dye we call Blue interacts with wood, with plastic, with paper, with man-made and natural fabrics, with waxes … with anything that contains organic materials. Most importantly, for what we are here to discuss today, the blue dye interacts with skin … not just leathers but human, living skin. It interacts with hair. It interacts with fingernails and

216

toenails. It interacts with anyone who applies it to themselves. "Further, it has effects. It makes hair brittle. It makes nails brittle. It thickens skin. It makes skin calloused where the skin is ordinarily thick, such as on lips. It is damaging human beings throughout the world."

One of the reporters raises his hand. Les recognizes him. "What about dogs?"

Les feels shocked. "If the dog is dyed, there's a problem. Have people really dyed dogs?"

The man nods, looking alarmed.

Les waits a moment before continuing.

"Which brings me to the building behind me. This building contains equipment to correct the problems caused by Bleu Glo cosmetics. It is set up to treat clients who want the effects of Bleu Glo corrected."

He looks at the reporter who was worried about dogs. "It will work on dogs too. I have already used it to cure a rat."

He looks away from the man and addresses the camera. "The process involves the use of a laser that scans the damaged areas breaking the bond the blue dye has with the skin and allowing the dye to be removed with abrasive creams. It requires multiple treatments to thin the skin and bring the Blue to the surface for thick, damaged skin. It does not repair hair or nails. It treats the Blue and allows the hair and nails to naturally grow back."

Suddenly, the reporter with the blue hair blurts out, "My god, I'll lose all my hair. I'll look like a blue cancer victim."

Les is startled. "Yes, but the hair will grow out, and we'll remove the Blue from the skin."

"You'll do that in this building?"

"Yes, that's what this building is equipped to do."

"Do I have to sign up?"

"Yes, you'll have to make an appointment. We'll give you our phone number."

"You're going to give it to us today?"

"Yes. We have a flyer to give you."

One of the men asks, "Is this the only place this can be done?"

"For now, yes. The equipment is available for other people to purchase. It's not magic. Others can do it, but they'll have to get set up."

"Are others setting up?"

"Not yet."

"Man, it seems like you've got a monopoly."

"Only until others are set up. We're not stopping them." Les tries not to grin. He is afraid to look at Berty. "We'll work with them to set up if they wish."

The Times reporter looks coolly at Les. "I assume you will charge for this treatment."

"Yes, of course."

"And how much will the treatment cost?"

"It will depend on the case."

"Yeah, and when will the patients learn the cost?"

"Clients. We call them clients. This is not a medical procedure. But to answer your question, we will evaluate the clients and discuss the fee when they arrive here."

"So they're here, ready to be treated, and you give them the price. Then they must decide whether to stay or fly back to where they came from, San Diego or wherever."

"Considering the significance of the problem, I believe clients will find we are reasonable. Certainly, what we charge will become common knowledge as time progresses."

The New York reporter continues, "When will the facility open for business, and how do I sign up?"

The Blue-haired reporter shouts, "Hey, get in line!"

Les intervenes, "Please stay calm. We'll take care of signing you up before you leave here today."

The dog man exclaims, "What about Bojo?"

Les grins. "I assume Bojo is a dog. We'll sign you up too. Nothing about this process will hurt Bojo." He turns to Berty. "Will you please get one of the answering-phone people to come out and sign these people up?"

Les turns back to the camera. "Let me emphasize that treatment here will require an appointment. Those with appointments will be given specific times. The telephone numbers for appointments are listed on the flyers we have stacked on the table in the middle of the room. Please take one. For those needing accommodation for overnight stays, arrangements can be made when you make the appointment. Please don't come unless you make an appointment."

Next to him, Beverly Knowlton asks sotto voce, "I assume you'll take care of me without signing up."

Les smiles. "We'll take care of you after lunch so you can fly back this afternoon."

She smiles back. "That's good. I won't ask for my money back."

Chapter Sixty-Nine

After lunch, Les and Berty drive back to their building. A dozen women are gathered at the gate. Les stops outside the gate, gets out of the car, and addresses them, "Ladies, how can we help you? If you want an appointment, we'd appreciate your calling to make one."

A red-haired woman with Blue eyebrows and light smudges of Blue on her cheeks snarls. "I did call. I've been on call waiting for over an hour. Appointments aren't for shit if you can't get through."

The other women join in shouting over each other.

Les holds up his hands for quiet. "Look, I'm sorry you can't get through. Tell you what we'll do. I'll send someone out here to sign you up. How's that sound?"

The woman glowers. "So what do you want us to do? Form a line?"

Les draws in his breath in relief. "That would help."

The woman looks at him, as if he had just kicked her in the chin.

He turns to the two guards he has hired from a security company, Hornacote Protective Services, and asks them to open the gate to let his car in. He gets back in the car and drives through.

He glances at Berty, who looks worried. "What?"

"Mate, by the time we get back to the gate, there are going to be fifty more women out there."

Les slams on his brakes, exits the car, and runs back to the gate. He tells the guards to let the women through and then to lock the gate. The guards look startled and a little worried. They can't understand why the guy who is their boss is acting frantically.

The women stream in, looking excited and expectant.

While Berty parks the car, Les leads the women into the building and into a bay outside a room where telephone-answering personnel wildly answer telephone calls. He waves over the room manager, Guy Mallory, from where he is helping an agent. "Guy, get one of your staff to sign up these women. They couldn't get through by phone."

"Hell, no one can get through on the phones. We're already booked up for nearly three weeks. This place is crazy. If we close tonight, I don't know what this place will look like when we return in the morning. All the electronics may be burned to a crisp."

"Damn, Guy, just take care of these women and send them back out. I'll go up to my office and phone the telephone company … see what can be done."

Berty intervenes, "I don't know what can be done. I just talked to a friend who has been trying to get through. She says the queue is full, and the system isn't even putting people on hold."

Les turns to his friend. "Yeah, when people do get through, Guy says they're screaming at the agents … giving them hell … venting about the phone system and about their predicament … about the evils of Bleu Glo … about the way they've been scammed … about that bitch Della B."

Les turns back to Mallory. "Tell the agents to do the best they can."

"Christ, I am. What do we do when the shift ends?"

"Send everyone home. Tell them to come back in the morning. They can only do so much."

Les and Berty hurry up to their offices.

The red phone, the security phone, is ringing when they open the office door. Les rushes to the phone. It's a guard at the gate. "Yes."

The guard sounds panicked, "Hey, we must have a hundred

women and a few men here demanding to come in. What do we do?"

"Tell them we're not open for business yet. The people who will do their work aren't even here today. Tell them we'll be glad to take care of them, but they need to make an appointment. We can only handle a few at a time."

"They're screaming that they can't get through to make an appointment."

"Tell them we're trying to fix the phone system, to please phone."

"Hey, don't you understand? They're not listening. They're just pushing at the gate. Those women you let in are coming to get out. We're afraid to open the gate ... afraid we'll never get it closed again. We need help."

"Stay calm. I'll phone your office."

Les turns to Berty. "I'll phone Hornacote. You phone the State Police. The guards are afraid to open the gate to let people out."

Les phones the security company. A secretary answers, "Hello, Hornacote Sec—"

Les cuts her off, "Get me your boss. Quickly!"

"And who may I say—"

"Les Warin at Bleu Regrets. We've got a crisis! Get me your boss! It's a damn emergency!"

Over the phone, Les can hear the woman shouting.

"David Hornacote here."

"Damn, David, we've got a crisis here!"

"Who is this?"

"Les Warin, Dave. Your gate security people are in panic! They need help! Hundreds of women are trying to get in the gate. Your men are panicking!"

"Yeah, yeah, are they in danger?"

"We're all in danger!"

"Well, I'll try to get a couple of men down there."

DELLA B'S BLEU GLO

"A couple of men, hell! Get everyone you can get! Get yourself! Get your goddamned secretary! Get everyone you can get!"

Les slams the phone down and looks at Berty, who throws his hands up in frustration. "They're sending a patrol car to check."

Les throws his head back and groans in frustration. "Are the doors locked?"

"All of them except the main door through which the women just left."

"Damn. I'm going to lock it. Call Guy Mallory and tell him to lock his room."

"Do you think they might get in?"

"Hell, Berty, I don't know a damned thing."

After locking the door, Les joins Berty back in their office, locking the door behind him. They both go to a window overlooking the parking lot with the gate in the distance. There are only a few cars in the lot. The women they had let in are hiding behind the vehicles. The guards are standing far away from the gate. The crowd is rocking the gate and the fence.

Les thinks, Thank heavens we're not open for business today ... We only have to protect the telephone agents ... Oh, shit, the equipment! The patient rooms!

He grabs Berty by the arm and turns him toward the office door. "Grab your master key! We need to lock the client rooms! Oh, shit, Beverly Knowlton is in room 1 getting worked on by Doctor Gmellin."

Out they run and down the stairs. Les sends Berty to the far side of the building to begin locking doors. He rushes to room 1 and pounds on the door. He hears it unlock. It opens. Torran Gmellin, the head project physician, looks out. "We're right in the middle of a—" He stops in mid-sentence when he sees the desperation on Les's face. "What, what's wrong? Has something broken down?"

"We're being stormed by a mob!"

Beverly Knowlton pulls her head away from the laser apparatus.

"What are you saying?"

"I'm saying hundreds of angry women outside are trying to break it, demanding help with their problems with Bleu Glo!"

Knowlton slips from the table she's lying on. She's wearing a client robe. "Are they going to break in?"

Les acknowledges that he doesn't know, but they're trying to knock down the fence.

Knowlton picks up her cell phone and dials. "Barry, get the chopper ready." She turns to the men. "Get your asses out of the room. I need to get dressed and get out of here."

The two men exit quickly. Les addresses Gmellin, "Take yourself to the telephone room and get locked in. I've got other rooms to lock up."

He hurries to the next rooms and begins locking doors. As he proceeds, it seems to take forever. He pictures hordes of women swarming into the building. He imagines himself trying to block hundreds of women methodically storming toward him, knocking him down, trampling him as he cradles himself in a fetal position while they surge over his body.

Les and Berty ran back to the office when all the rooms were locked. They can hear banging on the outside doors. They again lock themselves in their office and hurry to the window. Forty feet of the fence and the gate lie flattened. The mass of women is at the building's doors. Les is relieved as he sees no weapons, no crowbars, no battering rams. These people had not come ready to wage war as had the mob that invaded the U.S. Capitol a few years before. They had come to get appointments, but they wanted the appointments immediately. The repair to their bodies could not wait.

As the two men stand there, Beverley Knowlton's helicopter takes off from the roof, whirling above the women. Many shake their fists at the craft as if they think the men responsible for their plight are escaping.

Les is appalled to see several women lying or sitting in the parking lot, appearing severely injured. "Damn, Berty, call 911.

Get ambulances here! Get them here quick!"

While Berty is dialing, there's a crash as the entrance door gives way. Then they hear angry voices in the building. They go to the one-way mirror and look down on the client rooms. Women and a few men are streaming into the building and through the aisles. One man is smashing a door with a fire extinguisher.

Les cringes. He hadn't thought of that as a weapon. The door gives way. Les thinks, Thank God, everything is bolted to the floor. I wonder what damage they can do to the equipment with a fire extinguisher.

Les and Berty spend their time sitting helplessly in their desk chairs or peeking out the window. There's some noise outside their door. There's some knocking at the door. They think about crawling under their desks. Eventually, footsteps go away, down the stairs.

Out front, they see a Martinsburg patrol car arrive. The patrolmen sit in their car away from the flattened gate. Les hopes they're calling for help.

After twenty minutes, more police arrive, with lights flashing and sirens screaming. Les sees some West Virginia State Police getting out of their cruisers. They all stand around outside the flattened gate. Finally, they get organized. Batons have appeared in their hands. Some have riot shields.

Moments later, two vans with side panels emblazoned with "Hornacote Security" arrive. Seven personnel get out. One of them interacts with the police, and they stand back.

The police advance on the building and vanish inside. After a few minutes, women begin parading out of the building into the parking lot. Some stand around, but most head toward the cars they have left parked on the road and in the fields outside the fence. Eventually, the police come out. Dave Hornacote moves forward to talk to the police. His group has now grown to nine. They have been joined by the two gate guards.

Les wonders where they were when the building was being

invaded. He opens the office door nervously. All is quiet.

He and Berty descend the stairs. Berty knocks on the telephone room and gives them a tentative "all clear."

They step carefully over and past the damaged reception room doors. Les is met by a police captain. "Thank you."

"You the boss here?"

"Yeah, I own the business."

"What the fuck did you do to piss them off?"

"We've set up a business to help them eliminate their Bleu Glo cosmetic issues."

"And they stormed the place because of that?"

"Because they couldn't get to us on our phone system to make appointments."

"Buddy, it sounds like you need a bigger phone system."

"Unfortunately, I don't think they've invented that system."

"Well, you had better figure out something. You were lucky. These people didn't come prepared for a fight. Next time, who knows? You can't depend on the police to bail you out. We'll be unhappy if we have to come again."

The captain gathers his police personnel together and walks off complaining about Les and his damned business.

***

Late that night, Les and Berty sit at a table at the bar in the Liberty Motel, one of the motels they have bought for their clients.

Berty cups his Scotch in two hands.

Les looks at him. "Are you sure you need to start with a double?"

"Mate, I'd have a triple if the glass was big enough. I need to get pissed."

"No reason to get mad. We'll just be set back a little."

"Not mad … pissed … snockered."

"Man, I forget you're English … speak a different tongue. No, you don't need to get drunk. We have work to do tomorrow."

"Shite, mate, you take the fun out of being miserable."

"There's no time for that. Hornacote is working tonight to get the fence put back up. Tomorrow, he's having a Jersey wall brought in to set along the fence, so it will be harder for people to get a footing to push the fence. Over the next few days, he'll have the fence posts replaced with longer ones he can set in concrete."

"Meanwhile, we just sit."

"We have to wait anyway. We need to get the outside doors replaced with stronger doors and two doors to client rooms replaced. It won't stop us from opening the business, but the lasers in those two rooms must be replaced. We also need to get painters to cover all the ballpoint and felt-tip pen scribbling on the walls. The place looks like hell. The biggest deal will be the mechanical work, fixing the heating and cooling systems. They were battered badly. Hope we don't have to order parts that will take time getting here."

"Mate, it all sounds like things you can order from your phone in our penthouse office. You can sit there with your phone in hand and supervise the whole thing while I sleep it off."

"Damn, Berty, are we partners or not? In addition to all the stuff I just talked about, we need to do some public relations work. I can't be in two places at once. We need to do interviews and explain that our whole operation has been screwed up by an undisciplined mob. We need people to understand that if they don't play by our rules, they will stay Blue."

"You think that will hold them off?"

"That and thirty security people with long guns."

"Is that what Hornacote says he's going to supply us? I thought he was short people when we needed them."

"He's training more."

"So is that another two weeks we have to wait?"

"He says it will take a couple of days."

"Blimey, I hope he doesn't load their weapons. He could put us out of business if we have some wanker shoot a little, old blue-haired woman at the gate."

"He assures me he's only getting people who know how to use the weapons."

"Just men dusting off the AKs they bought at the last gun show?"

"Probably some of those, but hunters too. After all, we're in West Virginia. Everyone has a gun. It's part of life away from the big city."

"Where they have short guns."

"All I'm saying is that finding people who have handled guns is not hard."

"Can't your national guard protect us?"

"I don't think we qualify. The guards are busy protecting capitols."

"So I should pray?"

"You might try that."

PART FOUR

Cathy's Dream Slips Away

Chapter Seventy

Cathy wakes up, leaves the bedroom still tying her robe, and is surprised to find Etienne pacing in the living room, looking distressed.

"Jeez, Etienne, you startled me. Why are you home?"

Etienne waves a newspaper at her. "Did you see this damn paper?"

"Etienne, I've been sleeping."

"Shit, yeah. You're always sleeping."

"You've never cared about my sleeping in."

"Well, you're useless anyway."

"What am I supposed to be doing?"

"Helping."

"Helping you do what?"

"Saving me from this goddamned newspaper."

"The newspaper did something to you?"

"The damned stock market report did."

"The stock market? I thought Mallet was private."

"Honey, you don't pay attention to business. We went public when we got into the cosmetic business … Needed cash to expand."

"So what happened to the stock market?"

"Stock in Mallet Pharm has dropped 90 percent. It's worth only twelve dollars a share … may be less than that by now. We're recalling everything … all Bleu Glo cosmetics from around the world. The government is making us. We don't know how to pay for it. We don't know where to put the stuff. We don't know what to do with it after we get it. I'm afraid to listen to the radio."

Cathy suddenly has an uneasy feeling. "Because of the riots at Les Warin's place yesterday."

"Yes, this damned Les Warin." He suddenly turns to Cathy. "Jesus Christ, you sound like you know the bastard."

"Uh, I … I just heard his name on television last night. Uh, the riots were on television. How did that hurt you?"

"Not the goddamn riots. The bastard deserved the riots. It's the news conference he had in the morning. He said that our cosmetics had never been tested properly, that they are doing terrible things to users, cracking their nails, thickening their eyelids and lips, making their hair fall out, all kinds of shit. It's going to ruin us."

"Us?"

"You and me, babe."

"How can that happen?"

"God, don't you know? My parents pay me mostly in stock. Two hundred thousand a year in cash, but that goes fast. I only have twenty or so thousand in the bank, and the stock may be worth nothing."

"Well, can't we live on two hundred grand?"

"We probably won't get paid in cash anymore."

"Why not?"

"Because the damned company may not survive."

"You're kidding me."

He turns on her. "I'm not. And get that damned blue crap off your eyelids. I don't want to see that stuff ever again."

Suddenly, Cathy realizes she has problems other than money. She reaches up to feel her eyelids. Lord, I've been having trouble blinking. A bug hit me the other day. Crashed right into my eye.

She runs her fingers through the blue streaks in her hair and finds four strands in her hand, pieces of hair that just broke off. She looks at her fingernails. They are cracked. They need redoing. I just did them yesterday. I now do them almost every day.

She holds out the strands of hair to Etienne. "My hair is falling out, breaking off in bits."

"Yeah, that's what this guy says. That's nothing compared to the money."

"What do you mean, nothing? My hair is falling out. Maybe my eyelids will break off. What's going to happen, Etienne? What's going to happen to me? Les is screwing me over."

"What do you mean, Les?"

"Uh, this guy Warin."

"You sound like you're taking it personally."

"No, damn it, Etienne. I just don't know what's going to happen to me."

"You and a few million other women. You were all stupid and used the stuff."

"You sold it."

"The cosmetic people said they tested it. God, woman, be serious. You damned stupid women and your fads are going to ruin us. We may be broke. We may be out on the street."

"Your parents will take care of us."

"Just enough to keep from embarrassing themselves. Money and reputation matter to them."

"Well, what are we going to do?"

"I'm going to stop spending money and see what happens."

"No, what are we going to do about me? How am I going to be cured? Doesn't this guy say he can fix women? Isn't that what the riot was about?"

"Yeah, he claims he can. But I bet he charges a fortune."

Cathy screams, "The man has ruined me," and runs to the

bedroom bathroom. She stands at the sink and looks at her hair and eyelids in the mirror. "Damn you, Les Warin. You knew it. You knew it all along. You knew what the stuff would do. You did it all because you hate me."

<u>Chapter Seventy-One</u>

Les arrives at work and studies the collapsed tent lying in the parking lot where the mob had left it. He doesn't think his telephone agents have the ability to put it back up. They're the only labor he has.

He hurries to the office and calls the tent rental company. "Sorry, your tent has fallen down. I need help getting it back up … Yeah, I understand … I'm not scheduled today … but it's an emergency … I need to use it today … overtime? … Yeah, okay, whatever … By what time can you get it up … two o'clock? … okay."

He looks at Berty. "The bastards are screwing us."

Berty leans back, a slight smile of resignation on his face. "It's only bloody money. Our investors are in too deep now. Besides, we've never finished working on Beverly Knowlton. She's more than invested in our succeeding."

Les sets up a news conference for four o'clock, trusting the tent company. That's a little later than he wants, although he does want it up by the afternoon. He had picked up The Washington Post, The Baltimore Sun, and The New York Times on his way to work and had read what they said about the previous day's riots. He wants to make sure that the papers' reporters have time to make his news conference today.

He puts the word out far and wide about the news conference and settles down to think about what he will say.

***

When the news conference is to begin, the tent is more than half full. There are three TV cameras. National news services have preempted the front rows, and the disgruntled local reporters are relegated to the third and fourth rows. In addition to his own microphone, he has a half dozen additional microphones set up before him on the table.

Les also notes that a few hundred people are standing outside the gate behind where twenty or so security personnel are positioned.

Berty sits beside him. Les had made sure he would be there.

Les taps his microphone and begins, "Thank you all for coming. As you can see from the large sign displayed next to the damaged entrance door to the building behind us, our company, Bleu Regrets LLC, has been temporarily closed due to damage received during the well-reported storming of the building by men and women seeking to obtain our services. As we have previously said, this building has been built to house the equipment needed to correct the damage done using the cosmetic line Della B's Bleu Glo.

"As the press has thoroughly reported, our telephone scheduling system was overloaded by the many calls for reservations when we opened the system yesterday. In frustration at not being able to get through on the telephone lines, many people came to this building demanding to be served and, in the process, stormed the building and did significant damage, especially to our HVAC equipment. Our intention was to open the business to help those needing our services beginning this morning. However, the opening will be delayed an estimated two weeks because of the damage.

"Our telephone-answering service will be upgraded over the next ten days and will be back in service ten days from today. We would like to ask those interested in our services to recognize that many people require our help and that we must queue those desiring the services. We invite everyone to please use the telephone system. We ask that they not come to the building without an appointment. Doing so disrupts our ability to serve the people who need us and delays our ability to serve their needs. We, and you, have already lost two weeks. Again, I ask everyone to please help and use our system. Does anyone have any questions?"

Les points to a woman in the front row.

"How many people can your facility handle a day?"

Les replied, "We have fifty treatment rooms and hope to handle four or five hundred people daily."

The woman fingers a handheld calculator. "Let's say there are a million women who need help. At four hundred a day, that means it will take twenty-five hundred days to do everyone. 6.85 years. And if there are a hundred million women, it will take 685 years. Is that about right?"

"Uh, no. We're planning to build more facilities. And we will license out the equipment and procedures so that others can create facilities." Another reporter asks, "How many of these are under construction?"

"There are none under construction."

"So none are currently being built?"

"That's correct, but they'll be started very soon."

Now everyone is joining in. "Why weren't more buildings started when you started this facility? You must have known the need. Joannie over here did the math on her calculator. It's simple math."

"Well, yes. But you don't finance these things overnight. People have to learn of the need before they act."

"Well, you must have known the need. You and the people who provided the money for the construction must have known it. Can you explain why you didn't make the public aware of the need until yesterday?"

"Because there were no answers as to what to do. I didn't want to panic people."

Someone groused, "That's what Trump did about the pandemic."

Les ignored the implication. "I wanted to be able to answer the need."

"A shot glass instead of a bucket to handle a ceiling leak."

"Gosh, people, the covid vaccine didn't roll out instantaneously. And besides, it had government funding."

DELLA B'S BLEU GLO

"Do you think there should be government funding to address the Bleu syndrome?"

"Maybe, and national guard security too, if people can't behave."

A woman in the second row to the left stands. "Isn't it true that Bleu Glo is a domestic terrorist weapon?"

There is a lot of commotion as reporters stand and try to see the woman talking.

The woman continues, "Isn't this a right-wing, male conspiracy to make women look like fools? A kind of scarlet ribbon for vanity."

Suddenly, Berty is on his feet. "What a bloody fool statement. This is about a wanker pharmaceutical company wanting to make money. It's about capitalism. It's the way it is. It's got nothing to do with pondering navels to come up with conspiracy theories."

There is some snickering in the crowd.

When the noise settles down, a man in shirtsleeves who has hung his jacket at the back of his chair rises to speak, his hair loose and hanging down over his forehead. "Mr. Warin, is it true that you once held the patent to the dye known as Blue? And, if so, are you not responsible for the nightmare it has become?"

Again, there was stirring and talking. Finally, the crowd settles and looks at Les in apprehension.

Les's eyes shift from one face to another. They are not friendly.

Finally, he speaks, "Yes, I owned the patent. I discovered the dye while working for Mallet Pharmaceuticals before they owned Vincent Cosmetics, the maker of Bleu Glo cosmetics. After discovering the dye, I left Mallet and worked on the material in a small lab I set up in my bedroom. I learned how to mix it with other materials to make them glow. I created a paint I used on my front door. I also gave some to a neighbor's son who used it on his soap box derby car. The door and the car were noted in an article in The Washington Post. My connection to Blue was documented early on.

"One of the things I learned about Blue was that it had a half-life of about twenty years. That is, in that period, half the molecules of Blue will change into a different configuration—a configuration that will not glow. Another way of saying it is that Blue will be half as bright after twenty years. This I knew. In today's society, twenty years is a long time, more than the lifetime of most products made.

"Based on my studies, I patented Blue. However, because I discovered Blue while working for Mallet Pharmaceuticals, their lawyers took the patent away from me. At that point, I knew Vincent Cosmetics was considering making products using Blue, although they indicated they would thoroughly test Blue before using it. As I understand it, they did around six months of testing. As it turns out, six months was not long enough to test something that has a half-life in years.

"Even after I no longer worked for Mallet, I continued working on Blue, including hiring a professor at the University of Maryland to do research for me using equipment I could not afford. I learned two important things. First, I learned that when Blue is associated with organic materials, it stabilizes itself not by reconfiguring itself but by latching on to the materials it has become associated with. There are an enormous number of things that are organic. Among them are skin, hair, and fingernails.

"What really proved significant was the second thing I learned. It was that when Blue interacts with organic materials, the half-life for the interaction is only seven years. This means that Mustangs coated with Blue paints in an organic paint base become half as bright in seven years. It also means that skin interacting with Blue will suffer a significant impact in very few years. I could have warned people at that moment, although I didn't believe they would have believed me. I felt I'd be accused of sour grapes because of losing the patent. Instead, I decided to see what I could do about the problem. The result is the building you see behind us."

The man asking the question has rolled up his sleeves. "I see you found a way to get revenge against Mallet Pharmaceuticals and put yourself in a position to make a lot of money."

Les sits down and takes the microphone in his two hands. "If I had wanted revenge, I could have announced the problems much sooner."

"But that would have lessened the impact of announcing it now," the man continues.

Les is growing tired. "Maybe," he acknowledges, "but my mind was on finding the solution."

"And making money."

Les is seething. "Sir, may I ask your name?"

"Uh, Arnie Paynel."

"And, Mr. Paynel, who do you work for?"

"The New York Times."

"Mr. Paynel, until a moment ago, I had never heard your name. Yet you have a hell of a platform. Until yesterday, no one had ever heard of me, and I had no platform. Yesterday, five people showed up to sit in this big tent. Maybe I could have said something earlier, but who would have listened? Now I have a platform. Now people will listen. So say what you want to say about me. It doesn't matter. We are where we are. So tell me, what do I do with the building behind us? Should I close it down?" There's silence.

Les rises, followed by Berty, who looks shellshocked.

Les turns back and picks up the microphone from the table. "Two weeks … We'll be open in two weeks as long as everyone behaves. And, yes, there will be a charge for the service."

Chapter Seventy-Two

Berty settles in a leather lounge chair overlooking the empty floor of Bleu Regrets LLC and speaks as if in a daze, "Lord, Les, you just told the national press to go fuck themselves."

"Not quite, Berty. I just told them we were going to go on with business no matter what they think or write."

"Yes, but they're going to say that you created this problem so that you could make a fortune correcting it."

"Not true. I didn't produce cosmetics without adequate testing. I wouldn't have sold them if I had been involved. I would have tested."

"Do you think they give a shit about what you would have done? The simple fact is that the cosmetics weren't adequately tested, they were sold, and you invented the bloody stuff."

"I didn't invent it. I just noted it. It's part of a chemical research process."

"Details, Les. Just details. Do you think anyone gives a damn? The world just knows you're associated with its genesis and that you're going to make money from it."

"Okay, so what? Do you think women won't come to us with money in their hands? We needed to get the word out about what we offer, and now it's out … out on the front pages of the newspapers of the world. It's time to get us and others in line to build more facilities, both here and around the world. We need laser equipment built. We need workers trained. We need to hire people who have done these things to serve as our managers. We're on a roll, Berty."

"Lord, Les, do you think manufacturers can produce enough lasers?"

"Damned if I know. We're going to find out quickly and get other companies involved. If necessary, we'll ask the President to implement the National Defense Act. After all, we're going to have half the people in this nation demanding our help. It's a national crisis, Berty, and you and I are going to solve it."

"It sounds like we have a lot to do, Les. I don't know if we're up to it."

"We're going to get help, Berty. We're going to get lots of help. We need more facilities up and running in six to ten months. The reporter talked about almost six hundred years to do the United States. With more treatment facilities, it will be nowhere near that. Others will emulate us. I figure, at best, we have ten or fifteen years, Berty. Then it will be done except for a little cleanup. We have, at best, fifteen years, and then we're out of business. Fifteen years and then we can sit back with our heels up."

"Lord, mate, is this the same Les Warin I once knew? The one who lost a fortune and couldn't afford an apartment? The one who was worried about his future? The introspective scientist?"

Les frowned. "And the cuckolded husband? No more, Berty … no more."

Chapter Seventy-Three

Etienne returns from a few hours at the office. "We're finished, Cathy." He goes to the sideboard and pours himself a large glass of bourbon.

Cathy watches him from the sofa where she has been reading Harpers Bizarre. "Don't you want some ice and water with that?"

"Maybe for the second one."

"What the devil, Etienne?"

"The stock's down to seventy-nine cents. I sold at four dollars."

"So we have money?"

Etienne gives her a sick smile. "Seventy-eight thousand."

"So we're okay."

"Six months, maybe."

"But you'll keep getting paid?"

"No, the pay ended as soon as I arrived at work. Then things became worse after I sold. My father said I was abandoning the company, abandoning ship. The Mallet name would be gone forever. He blamed us for his buying Vincent Cosmetics. He said it ruined the company."

"Us?"

"Yeah, Dad said things have been downhill ever since I married you. After all, I made a big deal of your involvement when I proposed buying Vincent Cosmetics."

"Shit, Etienne, Mallet made a fortune from those cosmetics."

"And it's all going down the drain. Mallet's got so many class-action suits coming its way that all that so-called fortune is going to vanish. Dad's had to hire extra law firms to handle things. The lawsuit over the cosmetics has over fifty million people involved. It may be the largest class-action suit ever. Then there's the actors' guild suing over lost wages due to facial damage, the porn industry over layoffs, and I don't know what all. Mallet is not going to survive."

"What about your parents?"

"They're like the Sacklers ... They have all kinds of other investments."

"Who are the Sacklers?"

"They were sued over oxycontin."

"They lose?"

"Big time."

"Well, Bleu Glo didn't kill anyone."

"No, but it affected even more people than the narcotics, and they're all angry."

"Well, if your parents have other investments, don't you have some too?"

"No."

"No, Etienne? What planet have you been living on?"

"I figured all that would come later. I've been having a good time. You have to."

"So you're blaming it on me?"

"I'm not blaming anyone ... just trying to face reality. It's not easy."

"God, what's reality, Etienne?"

"I need a job."

"Damn, Etienne, you've never worked in your life."

"Well, you have."

Cathy looks at Etienne, aghast. "You're shitting me, aren't you?"

Chapter Seventy-Four

The business is thriving. Bleu Regrets LLC has been open for two weeks. Despite the bad press, the schedule is packed. Bleu Regrets is making an average of over five thousand dollars per client for the laser treatments, and the motels are full. If individuals want privacy, the fee can be as high as twenty-five thousand dollars. Those who can't afford the treatments are complaining. Television is running interviews with the poor. The publicity is not good. Les tells Berty the people can just wait. Money has its privileges. He says he'll drop the price when the wealthy clientele begins to dry up.

Les and Berty have moved quickly. They've hired internationally experienced managers from General Motors and Starbucks to run the international business and put Bechtel in charge of construction worldwide. They've hired another medical supply company, a manufacturer of eye surgery equipment, to manufacture the lasers. A university president has been hired to establish a personnel training facility, and recruitment is proceeding in earnest. Everyone is being paid triple wages or more, and everyone knows the job is only for a few years. They're after the money.

The company's penthouse offices have expanded the building's length to accommodate the expanded leadership. The new conference room is cantilevered over the client bay with mirrored windows on three sides.

Everything is fine.

Les's intercom comes alive. It's the receptionist in the entrance foyer.

"Yes, Margie?"

"Sir, there are two men here to see you."

"I'm not aware of any appointments."

"Sir, they say they're from the FBI."

Les reacts with a shiver of uncertainty, as he expects anyone does who hears those threatening words. "Oh, they want to talk to me?"

"Yes, sir."

"Er, I guess they need to come up. Will you escort them?"

"I'm by myself, sir."

"Okay, I'll get someone from security to bring them up."

After a few telephone calls, Les arranges for the men to be escorted.

The two men arrive at his office door, following Les's security guard. They look the way Les thinks FBI agents should look—smartly dressed in dark suits, standing erect, looking fit. He wonders if all agents looked that way or just ones sent to intimidate.

Les admits to himself that he is intimidated. He stands to greet them over his desk. He's damned if he is going to move from behind his desk. He extends his hand. "Les Warin. How can I help you?"

They shake his hand. "Agent Raby."

"Agent Montecaniso."

Les nods. "Have a seat, gentlemen. May I offer coffee, a soft drink, anything?"

"No," the agents reply in unison.

There is no "sir" after it. It's a business "no."

Raby speaks, "Mr. Warin, we're investigating some allegations made against you."

"Allegations?"

"Yes, it has been alleged that your negligence has resulted in extensive injury to millions of United States citizens."

"Hell, all the media have been conjecturing about that. Others say I'm involved in all kinds of conspiracies."

"That's been alleged too."

"So there's nothing new here."

"The Department of Justice wants to know if your negligence or conspiracy should be elevated to the level of a crime."

"Crime? My god, man. Negligence resulting in your killing or injuring someone might be a crime. I haven't done either."

"The allegation is that thousands of people have suffered severe injury from Bleu Glo Cosmetics because you didn't warn them not to use it."

"I didn't tell them not to get out of bed because they might be injured or killed, either. What makes me responsible? I didn't make the stuff. I didn't market it. The damned stuff is not my doing."

Raby looks through a file he has taken from a briefcase. "The cosmetic company says you are the inventor of this blue dye and that you were present in the office of an attorney"—he looks through his file—"an attorney named DeSilvo when the making of these cosmetics was initially discussed."

"Okay, yes, I was. And we discussed doing testing. And the whole thing was taken away from me before anyone did any testing or manufacturing. I wasn't involved."

"You didn't tell them the stuff was dangerous?"

"I didn't know it was dangerous."

"You've told reporters that you knew it had a half-life?"

"I did, but I didn't know it was dangerous."

"Don't you know that radium is dangerous?"

"This stuff is not radium."

"But you know radium is dangerous?"

"Yes, but that's not relevant."

DELLA B'S BLEU GLO

"Isn't it correct that you did know that this Blue stuff had a half-life?"

"Yes."

"Who did you tell about it having a half-life?"

"Uh, no one."

"No warning to anyone?"

"I didn't know it required a warning."

Raby eyes Les as if he thinks Les is evading the truth. "Whether it does or does not is not up to me to decide."

Les throws up his hands. "Are you saying you're not judging me? The questions are judgmental."

"I didn't write the questions."

"So you're just the messenger?"

"I'm just doing my job."

"Yeah, and what additional questions are part of your job?"

"It has been further alleged that you knew that Blue might damage people as early as a year ago and did not warn anyone about it. Is that true?"

"Yes, but I had no platform to put out that information, and I'm not sure anyone would have believed me anyway."

"Did you try to warn people?"

"No."

"But you could have tried?"

"Are you saying that because someone knows something and doesn't trumpet it to the world, he is criminally negligent?"

"Again, it's not my job to decide."

"Yeah, yeah, I know. But I feel that you're trying to define 'negligence' in some kind of new, legal, criminal way."

"Again—"

"I know, I know … not your job. Donald Trump knew covid was dangerous, that it would kill people, and he played it down. He told people not to worry … refused to wear a mask, which cost thousands of lives. Was he negligent? He not only knew, but he lied about it. However, I'm unaware of anyone suing him for negligence or indicting him for criminal activity. Let's make it very clear, Agent Raby, that I haven't cost anyone their lives. What people did, using those cosmetics, was done entirely of their own volition. I didn't encourage a damned thing and didn't make any money from it."

"Yes, but by not warning people, you set yourself up to make money."

"So did Walmart when they started building megastores and putting neighborhood stores out of business. Were they supposed to warn the little guy?"

"Are you saying you weren't thinking about making money when you held off warning people?"

Les knows he's guilty. "I'm not saying anything. As I said before, no one would have listened, and I don't believe I had any responsibility to issue a warning. It was not my product. Bleu Glo's sales were not my responsibility. I learned it might be dangerous, and I started to develop means to correct the damage it might do. Pharmaceutical companies do this all the time. When they discover a medicine, they make money from it. That's the way it works. They see a problem, and they make money by fixing it. I'm no different."

Raby closes his folder and stands up. "I guess that remains to be determined."

They don't shake hands.

Chapter Seventy-Five

Cathy has cut out her streaked hair and has swept her remaining hair over the gap. It almost works except where her hair meets her forehead. Something looks awry there, but it isn't too bad.

She had bought huge sunglasses years ago as a gimmick. They are no longer a gimmick. They hide her inflamed eyelids and the dark half-moons that have developed below her eyes. She never takes them off, even in the darkest of rooms. At home, she keeps most of the rooms dark.

She wears bright red plastic fingernails over her natural, shattered nails. Looking carefully, she can see the pattern of cracks under the polish.

Outside her house, she is not alone. Every woman is wearing sunglasses. Hoods and stocking caps are in vogue. There are so many people wearing masks that you would think the covid pandemic has returned. As a result, everyone knows who has dyed their hair and whose lips are thick and bleeding.

Cathy is better off than many, but that is little consolation. She cusses Les Warin every time she looks in the mirror. She knows he didn't develop the cosmetics and didn't market them, but who else is she going to blame? Not herself, certainly. She was duped along with everyone else.

If he only hadn't discovered the damned dye. It didn't matter that she had sent the email that incited all the following events. If only Etienne hadn't been gullible enough to buy in. If only … if only.

And now she's broke, except for a few dollars left in the bank from selling the Mustang.

Damn Etienne. Damn Les. Damn husbands. They don't produce. They leave you high and dry.

She opens the door to a store where she hopes to find work and goes in. It's another place on the list of stores she's visited to look for a job. She has been looking for ten days.

Her old hotel wouldn't have her. The old management was gone. The new people didn't believe she could interact with the public in her current condition. It didn't matter that the public looked just like her.

For other positions, she had been told she doesn't have secretarial skills. She had scoffed at that. Computers were word processors. Anyone can work them. But she was told she lacked experience. How the hell do you get experience if no one will hire you?

She was damned if she would be a waitress and stand on her feet all day. Maybe next week I'll feel different.

The managers at most stores rejected her. It was the same story everywhere, "You need to be able to look the customer in the eye." They told her she was damaged goods.

But everyone is damaged goods … at least most women … a few men, but most women. Are men going to be the only ones in the workforce? And Etienne … Lord, what a useless prick. He reads the paper every morning, looking for a job as a company president or vice-president, as if he's qualified. Hell, do companies advertise in the newspaper for presidents? I don't think so. The man's useless … useless, useless. And the name "Etienne" doesn't help. It's too damned effete.

Inside the next store, she looks around at a sea of mattresses lit by a ceiling of fluorescent lights. Despite the overhead lights, she feels she is looking through a fog. Through it, she sees the light of one incandescent bulb shining yellow through her brown sunglass's lenses from a desk in the far back left corner.

She heads that way. She strips off her coat as she weaves through the mattresses. She walks the walk. Hell, it used to work. Maybe he won't look at my face. He's clearly watching.

The man behind the desk rises to meet her. He's wearing a tie pulled loose from around his thick neck. He's in shirtsleeves, with his suit jacket draped over his chair. She guesses he's mid-fifties, already utterly bald on top with a fringe of hair grown long around the sides, combed to look like a duck in back.

"Hi, I'm Cathy, uh, Warin." Humiliation fills her consciousness at using her former name. Lord, help me. "Are you Jerry Brenner?"

"Yes ... yes, I am. How may I help you?"

"My husband, Les Warin, used to work here."

The man squeezes his eyes and frowns momentarily in thought. "Oh, yeah, smart guy ... too smart for this job, but he did well. I'm pleased to meet you. How's Les doing?"

"Very well. Thank you," Cathy responds, thinking, Well, like making millions.

"That's good to hear. Now, what can I do for you? We have a couple of items on sale today."

"Thank you, but that's not why I'm here."

"Oh?"

"I'd like a job. I'm good at sales."

Brenner looks over Cathy's body. He sees past her damaged face. "I bet you are."

<u>Chapter Seventy-Six</u>

Berty can't believe his ears. "Blimey, mate, the FBI, they're after you for negligence. How far can they extend that notion? You didn't kill anyone. I can't believe the legal system would ever consider what we've done as criminal. This is coming from nowhere."

Les has a worried frown. "Hell, if they take me to court, who knows what might happen? It will be up to a jury, and who knows what a jury might think?"

"Mate, if that kind of thinking goes on, we're all doomed to what other people think. Anyone can throw anything into the courts and maybe win."

"Frightening, isn't it?"

"If they were after you for conspiracy, I'd understand it better. You did conspire ... no denying it."

"Damn, Berty, I won't call you for a character witness."

"Well, you did."

"Man, I didn't conspire to do anything. There was a market, and I worked to fill the needs of that market. That took time. That's what business is all about."

"Yeah, but that market is a bunch of damaged people. It could be said that by not setting off an alarm, you added more damaged people to the market and let the damage to all the users of Bleu Glo get worse, get more damaging."

"Yeah, but at the time, I wasn't equipped to do anything about it."

"People could have stopped using the stuff, yes?"

"They still had Blue on and under their skin, in their nails, and on their scalps. It was still latching on to their flesh. Once it did, it wasn't going away."

"Yes, but more Blue was piling on over time, no?"

"Shit, Berty, you're no help."

"Just playing devil's advocate, mate. If there's a suit, it will get me too."

Les sighs and looks like a herd of wild horses is coming toward him. "So what do we do?"

"We spread our money out. Get the money out of the LLC. Buy ourselves million-dollar homes. Establish other nonrelated corporations. Get lawyers to help, but we do it quickly before any suits come down the road ... before the word gets out that the FBI is investigating."

"Damn, and I thought we were the saviors of the human race."

Chapter Seventy-Seven

There's a lot of excitement in the building. Della B is in the building being cared for. She has landed on the roof in a helicopter. It is not the first helicopter to land. Several celebrities have been there for treatment, but Della B is the one who had connected her name to Bleu Glo. Now, everyone knows she has broken off that relationship. People have sued her, and in turn, she has sued Vincent Cosmetics and Mallet Pharmaceuticals, all of which have added to the wealth of numerous attorneys.

Upon landing, she is escorted quickly from the roof. Her appearance is disguised, with several scarves wrapped around her head. It is assumed she is wearing dark glasses, but no one can see through the scarves. She looks like a walking mummy, although a colorful one.

Les always gets a kick out of the celebrities wanting to hide. Generally, everyone working in the building knows they are there, no matter how they try to cover themselves. The word spreads faster than a virus.

Les tries to ensure their privacy. Everyone knows not to talk outside the building. Les has made it clear that he will fire anyone who does.

Most days, the scheduling system runs smoothly, although there are a lot of anonymous clients. They are given secret code names. It makes them feel important—makes them think that their helicopters are flying under the radar.

Les will give them whatever they need. They pay for it. He doesn't understand a lot of what goes on. It seems to him that if you want anonymity, you don't arrive by helicopter or in a stretch limousine, but who knows how the "anonymous" of the world think?

Sometimes the proffered code and procedure aren't enough. Sometimes there are special requests (demands). If a client wants to be treated at two o'clock in the morning, that can be arranged, for a price. When there are special requests, they are referred to the management.

Thus, near the end of the third week of operations, when a call comes in from the scheduling room, Les braces himself to talk to a movie star or congresswoman. "Les Warin. How may I help you?"

"You bastard. Your damn people are giving me a runaround."

"Cathy?"

"Yes, damn it. How the hell does anyone get to you? You're all wrapped up in your management cocoon. I've phoned three times … waiting times twenty-seven minutes, twenty-two minutes, and thirty-two minutes respectively. Your damned people have refused to connect me to you. They've cut me off."

"Damn, Cathy, we get hundreds of calls. If there's the slightest question, people want to talk to me. I have to be insulated some way."

"Well, it's damn frustrating."

Annoyance is building in Les. "Well, you've got me now. What do you need?"

"I need to be fixed."

"I assume that means you used your Bleu Glo."

"What do you mean your Bleu Glo? You invented the damned stuff."

"Invented, nothing. I discovered the dye. I didn't make the cosmetic. I didn't sell it. I didn't advertise it. That's all your doing, Cathy. You're the one who sold me out."

"The crap I did. Etienne received an email telling him what you had done."

"Yeah, I bet he did. A clandestine email was sent anonymously from the only person who knew I'd discovered Blue. You did it, Cathy. I've always known it. You didn't get the money when we were married and were determined you were going to get it another way and punish me in the process. You're rich now, Cathy. You should be happy."

"Rich, nothing. You tanked Bleu Glo … stuck a dagger in its back. After all the suits, I haven't got shit."

"What? Etienne didn't have money stashed away?"

"The bastard hasn't got anything."

"So, as I understand it from this conversation, you've been married to two bastards. Neither of whom made you rich."

"Damn you. It isn't funny."

"Don't mean for it to be, Cathy. Let's get down to what you've called for. I assume you used Bleu Glo and want treatment."

"You owe it to me."

"I don't think so, Cathy, but tell me what you need."

"Eyelids, fingernails, a streak in my hair."

"Okay, if the streak is not too big, we can probably do it for three hundred. The nails will be twenty-five hundred and the eyelids, three thousand."

"Fifty-eight hundred!"

"The going rate."

"You fucker! I don't have fifty-eight hundred."

"Well, we'll probably drop the cost in a year or so."

"You son of a bitch!"

"Cathy, it's simple. You screwed me, and I don't owe you a thing. Pay the going rate, and we'll help you. Stand in line like everyone else."

"Fuck you, Les!" Cathy slams the phone down.

Les holds it out and studies it. Not even for old times' sake, Cathy. You need to pay for what you've done.

Chapter Seventy-Eight

After Cathy hangs up the phone call with Les, she sits alone in her new apartment, furious. She's furious at life and furious at Les. She has spent her day being stiffed by Les's company on the phone. That would send any sane human being out the front door and down the street screaming at the top of her lungs. And after all that, Les treated me like a worthless woman.

He took no responsibility. Christ, he developed the stuff. He won't even admit it, but I know from what Etienne told me that the initial idea for Della B's cosmetics was discussed by Les in a meeting at his lawyer's, Silver something. I know damn well it started with him. He claims he would have tested more than was done. That's a bunch of crap. He was out to make money like anyone else would be. And now I'm stuck.

He took my beauty, my lifeline. And he doesn't accept any responsibility … doesn't show an iota of sympathy and contrition … treats me like any other woman. Hell, I was his wife. I was a good wife for years. I was patient while he fiddled in his lab. He owes me. He owes me in more ways than one.

She is sitting in a folding chair, with her cell phone in her hand. She looks around the empty room. Shit, I shouldn't have just moved out on Etienne. I should have kept my wits about me, kept my cool, and arranged for some of the furniture to come with me.

Jerry Brenner had given her a damaged mattress and box spring set and written it off. He had helped her tie it to the roof of her Mercedes.

She had collected several 20 percent off coupons for one item at Bed Bath and Beyond. So far, she has made four trips and has gotten a pillow, a linen set, a blanket, and the folding chair she is sitting on. She'll get a card table next or maybe a cheap set of pots and pans.

She sighs, gets up, and puts on her coat. She needs to get to Brenner's Bedding. She has the evening shift. It will give her time to think. She'll decide what to do about Les. She'll do it tomorrow. She'll do something.

She locks the apartment door and heads for the Mercedes. It's in the company's name. She wonders how long she'll have it before it becomes part of a bankruptcy settlement. They'll have to find her. She's not giving anyone her new address.

***

At first, she had been alarmed at having left Etienne too compulsively, inadvertently leaving some of her property behind, which she now needs.

Cathy drops by her old apartment. Fortunately, Etienne has not changed the locks on the apartment and has not yet moved out. She finds what she is looking for in her bottom bureau drawer, underneath sweaters. She stuffs it all in a large shopping bag and quickly leaves. She doesn't know why she left the sweaters— perhaps to hide what was under them. She could use the sweaters, but what's important is the plastic bag of syringes and the small notebook to which the bag is attached.

Next, Cathy returns to the same library she had visited years before to take Blue away from Les. Then it was for financial gain. Today it's for revenge.

In the library, at a computer, she pulls a slip of paper from her wallet. She has written down the email address of the West Virginia State Police. She also opens the small notebook. On the computer, she enters the address of the police and then types, "You can find a body at the following coordinates." She then, from the notebook, copies the coordinates she had extracted from Les's cell phone years before.

Okay, you bastard. Let's see how you explain that.

Her next task is to plant the syringe that killed Godfrey at Les's apartment or in his car.

Cathy thinks, Damn, I can't believe it. I remember Godfrey's name. He was only a blip in my life.

Chapter Seventy-Nine

A couple of weeks have passed.

Cathy is sitting behind the desk in the mattress store. In the past three hours, there has been only one customer, a browser. Usually, she brings a book to read, but she forgot it and is incredibly bored. She's never learned to play games on her cell phone. She's reviewed the news and the weather but doesn't know what else to do.

When her cell phone rings, she jumps. She looks at the screen—E. Chisholm. God, what's this about? She realizes she has never changed her phone number and shakes her head. That was a mistake.

Reluctantly, she answers. "Eddie Chisholm, a ghost from the past. What's up?"

"Hey, Cat. Do they still call you Cat?"

"No, it's Cathy now ... at least most of the time. Why the hell are you calling? I know you have bad feelings toward me, and I haven't got much better toward you."

"Listen, Cathy. I thought I'd give you a heads up."

"Why's that?"

"We know too much about each other."

"So?"

"Thought you'd like to know. The police are coming around ... been here talking to Sanchez ... probably coming to see you."

"The police?"

"Yeah, they found Billy Covington's body."

"What?" The hair has risen on Cathy's neck. From now on, I need to be careful what I say. "His body? Do you mean he's dead? Why would the police come to see me? Why would they think I'd know anything about that?"

Chisholm ignored Cathy's attempt at misdirection. "They went to your old office. Peggy Sanchez told them Billy was in and out of your office a lot before he vanished."

"Hell, he was all over the building. He was in charge of maintenance, for God's sake. You'd know more about what he was doing than I would. What did you tell them?"

"I told them he was just here one day, and the next week he wasn't … Told them I knew nothing about it."

Thank God, Cathy thinks, he hasn't fessed up, and he hasn't said anything over the phone yet that's compromising. I need to hang up before he says anything. "Gosh, I don't see how I can help. I appreciate your calling, but I really don't know anything. You take care, Eddie."

She hangs up. Shit, shit, shit. How did they find Billy's body? What's happening with Godfrey? Were the two men buried in the same place? How could that happen? Maybe the discovery of Billy at this time is just a coincidence … or maybe not. I can't ask Wigram or Chisholm where they buried Billy … at least not over the phone … and I can't go see them. They might be being watched. Damn, this is a mess.

Chapter Eighty

There's a knock on Cathy's door.

Damn, she thinks. No one knows I'm here.

She has the security chain on her door. She opens it a crack. A big, tall woman holds a badge up to the opening. "Gertrude Sorenson, Alexandria Police. May we come in?"

"Yeah, just a minute."

Shit, thinks Cathy, as she unchains the door and opens it.

Sorenson motions her hand toward a young man with her. "This is my partner, Ben Metzinger. Are you Cathy Mallet?"

Cathy hesitates, wanting to deny who she is. "Yes, how may I help?"

Sorenson eyes the nearly empty apartment. "I gather you just moved in. Your husband didn't know where you were. I found your ex-husband in the marriage license file. He told us where you worked. Your boss, Mr.Brenner, told us where you live."

"So Les Warin knows I'm working at the mattress store?"

"He apparently talked to the owner. You trying to keep it a secret from the world?"

Damn, Brenner must have called Les to check on me. "Yes, my husband and I are going our own ways. I want privacy until I can settle down."

"You and your husband have problems?"

"You might say that. I'd offer you a seat, but I don't have any."

"That's okay. We just need to ask a couple of questions."

"About Mallet? About Bleu Glo?"

"Bleu Glo? That crap? No, no. About Billy Covington."

"Billy Covington? Gosh, I haven't heard that name in years."

"You worked with him at the Pleasure Hotel in Crystal City."

"Right, he was in charge of maintenance. Just didn't come to work one day."

"His wife says he didn't come home from work the previous Friday."

"Oh, I wouldn't know."

"Well, he's dead."

"What? Did he kill himself?"

"We don't think so. Suicides don't usually bury themselves."

Metzinger suddenly speaks, "We think he was murdered."

Cathy looks at him. He hardly looks old enough to be out of highschool. "Really? He was a big, strong guy. That's hard to believe."

Sorenson interjects, "Well, we don't really know that. We only have bones." Sorenson studies Cathy for a moment. "You don't know anything about him?"

"No, why should I?"

"We talked to Covington's ex-boss, Stanley Wigram. We were asking about all the people who worked with Covington. You were mentioned. He told us what your job was at the Pleasure Hotel, and from there, we went to talk to Peggy Sanchez, who apparently worked for you."

"Yes, that's correct."

"We understand Covington was in and out of your office many times."

"Yeah, of course. I was in charge of the banquet rooms. He did maintenance for me. We coordinated on that."

"We understand he left a brown paper bag for you once."

"What?"

"It had a camera in it."

Cathy is caught off guard. Sorenson is watching her face. She hurries to respond, afraid she has hesitated too long. "Oh, yeah, it was a camcorder, not a camera. I loaned it to him. He was going to take some movies of his kids. I don't know if he did. It wasn't on the memory card when he returned it."

Sorenson looks skeptical, as if she doesn't quite believe Cathy. "So you were friends with him, friends enough to loan him a camcorder?"

"I wouldn't say friends. We were acquaintances. We all worked together in the same hotel. We were acquaintances at work but went our own ways when we weren't there."

"But you felt you could lend him a camcorder?"

"Sure, why not?"

"Do you still have the camcorder?"

"No. It was old technology. I got rid of it."

"You didn't keep the memory card?"

"No."

"Not even of the movies you had taken?"

"I didn't take many movies. I wasn't particularly good at it."

"So you didn't keep them?"

"No."

"Sounds like you wasted your money buying the camcorder."

"Yeah, I did."

"How about Mr. Covington's other acquaintances?"

"What about them?"

"Were any of them shady … suspect? Did he argue with anyone?"

"Not that I'm aware of."

Sorenson pulls out a business card and hands it to Cathy. "Well, thank you for your help, Mrs. Mallet. Please phone me at the number on the card if you think of anything."

Cathy can't help it. She inquires, "You didn't ask me if he was depressed. Don't police always ask that?"

Sorenson looks at her, thinking, You smart aleck, cocky bitch. "We told you we don't think he killed himself."

"Then what killed him?"

"Do you mean, how did he die?"

"Is there a difference?"

"Could be."

***

That night, Cathy drives out the George Washington Parkway toward Mount Vernon. She parks in a pull-off, gets out of the car, walks to the Potomac River, and throws the camcorder as far as she can out into the murky water.

The memory card is in her glove compartment. She needs to get rid of it. That's a job for the morning. I can't wait long.

***

The following morning, she lays things out on her bathroom counter. There's the small notebook where she had recorded the coordinates of Godfrey's burial, the memory card of Wigram stealing from the hotel, and four syringes in two plastic bags. She never planted the syringes at Les Warin's. She thinks just as well. They found the wrong body.

She wonders what Billy Covington did with the memory card of their tryst. Christ, if they find it, I'm dead. She guesses that he didn't take it home. He wouldn't want to take a chance of his wife finding it.

She knows the police will do a thorough search to see if he hid it at work. She hopes he didn't. She hopes it's lost forever. She puts all the items in a brown paper bag.

She drives to the athletic club where she and Etienne share a membership. In the locker room, she finds an empty locker. She stores the paper bag in the locker, locks it tight, checks it again to ensure it's locked, and puts the key in her purse.

She feels like she's being watched but knows she isn't. She drives to the city library.

In the biography section, she finds a book, Geometric Approaches to Light Refraction, that looks like it hasn't been taken out in years. The adjacent books are similar. She tapes the key to the locker inside the back of the book and leaves.

She's not entirely comfortable, but she believes that if someone finds the key, they won't know where it came from. She's uneasy, but it will have to do. At least my apartment's clean. Let the damn cops search to their heart's content. There's not much there to find, anyway.

Chapter Eighty-One

Cathy's phone rings. She looks at the screen. What the hell?

The call is from Bleu Regrets LLC. She shivers and answers, "Yes?"

"Can you be here at eleven in the morning?"

"Les?"

"Yes, can you?"

"You're going to fix me after all?"

"If you can be here at eleven."

"I'll be there."

"Good. Enter door 1." The phone goes dead.

"I'll be damned."

***

Inside door 1 to the Bleu Regrets LLC building, Cathy is met by a receptionist. She gives the woman her name. The receptionist eyes her with undisguised curiosity.

Cathy intuits that the receptionist knows more about her than she would like.

"Please follow me, Mrs. Mallet. You'll be in treatment room 1."

As they walk into the cavernous bay, Cathy asks, "Is there something special about room 1?"

The woman speaks without turning her head back to Cathy, "It's where Dr. Gmellin works."

"Is there something special about Dr. Gmellin?"

"He handles our special clients."

So I'm special. I wonder what that means.

The receptionist opens the door to room 1. To Cathy, the room looks empty except for some heavy equipment, a chair that looks like it's from an ophthalmologist's office, a plastic chair, and a patient table.

She enters and hears the door close behind her. She jumps when she hears a voice coming from the corner behind the door. "Hello, Cathy."

She whirls to look into the corner. Les is sitting on a second plastic chair. He's looking at the floor.

"Jesus Christ, Les, you scared me. Where's the doctor?"

"Getting a cup of coffee."

"He's coming back, isn't he? He's going to treat me like you said?"

"Yes, Cathy. I said we'd do it, and we will, but I want to talk to you first."

"Okay, whatever, but you're going to have to look at me first?"

"I'd just as soon not."

"You don't want to see what you've done to me?"

"What you did to yourself."

"That's your opinion. Now, damn it. Look at me."

Les does and grimaces.

"Bad, huh. Remember this face, Les. It's what you did to the world."

"It's what the world did to itself. It's what vanity did."

"Your nightmare, Les. Yours and yours alone. You should have buried Blue."

"I didn't know enough about it. Besides, you took away my control … over money, Cathy … to make yourself rich. Put the blame where it belongs."

"I know where it belongs. Now, what the hell do you want to talk about?"

"Who the hell is Billy Covington?"

"Who?"

"Don't shit me, Cathy."

"Why should I know about this Billy Covington?"

"Because the police phoned me, asking about him ... asking about you. They phoned me because I was your husband ... your husband at the time Billy Covington vanished from the Pleasure Hotel."

"Again, why would I know about this man Covington?"

"Because we both know what you are capable of."

Cathy becomes irritated. "Is this place bugged, Les?"

"If it were, would I admit I know what you're capable of?"

"No, but I didn't kill your lab partner."

"You all but did. I know you could have done it. You made me your patsy."

"Hey, I've got a syringe with your fingerprints on it and Godfrey's blood on the needle."

"You didn't look at the syringe, Cathy. The needle's stuck in the asphalt at Godfrey's apartment, or maybe in the tire of some car that parked there long ago. Besides, how would you explain having the syringe?"

"Believe me, Les. I could make a case."

"I believe you, Cathy, but without the needle, it only means I used the syringe. That doesn't mean a thing ... not after all this time."

Cathy sits in silence.

Les asks again, "So who is Billy Covington, and why were the police looking for him?"

"Did the police tell you about finding this guy Covington?"

"They did, but I already knew. The finding was in the paper, both here in Martinsburg and in Winchester. This is West Virginia, Cathy. Things like finding bones in the neighborhood make the news."

"So again, what's it got to do with me?"

"Cathy, I don't know the why or the what for, but it has to do with you. This guy Covington worked with you, the police phoned me because I was your former husband, and the police evidently found this guy near where Godfrey is buried. They went there because they received an anonymous email tip providing the location and traced the email back to an Alexandria library. I never told anyone the location of Godfrey's body, but you could have traced me. My guess is that you did and that you gave the West Virginia Police the location because you wanted them to find Godfrey and pin it on me, all because I gave you grief about what you had done to yourself with Bleu Glo."

"That's a lot of guessing, Les."

"What I can't figure out is why you buried this guy Covington in the same place?"

"Maybe, because I didn't bury him."

"No, right, you didn't bury him. You had someone else do it. That's a mistake, a bad mistake, Cathy. A bad, bad mistake. You had better pray your cohorts don't talk."

"Where's the doctor, Les? Let's get on with this. If it's still fifty-eight-hundred dollars, you'll have to catch up with me down the road."

"I could stop the whole procedure right now if I wanted to."

"You could, but Godfrey's still out there."

Chapter Eighty-Two

The procedure is complete. Dr. Gmellin has left the room. He's told her she has ten minutes. The next client is on her way.

Cathy stands in front of a mirror, with her mind wondering. Torran Gmellin. I've never known a Torran before. Wonder where that name comes from.

She finally focuses. She takes her fingers and pulls down one eyelid. It stings to the touch. It's flaming red, but it's not blue. She sighs with relief. The doctor has told her the inflammation will be gone in ten days. She prays it will.

She takes a brush from her purse and works on her hair to cover where the missing strands were, and the reddish spot from which the blue hair has been removed. If I have to, I can wear a scarf for a while.

Finally, she studies her fingernails. Almost all of the nails are gone. She has been told they will grow out in four or five months. God, what do I do until then … wear slacks with pockets … keep my hands in the pockets? I don't even have anything left to which to attach fake nails. What do I do at the store when I have to write receipts? I'm going to have to bandage my hand … make them look like I'm wearing mittens. Thank God I never did my toenails.

The door opens, and the receptionist comes in. "Mr. Warin would like to see you."

Damn, what now?

The receptionist leads Cathy to the front of the building, up a stairway, and down a hall. She knocks on a door. Cathy hears Les say, "Come in."

Cathy enters an elegant conference room and looks out through the one-way glass. "God, is this the place from which the king surveys his kingdom?"

Les gives her a pleased smile. "Sometimes."

Cathy turns toward him. "Didn't we talk enough downstairs?"

Les becomes serious. "There's something I think you need to know."

"What's that?"

"People are searching the mountain where this guy Covington was buried. I assume it's the same mountain where Godfrey Trainham is buried."

"Lord, what kind of people are they?"

"Ghouls, fans of The Walking Dead. Hell, I don't know."

"Oh, shit, you mean they might find him?"

"Hell, it wouldn't be hard. If they do, you're going to have two bodies connected to you."

"And one to you and me to you. You can't avoid being involved."

"That's what I'm afraid of. Goodness knows I've wished I wasn't connected to you more than once."

"Well, what are you going to do?"

"It's not 'you,' darling. It's 'we.'"

"Yeah?"

"You and I are going to move the body."

"A bunch of bones?"

"We'll take some shopping bags."

Chapter Eighty-Three

Charlie Scruggs and Billy Kominski meet in the high school parking lot after school and get into Charlie's Plymouth Neon. Billy is always amazed that the car still runs. Charlie tells him his father loves cars and views the Plymouth as a challenge.

They drive into Alexandria, talking about girls, particularly Cyndi McKnight. Billy sits behind Cyndi in chemistry, and when the girl gets bored, she turns and scribbles a tic tac toe pattern in Billy's notebook. Billy usually lets her win. He's perfected the art of losing. Losing is worth it because he gets to look at Cyndi and gets her to smile. It's his only interaction with Cyndi, but it's worth it.

Soon, they arrive at the Alexandria Library, the Kate Waller Barrett Public Library on Queen Street. Charlie pulls into the parking lot next to the library and finds a slot near the rear. Sometimes the lot is full, and he has to park on the street. Sometimes the librarian Mrs. Corbet tells him to move his car when the library becomes full. He always thinks, If I have to, I have to.

Charlie and Billy go past the registration desk and eye the carts piled high with books returned or left on the tables by visitors. It's their job to return the books to their rightful positions in the stacks. They work three hours after school, three days a week. They go to Mrs. Corbet's office to check in.

Billy gives a tentative hello.

The woman looks up from her desk. "Good, you're both here today. I have a project for you. After you finish putting away the books, I want you to start going through all the books and separating out all those that have not been taken out by anyone in the last ten years. We need to weed things out to make room for new books. I want you to stack the books you identify in the storage room. I'll have the other librarians review them to see if any should be retained. You'll need iPads to compare them to the files. Do you have any questions?"

As they leave to get the carts of books to stack, Billy grouses to Charlie, "There goes our break time."

After the books have been returned to the stacks, they are accustomed to having time to sit and read magazines or get ahead on homework. Tonight, they are going to have to work.

***

Charlie is growing tired of the task. It's been boring enough putting the books back in the stacks. After that, he'd pull an empty cart behind him into the stacks and begin the task of searching the books and reviewing their histories in the library files. After a while, he concludes that he's probably been through a thousand books and has twenty-eight stacked on the cart. Some seem to have hardly ever been used, with their spines still stiff. He guesses some people author books about subjects that are only interesting to themselves.

He reaches high, takes out a book, checks it, and puts it on the cart. The next book looks similar, but he notes the back is not closed when he pulls it down. He looks at the back of the book to see what's keeping it from closing and is surprised to find a small envelope taped there. Intuiting that something is strange, he pulls the envelope loose, unseals it, and shakes out a key.

"Psst, psst," he tries to get Billy's attention. He hurries over to Billy, who only has six books on his cart. "You look like you're not doing anything. I've got almost thirty books on my cart."

"Shit, Charlie, I'm working fiction. I guess people read these books. What are you whispering about?"

Charlie holds up the key. "I found this in an envelope taped inside an old book."

Billy squints at the key. "It looks like a locker key for the lockers at Jason Quigg's Health Club."

He reaches in his pocket and pulls out some keys on a ring. He fingers through them. "See, it's got the same blue and yellow plastic cover for the head of the key."

"You're a member of the health club?"

"My dad is. We share a locker."

"You never take me there."

"Gosh, I don't know if I'm allowed to. I'm usually the youngest person there. I always feel like they might throw me out at any minute."

"Could you get me in to see if this key works in a locker?"

"Yeah, I guess. The place doesn't close till ten."

***

Charlie parks in the lot outside the health club. Before they leave the car, Billy puts his hand on Charlie's shoulder and gives him a stern look. "Look casual. Look like you belong. There's a gate inside. After I hold my membership card up to a reader by the gate, I'll be able to open the gate. Follow me in through the gate before it has an opportunity to close."

"Won't they be expecting us to be wearing athletic gear?"

"No, a lot of people work out in jeans. Only the really serious, or the ones with good builds, wear athletic gear."

The two hurry across the lot. The woman behind the counter is helping someone. They quickly rush through the entrance gate while she is preoccupied. Watching the gate is only a peripheral part of her job, and she pays no attention.

Charlie doesn't look at her. He tries not to look at anyone. He stays close to Billy, who is moving briskly toward the men's locker room.

Inside the locker room, they find one man changing his clothes. Billy goes to his locker and fumbles in it until the man leaves.

He then quickly begins trying the mysterious key in other lockers. He fails to open any. "Damn, it doesn't open any locker."

Charlie is trying to look inconspicuous. "Okay, I guess we need to leave."

"Not yet … it could be a locker in the women's locker room."

"Then we're screwed."

"No, we're not. I'll go on the women's side."

"What if we're caught?"

"You're going to guard where the two locker rooms separate."

"I can't stop a woman from going in."

"You can warn me."

"Yeah, but then I'm going to run."

"I'll be damned if you will. After you warn me, I'll walk out casually … say I'm checking on someone."

"Jeez, okay, but how do you know someone's not already in there getting dressed?"

"I'll shout a warning before I go in. If there's someone there, I'll just say I'm looking for my sister."

"Okay, but don't get us arrested."

Billy moves before Charlie can change his mind. Charlie stands almost shaking outside the door. The minutes pass. The building is hot, and he begins to sweat. Finally, Billy bursts out of the door holding a brown paper bag.

Charlie gapes. "That's it? That's from the locker?"

"Yeah … all there was."

A woman passes, glancing at the two boys uncertainly, and enters the locker room. Billy has hidden the bag behind himself.

Charlie leans back against the tile wall when the woman is out of sight, with his head tight to the wall, and sighs.

Billy grabs Charlie's arm. "Let's get the hell out of here."

Back in the car, Billy sits for a moment, breathing as if he's just run a mile.

Charlie flips on the dome light. "Okay, let's see it."

Billy pulls the bag open and pulls a plastic bag out. "Jesus, four syringes. You think she's dealing drugs?"

"Shit, I hope not. Let's not get involved. This could mean trouble."

"You're right. Drop me at my house, and I'll figure out what to do with this shit."

Billy knows Charlie is scared that the bag could be trouble, but he can't help being curious. Maybe the woman is into dope, but perhaps she's a diabetic. He has not only seen the syringes but also a small notebook and a computer memory card. Maybe it's innocent, and maybe it isn't. He wants to check the memory card before he rids himself of the bag.

Chapter Eighty-Four

Billy's parents are in the kitchen. His mother calls into the hallway, "Billy, is that you?"

"Yes, Mom."

"Your supper's ready … been ready. You're late."

"I'm sorry. I was talking to Charlie in the car. Let me put my books in my room. I have homework to do later."

"Okay, but hurry. Don't let supper get cold again."

"Be right back."

Billy rushes up the stairs and hides the bag in his bureau drawer. He's relieved to be rid of it, even if it's only for a few minutes.

He hurriedly returns to his supper, trying to look innocent and twitching internally as he thinks about what might be on the memory card. He pictures details of drug shipments. After all, Interstate 95 is a major traffic route from Florida, isn't it?

***

Charlie texts Billy an hour later. "What's on the memory card?"

Billy phones Charlie in reply. "It's a movie of some guy sitting at a desk, counting money and slipping some of the money into a briefcase."

"You think he's stealing the money?"

"Kind of looks that way."

"Do you know who he is?"

"No. There's no way to tell."

Suddenly, Billy hears, "What are you watching, son?"

"Charlie, got to go," Billy says as he hangs up and tries to place his body between his father and the laptop screen. He curses himself for not closing his door.

"And what's in the plastic bag?"

Oh, sweet Jesus, Billy thinks as he leans back while watching his dad pick up the bag of syringes.

"It's a long story."

His father studies Billy with alarm. "It had better be a good one."

Billy tells his tale; his father looks tense and disquieted the entire time. After he has finished, his father castigates him, "For goodness' sake, Charlie. You don't get yourself in other people's business. You should have left the key where you found it. It had nothing to do with you. You were just looking for trouble, and now you have it."

"Yeah, I know, Dad. Charlie and I were just playing detective."

"Son, detectives are professional. They carry guns. Their business is dealing with trouble. What they do is serious. There's no telling who's involved with this stuff you've found. It could be some really nasty people."

"Yeah, I know now. It just didn't dawn on me. What do I do now?"

"We go by the police station in the morning on your way to school, tell your story, and get rid of this stuff."

"What do we tell Mom?"

"Nothing. She worries about you enough without this adding to it."

Chapter Eighty-Five

Billy and his father arrive at the Alexandria Police Department a little after seven in the morning. His father figures they'll drop off the bag of syringes and then head up Quaker Lane to get Billy to TC Williams High School with a cushion of time to spare.

They are met by a police sergeant sitting behind a glass window.

Billy's father squints, reads the sergeant's name tag, and then speaks through a window, "Good morning, Sergeant Eastham. I'm Dominic Kominski, and this is my son, Billy." He waves his hand in the direction of Billy, who is hanging back behind him. "My son found this bag yesterday. It looks suspicious to us, and we thought we should turn it in."

He slides the bag through a slot under the window.

Eastham pulls the bag a few inches toward him, flips down his glasses from the top of his head, and looks the bag over. He then secures a box of latex gloves from somewhere low behind his desk and slips on a pair. "Found it, huh?"

Billy's father nods. "Yes, yesterday."

Eastham looks at him appraisingly. "Kominski, huh?" He starts writing. "You said Dominic, and the youngster is Billy?"

Billy's father seems to be becoming unnerved. "That's right."

"And your address, sir?"

Dominic Kominski gives it to the sergeant, who, after writing it down, directs them to have a seat.

"Someone will be out to talk to you in a moment."

The Kominskis sit. Billy whispers, "What's happening?"

"I guess they want to know more."

"They're going to question us?"

"I guess. Just tell the police the truth … every detail."

"Jeez, okay."

They note a large woman in a civilian suit joins Sergeant Eastham behind the window. She too dons gloves and then picks up the bag, studies it for a moment, and says some words to the sergeant who nods. The woman then leaves. The Kominskis hear buzzing. A door then opens to the left of the window, and the woman appears in the doorway holding the bag. "Gentlemen, please come in."

They follow her down a hallway and into a small conference room. She tells them to have a seat and then addresses them, "I'm Detective Gertrude Sorenson." She studies the paper that Sergeant Eastham had written on. "And you are Dominic and Billy Kominski?"

They both nod.

Sorenson looks at Billy. "You found this bag?"

"Yes."

Sorenson sits down with a ballpoint pen and a pad of paper in front of her. She methodically positions the pad so she can write on it. "Please tell me where and when you found it?"

Billy thinks, Oh god, I'm going to be late for school.

"Well, you see, my friend and I work at the Alexandria Library, the one on Queen Street, after school on the days it's open."

He then proceeds with the story. After he finishes, he waits for the detective to finish writing. She then looks up. "What is your friend's name?"

"Er, Charlie Scruggs."

"Do you know Mr. Scruggs' address?" Billy gives it to her.

She writes it down and looks back up at Billy. "And Mr. Scruggs can confirm your story?"

"Y-yes, ma'am."

"And you say this memory card has a movie on it that looks like someone stealing money?"

"Yes, ma'am."

"Okay, I don't know what any of this means, but we'll have a look at it. I would caution you that you shouldn't have gotten involved with this. You could be accused of stealing. I must admit though that finding a key in the library is a little strange. Before I let you go, I'd like to get your and your father's fingerprints so we can separate them from other fingerprints on the bag and on the items inside. Did you touch the items inside?"

"The memory card and the notebook. I was afraid of the syringes."

"As you should be."

She twists around the bag on the table, as if pondering the situation. "We'll probably have to get your friend, Charlie Scruggs, in to give us his fingerprints. You might warn him so his parents don't get too upset."

Chapter Eighty-Six

Cathy has decided that they should take Les's Lexus ES. She says it would be less conspicuous than her Mercedes S Class. Les knows his car is less expensive, but he isn't so sure about the "less conspicuous" claim if the car's front grill is considered.

She parks in the driveway in front of Les's house in the small town of Millwood, Virginia, and gets out of her car. Les is waiting for her, standing by his car next to where she has parked.

She gives the house a look over. "Gosh, Les, how much did you spend on this place?"

"More than makes sense."

"All from fixing Blue people like me?"

"You made a disaster, and I fix it."

"You know we have a different opinion about the who 'made.'"

"Yeah, Cathy, whatever makes you happy. I'm not the one being sued. How come you still have the car?"

"Corporate car … they haven't caught up with me."

"Well, the marriage had some benefits."

"For a while."

"Yeah, and you didn't have to wait like you did with me." She smiles sadly. "You win some, and you lose some."

"Well, you'll rise again. You're too beautiful not to."

Cathy chuckles. "A phoenix with two black eyes."

Les assures her, "They'll go away. That's part of the cure."

He opens the passenger door of the Lexus. She starts to get in, looking into the back seat.

"Where's the shovel?"

"In the trunk. It's a short one."

"You'll be able to dig with that?"

"Sure, he's not buried deep."

"He's not? Do you think he'll still be there? You think no animal has gotten him?"

"We'll find out. Back then, I couldn't dig through rock."

They drive out of the driveway and head west.

Cathy inquires, "How'd you find this burial place?"

"Drove west on U.S. 50 till I found someplace a little remote."

"Yeah, I followed your cell phone."

"Which is why we're screwed up now."

"Seemed smart at the time. I didn't know other people would follow the same route."

"'Other people' being some men you know?"

"Just 'some men,' Les."

"Yeah, I guess all men think alike … or is it just the men you know?"

"Cut the shit, Les. Let's get on with what we have to do."

"I wish I knew if it was something 'we have to do.' Maybe Godfrey will never be found."

"Maybe, maybe."

"Maybe."

***

Les and Cathy drive in silence for a long while. He points to the left as they cross the bridge over the Cacapon River. "I threw the shovel in a little way up that river."

"Are you giving a guided tour?"

"A history lesson."

"So this town is Capon Bridge."

"Yeah. You know it from following me on a phone."

"I know we're close."

"Yeah, I'm sure you do."

She hits him on the shoulder. "No sarcasm, Les."

"And no hitting the shoulder. We're not married."

They proceed through the town, follow the road around a bend, and head southwest. They pass the Jesse James Outlaw Bar & Grill, and Les says, "The turn's coming up."

They pass a turn for Terp Road, and Les says under his breath, "That's not it."

They next pass over a small creek, and Les immediately turns right onto a dirt road. At the bend in the road sits a police car. It's too late to turn around. A policeman steps out of his car as they start to pass. He flags them down. Les rolls down his window as the policeman approaches. The man leans down to the window. "May I help you, folks?"

Cathy doesn't look at the man as Les tries to stay poised. "We understand a body was found here and that people are searching the woods. Thought we'd give it a shot."

"Don't you think that sounds ghoulish?"

"Just an excuse for a walk in the woods."

"Well, I'm sorry you wasted your time, but the sheriff decided he didn't like strangers walking around a crime scene. He's afraid some evidence might get messed up. I'm here to turn people around. You'll have to take your walk someplace else."

Les tries to sound casual, "But we might find some evidence … help you out."

"The sheriff says no."

Les shakes his head and sighs in disappointment. "Do you have any other suggestions? We've driven a long way."

"Any other turn off this road ... just not this one."

Les pulls the car forward and turns around. He enters the highway and drives back to the bar and grill where he pulls into the parking lot.

Cathy throws her head back and sighs. "So what now?"

"The sign says Grill, so that implies food. Let's get something and think."

They enter and find a booth in the far corner by the front window. Les orders coffee and a burger, while Cathy orders iced tea and a club sandwich. While they wait for their meals, they sit in silence. The coffee arrives first. Les picks up his spoon and starts stirring.

Cathy watches him. "What are you stirring? You didn't put anything in the coffee."

Les looks at the cup as if he's just discovered it. "Cooling it down, I guess."

While they wait for their food, Cathy studies Les. "Are you happy, Les?"

Les snaps out of his reverie and purses his lips in thought. "Yeah, I guess."

"You guess? That's not much of an endorsement."

"Well, I stay busy."

"I don't think 'busy' equates to happiness. How come you never got married again?"

Les's face becomes serious. "Maybe because I can't match you. Maybe because I don't trust women."

Cathy grimaces and sighs. "Yeah, I understand that. But you're not bad looking."

"Not tall, dark, and handsome, though?"

"No, but you're the best lover I ever had."

"Shit, Cathy. That doesn't say much for the men you've been with."

"No, I guess it doesn't, but you were good. You had your heart in it. At least you did until after Godfrey."

"Yeah, that did change things."

Cathy looks soulfully at Les. "We did it for us."

"It was for you, Cathy. I needed to please you. I always needed to please you."

"Yeah, you tried. I know you tried."

"Did you kill that guy Covington too?"

Cathy answers dolefully, "Do you need to know?"

"No."

"What happened was not for money, Les. It was for survival."

"Okay. Whatever you say."

Cathy sighs. "You're a good guy, Les. You're not good at retribution."

"I think I've lived and learned. But retribution, revenge, or whatever you call it, I'm not good at. What I'm good at is not suffering remorse ... at getting on with life ... at building on other's greed."

"On my greed?"

Les nods. "Yeah."

Cathy chuckles. "Well, you're not above water yet."

"Godfrey?"

"Yeah."

The food arrives. While Les takes a bite out of his burger, he catches movement out of the corner of his eye. He quickly turns to look out the window. The patrol car is passing, headed for town. He takes another quick bite, and through a full mouth, he says, "Eat quick. The cop just abandoned his post."

"Darn, Les. The food just got here."

"Eat fast."

"What if he comes back?"

"We just play it innocent. We'll say we saw he had gone and thought the blockade was over for the day."

"You think he'll buy it."

"No, but I don't think he'll arrest us. After all, he abandoned his post."

***

They drive down the dirt road. Cathy's eyes search the woods, as if Godfrey's grave will suddenly materialize from among the trees and undergrowth. "How are you going to tell where you buried him?"

"I'm not sure," Les says apprehensively. "It all looks the same. It's been years."

"What do we do?"

Les pulls off onto the shoulder and turns off the engine. "We go into the woods and find the creek. He's buried next to the creek."

"Which way do we go when we find the creek?"

"Flip a coin and go a quarter mile one direction and then back the other."

"God, I guess that's a plan. You'll have to pick the ticks off me when we get out of here."

"Be my pleasure."

"Maybe I shouldn't have said that."

They leave the car and head into the woods, with Les sweeping the underbrush aside with the shovel he's retrieved from the car's trunk. "Damn, brush is worse than I remember."

Cathy protects herself with the shopping bags.

Suddenly, Les spots the rock outcropping where he initially tried to dig a grave. "Thirty or forty yards ahead to the creek and then a little to the left."

Cathy is suddenly animated. "No shit?"

"Yeah, I've been here before."

They find the location of the grave. Les looks at it in awe. "The damn ferns survived."

"What, you planted ferns?"

"On top of the grave."

Cathy points. "Right there?"

"Yeah, doesn't look like he's been dug up."

"Is that good or bad? Might have been nice if he'd been dragged off and we couldn't find him."

"Sorry, we're going to find him. Get the shopping bags ready."

Les waits as Cathy fumbles with the shopping bags. He knows digging won't take long. He didn't bury the body very deep in the ground.

He scoops up the ferns and sets them aside. Then he starts to dig.

He hits a bone, moves the shovel to the side, shoves it deep into the ground with his foot, and lifts up a shovel full of dirt and bones. It looks like an arm. He knows where to dig next.

When the dirt is all loosened where he is sure the body is, he drops to his knees and starts pulling the bones from the loose soil.

Cathy springs forward and holds a bag open. Les throws the bones into the bag, breaking them apart as he needs to in order for them to fit the bag's opening.

Les thinks, this sure is not like television where they carefully brush the dirt away from the skeleton.

After pulling out the rib cage and backbone and breaking them apart, he knows where the head should be.

He takes his shovel and pries up the skull. He picks it up and drops it unceremoniously into Cathy's bag.

Cathy shudders and drops the bag. "Geez, Les, that was a human being."

"Not anymore."

"Damn, Les, you worked side by side with the guy."

"Don't remind me. We need to get on with this. Let me shovel through the loose dirt one more time for small bones. Then I'll smooth the dirt and replant the ferns. They've gotten big and hopefully will cover the fresh dirt."

"Okay, Les, but let's hurry. I want to get out of here before someone drives down that road."

Les picks up the two bags, one on each side to keep his balance, and heads for the road.

From behind him, Cathy says, "Damn, Les, look at this."

Les turns and sees Cathy holding up a filthy cell phone. She looks at him. "Is this Godfrey's?"

"No. I took his away … disposed of it … nowhere near here."

"You think it's Covington's?"

"No idea. Let's get a move on."

When they get to the car, Les hurries to conceal the shovel and the two shopping bags in the trunk. Then he climbs into the driver's seat. Cathy is already in the passenger seat, working with the phone. "The screen's all shattered, and the phone won't turn on. Do you think the police can get anything from it?"

Les takes the phone from her and opens it. He pulls out the battery and the SIM card. "The battery contacts are all green. No wonder it doesn't work."

He puts the battery back in, closes the case, and puts the SIM card in this pocket. "They can't get anything from it now."

"Fingerprints?"

"I don't know. Wipe it off."

"With what?"

Les pulls a handkerchief from his pocket and offers it to Cathy.

She takes it carefully. "It looks messy."

"I've just blown in it a couple of times. It'll be worse after you wipe the phone down."

Les turns the car around and heads down the dirt road. As they approach the intersection, they see the police cruiser ahead.

Cathy freezes. "Oh, shit. What if he looks in the trunk?"

Les draws in a deep breath of air. "If he does, we say we found the bones and are taking them to the police station in town like any good citizens."

"Won't we be incriminated?"

"Not as much as if we don't have a story."

Les pulls in next to the cruiser. The policeman is already getting out. He doesn't look happy. He walks around Les's car, slapping his hand on the hood.

Les rolls down the window.

The policeman says, "Get out of the car."

Les picks up the found cell phone and gets out.

The man snarls, "Put your hands on the hood."

Les does so, with the phone still in his hand.

The man walks up beside him. "What have you got there?"

Les stares ahead at the hood. "A cell phone we found in the woods. Thought it might help your case."

The cop takes it with two fingers and sets it aside on the hood. "Damn it, I told you this road was off-limits … a damn crime scene. You may have screwed up the place by stomping around."

"Hey, we found the phone."

"Yeah, maybe it saved your hides. Get back in the car and drive back to where you found it. I'll follow you."

He puts gloves on, picks up the phone, and takes it back to his cruiser.

Les leads him back up the road and stops two hundred yards short of where he'd stopped before. He gets out of the car and is joined by the cop. "It was by that big poplar tree over there in the woods."

The policeman instructs, "Okay, show me."

They walk to the tree. Les points to the ground. "It was right there."

The policeman frowns. "Damn, it's a couple hundred yards from where they found the body."

Les shudders. That's too close for comfort. "You think it might help the investigation?"

"Don't know. You didn't go to the burial site? Did you … mess it up in any way?"

"No, we didn't see any burial site. Is it near here?"

"You don't need to know."

They return to the cars. Les asks innocently, "Is there anything else I can do for you?"

"Yeah, you can give me your name, address, and phone number. Get out your driver's license while I write you a ticket."

Les pulls out his driver's license. "Ticket? What for?"

"For illegally trespassing on a crime scene."

"But we found the phone."

"Tell that to the judge."

After he writes the ticket, he asks for Les's other ID. Les gives him a business card. He compares it to the license before handing the license back to Les.

He leans into the car window to speak to Cathy. "And what about … Damn, what happened to you? This guy beat you up?"

Cathy tries not to look at the policeman. "No, I'm being treated for damage done to my eyelids by Bleu Glo cosmetics."

"Damn, is that how my wife is going to look?"

"Yes, if she used it on her eyes."

"Hell, she used it on her lips too."

"Then she'll be a mess for a while."

"Oh, shit."

The policeman hesitates and then asks Cathy for her driver's license. He copies the information onto the back of Les's business card. He hands the license back to Cathy. "So you two are not married?"

"No."

"Traipsing around the woods with a guy who's not your husband?"

"Yes."

"Okay. None of my business."

Cathy doesn't comment.

Finally, the policeman looks at Les. "If I catch you here again, you will be in big trouble."

Les nods. "I understand. May we go now?"

"Mind your p's and q's."

Chapter Eighty-Seven

"Les, drive slowly."

"I can't drive slowly. I have to look normal ... drive the speed limit."

"Jesus, we've got to get rid of the bones. What are we going to do?"

"Find a river."

"We just passed one."

"Cacapon River's not big enough."

"So where's a big river?"

"The Potomac."

"How close is that?"

"North of Martinsburg."

"Oh god, that will take forever."

"Nearest I know of."

"How about the Shenandoah?"

"Not much closer and not big enough."

"Shit. How about dropping me off?"

Les laughs. "And leave me holding the bag ... the two bags?"

"It would be the chivalrous thing to do."

"Ha, that's a joke. Chivalry went out with Trump ... maybe as early as the sinking of the Titanic. Every man and woman for themselves. You're with me right up to your neck."

"You used to say 'pretty neck.'"

"Yeah ... used to."

"Very funny. At least get me to Virginia."

"You think Virginia is better than West Virginia? Hell. Virginia's where they're looking for the killer."

After that exchange, they sit in silence, driving across the state line, in and out of Winchester, on Interstate 81 north, back into West Virginia, past Martinsburg, and the Bleu Regrets facility. They leave Interstate 81 at the Hammond Mills Road exit, get on U.S. 11 north, get off on a side road, cut under a railroad overpass, and find themselves driving along the Potomac River.

Les smiles happily. "It's right where it's supposed to be."

Cathy grunts. "Good thing nobody moved it ... didn't screw up the emptiness. Did you really know where you were going?"

"Read the map last night. It's known as planning."

"It's good to be with a smart ass."

"You just didn't recognize it soon enough."

"Yeah, stick it to me."

Les stops by the side of the road, pops the trunk, and gets out of the car. He leans back into the door. "Come over to the driver's seat while I run the bags to the river. If anyone comes along, drive down the road until you can turn around and come back to pick me up."

Les runs through some brush across the path of a power line and finally reaches the river. He looks around, sees no one, and dumps a bag of bones as far out into the river as he can throw them. He then goes a hundred feet upriver and discards the other bag. He studies the water. There are no bones in sight. He wishes he could have gotten them farther away from the riverbank, but he's done his best. He hopes no little boys come fishing.

He hurries back to the car, throws the empty bags in the trunk, jumps into the passenger seat, and says, "Drive."

***

Les and Cathy arrive back at Les's house an hour later.

Cathy asks, "What are you going to do with the bags?"

"I'll go into town tomorrow and stick them into a couple of dumpsters … dumpsters separated by a mile or so."

"You going to keep the shovel?"

"I'm not keeping anything. I'll find another river."

"So I've got nothing else to do."

"Stay low and keep your mouth shut."

"I can do that. How about my using your bathroom and maybe have a drink before I go."

"If the drink's water, I'll let you in. We don't want you picked up on the way home."

"Okay, how about a soda?"

"Lemonade?"

"That'll do."

Les unlocks the front door and reluctantly lets Cathy in. "I told myself I'd never do this."

"Do what?"

"Let you into my house or anywhere near me."

"Shit, Les, what do you think is going to happen?"

"Somebody I know might get killed."

"Pfft, Les, I don't do that anymore."

"I don't know, Cathy. It might be like giving up cigarettes."

"Very funny."

Cathy leans against the kitchen counter and sips her lemonade. She peers over her glass at Les, trying to draw his attention, with her sunglasses raised to the top of her head. She wishes her eyes weren't circled in red. She misses their being seductive. She does her best.

She lowers her drinking glass, still looking at Les. "Do you still think I'm beautiful?"

Les walks over to her.

She looks up expectantly.

Les pushes Cathy's sunglasses further to the top of her head and takes her cheeks in his hands to turn her face toward him. He looks sternly into her eyes. "Listen, Cathy. You're still beautiful. You've always been beautiful. But remember, the police have both of our names. They've seen our driver's licenses. There's a good chance someone is going to follow up. Our story is that we got to talking, as an ex-couple, when you got your treatment for Bleu Glo, and you mentioned you had worked with this guy Covington, who had been found in West Virginia, and out of curiosity, you suggested we ride up to the area where he was found ... that we never had an idea that we'd be messing up a crime scene ... that it was just a lark. Does that sound right? You got it?"

Cathy flashes anger and shakes her head loose from Les's hands. "I got it. Cut out the rough stuff."

"It's important we're on the same page."

"Yeah, I get it."

"And we don't talk again, ever."

"Yeah, yeah, okay. It was just a one-off. A lark by two exes. Then we went on with our separate lives."

"We don't really like each other anyway."

"Yeah, bordering on hate."

"Don't get carried away."

"Remember, Les, I know where Godfrey's bones are."

"I do too. I also have the SIM card."

"There may be nothing on it."

Les smiles. "True, but there's no way you're going to tell the police about Godfrey ... No way you're going to admit you participated in a premeditated murder. You're not crazy."

Cathy brushes by Les and leaves his house. "Bastard."

Chapter Eighty-Eight

Sorenson sets the bag on her desk.

Arley Masterson, her partner when she isn't breaking in Ben Metzinger, looks across the two desk widths that separate them. "What have you been doing, scavenging the back alleys of town?"

"Nah, just some stuff a kid and his father dropped off at the front desk."

"They were using?"

"No, the kid says he found it in a locker."

"What was he doing in a locker?"

"Long story."

"Well, I could listen."

Sorenson, with her gloves still on, pulls out the memory card. "If you need entertainment, look over my shoulder, and let's see what we've got ... maybe a cartel snuff movie."

"Fat chance."

Masterson gets up and moves behind Sorenson as she plugs the card into her computer. The recording of Stanley Wigram stealing money begins to play. Sorenson's eyes open wide as she shouts at Ben Metzinger, "Ben, get over here."

Metzinger hurries over to Sorenson's desk.

She points at the screen. "Isn't that the hotel manager you and I interviewed?"

"Gee, it sure looks like him. What's he doing?"

"Looks like he's skimming some money and stuffing it in his

briefcase."

"Looks that way to me too."

"Gosh, what do we do?"

Just then, Lieutenant Givens, their boss, comes out of her office. She is followed by two men in suits, faces hardened by their self-importance. Givens walks up to Sorenson's desk. "Gert, Arley, Ben, these gentlemen are Agents Arroyo and Maddox from the FBI." Before going further, she glances at Sorenson's computer screen. "What are you looking at?"

Ben answers, "A guy apparently skimming money. The same hotel guy we interviewed about Covington's death."

Agent Arroyo's face suddenly becomes animated, and he exclaims, "Covington? Billy Covington?"

Givens explains to her detectives, "The agents are here about Billy Covington. They interviewed his wife, Adele. She didn't know anything about Covington going to West Virginia … Doesn't think he ever went there in his life … Makes it look like his body was transported across state lines … Makes his murder a federal thing … puts it under the jurisdiction of the federal government."

Masterson groans, "Just when it was getting interesting."

Maddox doesn't laugh. "We'll take over from here." He points at the computer. "We'll need that movie."

Sorenson points at the bag containing the syringes and small notebook. "You'll need this too." Maddox looks at the bag and frowns. "What's that?"

"The bag the movie came from … what you would call a mixed bag."

"Yeah, where did that come from?"

Sorenson tells the whole story. Maddox and Arroyo listen with little expression.

Finally, Maddox says, "Hell of a story. Hell of a coincidence. We'll need the boys' information."

Sorenson gives the agents the boys' names and addresses. "So we're off the case. What are you going to do next?"

"Go to West Virginia."

Masterson grins. "You want some company?"

Maddox gives Masterson a look as if he can't comprehend what the man is saying. "We'll handle it from here, detective."

Chapter Eighty-Nine

Dwayne Maddox and Ramon Arroyo leave the Alexandria Police Station, shaking their heads. They have copies of the interviews the police had done with Stanley Wigram, Peggy Sanchez, Les Warin, and Cathy Mallet.

Maddox mumbles, "Bunch of dumb cops with evidence falling on them out of the sky."

Arroyo muses and holds up the bag. "You think this stuff is related?"

"Coincidence?" Maddox replies. "You know what all the cops say on television. I don't believe in coincidences."

"Yeah, but it's still possible."

"Yeah, well, let's see where those coordinates in the notebook and fingerprints off the syringes lead. Maybe they'll be related. If they are, we might be dealing with more than coincidence."

***

The next day, the agents drive to Capon Bridge, West Virginia. They enter the police station and find a young, overweight woman in an overly stretched uniform sitting behind a desk in a room that holds two other desks, presumably for other policemen. The building isn't big. There seem to be some restrooms and a break room to the back on the left and on the right an office door with opaque glass on which is stenciled Sheriff Linerman.

The agents approach the woman's desk.

Maddox points to the door. "Is that Line or Len?"

The woman looks perplexed. "What?"

"The sheriff's name."

"Oh, Len."

The agents hold up their badges. "FBI. We'd like to see him."

The woman is suddenly flustered. "Oh, oh, sure." She struggles to her feet, goes to the door, and knocks.

From within the office, the agents hear, "Shit, Sally. I'm on my coffee break."

Sally opens the door and sticks her head partway in. "Sorry, sheriff. There are two FBI agents here to see you."

The agents hear some scrambling while Sally stands at the door and waits.

A voice finally comes from behind the office door, "Okay, don't leave them waiting."

Sally ushers the agents in.

The sheriff offers his hand for a shake. "Sorry about that. Hope you didn't have to wait long. Close the door, Sally. I'm Sheriff Myron Linerman. You like some coffee or anything? Sally, bring some coffee. Damn woman should have thought of that."

Maddox shakes the sheriff's hand. "Agent Maddox and this is Agent Arroyo. And no, no coffee. Thank you."

The sheriff shakes Arroyo's hand and shouts, "Sally, forget the coffee. Have seats, gentlemen. This about the guy we found in the woods? Sally, get Sergeant Billops to drive back here." He looks at the agents. "Billops dug up the bones."

The agents nod. Maddox says, "Sounds like the man to talk to."

"Yeah, he is."

Maddox continues, "How'd he find the body?"

"CiCi Hernandez found it and phoned it in. Just got cell service here. Matter of luck."

"CiCi Hernandez?"

"Yeah, she's just back from the earthquake in Peru. Member of our volunteer fire department. Owns a cadaver dog. Travels all over. She was giving her dog a run along a dirt road when the dog vanished into the woods. By the time she found Ginger, the dog already had a couple of bones dug up. CiCi stopped Ginger and phoned in. Billops went to the site and dug up the rest of the bones."

"Were forensics people involved?"

"Haven't got no forensic people. Just Billops. I called the state, and they sent some people over, but we just had a pile of bones by the time they arrived. They found a few more bones and took the pile away. They called a couple of days later and said they'd identified the bones ... belonged to some guy in Virginia."

"That's right. Did you do anything else?"

"Searched the area. Bunch of folks showed up and searched a lot too. Guess they were hoping we missed some bones. Finally, had to stop them from coming, trampling the crime scene and such."

Arroyo sighs and says facetiously, "Sounds like the right thing to do."

"Yeah," the sheriff concurs. "No walking dead up there anyway."

The door to the outer office bangs, and the sheriff grins as if he has achieved great things.

"There's Billops now."

There's a knock on the door, and Sergeant Billops comes in. The sheriff introduces everyone, and they sit. Maddox addresses Billops. "I understand you found Billy Covington's bones."

"Covington, huh. Just knew the guy was from Virginia. Nah, I didn't find him. Ginger, CiCi Hernandez's dog, found him. Amazing dog. Finds bodies all over the world."

"Right, but you dug up the bones?"

"Some of them—rib cage, skull, and the like. Just wanted to know what I had. Left it to the state to finish up."

"Did you or the state look all around for other evidence?"

"Oh, yeah, but we didn't find anything. About fifty people showed up the next day and went all over the woods. They didn't find anything either."

"You asked them?"

"No, there were too many, but no one volunteered anything."

"So nothing was found?"

"A couple snuck in there yesterday while I ran for lunch. They found a battered cell phone."

"Yeah, you have it?"

"Yeah, at my desk. Let me go get it."

He is back in a moment, holding the phone and a piece of paper.

Maddox takes the phone. "Filthy and really battered."

"Yeah, and it's missing the SIM card," volunteers Billops. In alarm, Arroyo asks, "You opened it and checked?"

"Yeah, looking for evidence to see if it was related, but no SIM card, no information."

"Damn," is all Arroyo can say. "What's the piece of paper?"

"Copy of the card the guy gave me with his phone number."

Maddox takes it from Billops and looks at it. "Leslie Warin."

He turns the card over, and then he looks at Arroyo. "Catherine Mallet."

Arroyo smirks. "I thought they were exes."

"Don't make assumptions."

Chapter Ninety

Arroyo and Maddox arrived back in DC in time to get the syringes, notebook, and cell phone to forensics.

The following morning, they eat breakfast at a King Street restaurant in Alexandria. They sit in a booth away from the entrance door. Both sit on the same side of the table with their backs to a wall. They look ridiculously conspicuous, but neither one is willing to put his back to the door. They have been taught not to.

Arroyo has a large stack of pancakes with blueberries and whipped cream. Maddox eats a poached egg over toast. They both sip from mugs of coffee.

Maddox eyes Arroyo's pancakes. "God, Ramon, don't you Mexicans ever get fat?"

"Mexican two times removed. I'm no more Mexican than you are."

"Damn, don't be sensitive. You got your skinny build from somewhere."

"My mother was Bulgarian."

"I thought Bulgarian women were short, heavy peasants wearing babushkas."

"Shows what you know."

"Whatever. Let's go over where we stand. We know that we've got a bunch of disparate evidence that may be related to Covington's death and probably is."

"Why do you say 'is'?"

"Because the coordinates in the notebook turn out to be where

Covington's body was found."

"No kidding."

Maddox nods. "Yeah, things are beginning to connect. We have five names up on the whiteboard at the office, Billy Covington in the middle, Catherine Mallet, Stanley Wigram, and Arlene Covington across the top, and this guy Leslie Warin down on the left. There's a connection line between the two Covington, a triangle connection between Billy Covington, Mallet, and Wigram, who worked together, and a connection of some kind between Mallet and Warin. Now we have this notebook and video in the same bag strongly connecting Billy C and Wigram."

"A lot of connections to learn about," Arroyo concludes. "So we start with Wigram because we have the movie along with the coordinates of Covington's body, information the cops didn't have. Should produce some excitement."

"Wigram this morning, and I've set up our going to Mrs. Covington this afternoon."

"Are we going to question her? When someone disappears, it's usually the spouse who's guilty."

"Yeah, but it's usually the woman who's disappeared, not the man. Today, I'd prefer not to alienate the woman. I just want to search the place, search the man cave, garage, tool shed, and such. If Covington was involved in something, we might find some clues. We can always question later."

***

The two agents arrive at the headquarters of Pleasure Hotels on Duke Street, near the railroad station.

They ride up the elevator to the fourth floor. The elevator is paneled. It looks like natural wood. Maddox taps it. "Better than the Formica panels in headquarters elevators."

"Not GSA, I guess."

They arrive at the fourth floor and enter through a door in a glass wall separating the reception area from the hallway outside the elevators. Behind the receptionist desk is a grass-cloth-covered wall with PLEASURE HOTELS NATIONAL HEADQUARTERS emblazoned across it in brass lettering. As Arroyo leads the way through the door, he whispers out the side of his mouth, "Guess it's not international."

Maddox, following behind, replies, "Don't know where you'll stay when you go home to Mexico."

"Shit, Dwayne, I've never been to Mexico, and you know it."

The agents approach an attractive receptionist. Maddox wonders if receptionists age out of the job when the first wrinkle appears.

He holds up his credentials and looks sideways to see if Arroyo is doing the same. "Good morning, FBI. We'd like to see Mr. Wigram."

"Do you have an appointment?"

"Is he in a meeting?"

"No."

"Then he'll see us."

The receptionist looks uncertain only briefly and then picks up a phone and calls Wigram. She explains the situation. She hangs up. "He'll see you."

"Of course, he will."

The receptionist leads the agents back through a labyrinth of offices and knocks on a door.

Wigram quickly puts away a comb he is using on his hair. "Yes, gentlemen, come in and have a seat. What can I do for you?"

Arroyo sets a laptop on Wigram's desk, turns it on, and starts the recording of Wigram, who's apparently skimming money and putting it in a briefcase. As he watches the computer screen, the agents sit down and observe Wigram, with their mouths slightly open.

Finally, Maddox speaks, "We know the police have talked to you about Billy Covington's bones. We don't know if your skimming money from the hotel is connected. We don't know who took this video or who owned it, but it's interesting. If I were to guess, I might think, since the video has never previously come to light, that someone might have used it to blackmail you."

"What do you mean 'skimming'?"

"Pocketing some of the hotel's money."

"Yeah, so now I understand what 'skimming' means. I wasn't. I had put some of my money in the cash drawers because the people at reception had a run-on cashing check and were short cash. I was just taking my money back."

"If we were to check your bank account, would we find some random cash deposits?"

"Gentlemen, I don't have to listen to these kinds of accusations."

"Were you being blackmailed, Mr. Wigram?"

"I don't have to reply to wild conjecture."

"Is that a 'no comment,' Mr. Wigram?"

"Yes."

Maddox pulls out the notebook. "Do you know what this is, Mr. Wigram?"

"A notebook."

"Right, a notebook, in which the coordinates of where Billy Covington's body was found are written. Strangely, the notebook was found in the same bag in which the video was found. Don't you think that's strange, Mr. Wigram?"

Wigram looks bewildered. "I haven't got the foggiest, and I have no comment."

"Right, we already went over 'no comment.'"

Maddox and Arroyo rise from their chairs, with Maddox nodding to Wigram. "Well, thank you, Mr. Wigram. We'll look into this further, with your help or without it."

* * *

Wigram arrives at the law firm of Dedham, Wilcox, and Braun

at three o'clock in the afternoon and is escorted into the office of Stephen Wilcox, who offers him a seat in a grouping of chairs and sits facing him. "Mr. Wigram, I believe this is the first time you've been to our offices. How can we help you?"

"Yes, well, there's this video of me that seems to show me apparently skimming money from the receipts at my hotel."

"Oh, what hotel is this?"

"The Pleasure Hotel in Crystal City, where I used to work."

"Used to work?"

"Yes, I'm at corporate headquarters now."

"You said 'apparently.' Is it not true?"

"Is what I say confidential?" "It is."

"Yes, it is true."

"You did skim money?"

"Yes."

"And there is a video of you doing it?"

"Yes."

"And when was this?"

"About eight years ago."

"Where has this video been for all this time?"

"I'm not sure."

"That sounds like you have an idea."

"Yes, the video was made by a woman who worked with me."

"And what did she do with it?"

"She blackmailed me."

"You paid her?"

"No."

"If not for money, what did she blackmail you for?"

"To do anything she wanted me to do."

"And what did she want you to do?"

"Bury a man she had killed."

"What?"

"Bury a man."

"Yeah, that's what I thought you'd said. What are you asking of me?"

"The FBI has the video, and I think they might charge me with skimming from hotel receipts some eight years ago."

"Well, you may be beyond the statute of limitations on the skimming."

"If I'm not, can I get a plea agreement if I testify about the murder?"

"Get a plea deal by admitting you abetted a murder?"

"Well, I was blackmailed."

"I don't think that will help, Mr. Wigram. There's no statute of limitations on murder."

"So confessing won't help?"

"I don't think so."

"So if I get charged for skimming, I don't say anything about the murder?"

"You'd be a fool if you did."

"Really?"

"Really."

"So what do I do?"

"Don't talk to the FBI. Don't talk to the police."

"What if they charge me with stealing from the hotel?"

"If that's all, you can come back to me, and we'll talk about why you might have done what you did, the statute of limitations, and so forth. But, if the subject of murder comes up, please find another attorney."

***

Later, Wigram walks back into the hotel office suite.

The receptionist looks up from her desk. "Those FBI agents phoned again. Should I dial them back for you?"

"No. If they phone again, tell them I can't help them."

"You're in a meeting?"

"No, I'm not talking to them."

Wigram hurries to his office, worrying about how long he'll stay employed. He knows that there are situations outside the law in which "statute of limitations" has no meaning.

Chapter Ninety-One

The agents knock on the door of a green shingle-clad, two-story house just off Commonwealth Avenue near the intersection with Mount Vernon Avenue. They know it is the same house Arlene Covington lived in when her husband vanished. The lawn is mowed, but weeds edge along the sidewalk. Weeds are growing among the bushes across the front of the house. Maddox concludes that the place is cared for but at a minimum of effort.

They knock a second time. A woman with salt and pepper hair tied back in a bun answers, "Are you the FBI?"

The agents hold up their identification. "I'm Agent Maddox, and this is Agent Arroyo. I'm the one who phoned."

"Whew, good. I just made it home in time."

"Oh, you were out?"

"At work. I took the afternoon off."

"Oh, where do you work?"

"At the Pleasure Hotel. Ms. DuChant got me a job there after Billy vanished."

"Ms. DuChant?" Maddox asks, as an unfamiliar name appears on his radar.

"Yes, I think she was married after that and left the hotel. Married someone named Mallet."

Both agents say, "Oh."

"So you want to see if Billy left anything behind. I can't imagine what. I've cleaned this place a million times since then."

Arroyo tries to assure her they aren't questioning her cleaning.

"Sometimes men have places women don't go, simply because their interests aren't the same. Toolboxes, fishing boxes, hunting gear, and such. Did Mr. Covington have a den, a man cave, an area in the basement where he worked, a shed for garden tools, or such?"

Arlene chuckles. "A man cave? No, we didn't quite live at that level … No den either. We only have part of a basement where the furnace and hot water heater are, a crawl space under the rest of the houses, and the tool shed where we keep the lawnmower, shovels, rakes, and the like." Arroyo smiles hopefully. "Sounds like there are places to start. When's the last time you were in the crawl space, Mrs. Covington?"

Arlene appears repulsed by the thought. "Is that a joke, agent?"

"No, ma'am. If you don't go there, I'd say it's the place to start."

Arroyo turns to Maddox. "I'll get flashlights from the car and meet you in the basement."

Maddox nods. "Get your coveralls and gloves too."

"My coveralls?" Arroyo grimaces.

Maddox snickers. "Of course, you're junior." He turns to Arlene. "Which way, Mrs. Covington? I'll get the spider webs out of the way."

Arlene doesn't deny that there are spider webs. She hasn't been in the basement in several weeks. "Follow me, agent."

She leads Maddox through the kitchen, opens a door, and flicks on the basement lights. "Watch your step."

Maddox descends steps that have, at some time in the past, been painted battleship gray but are now worn to the bare wood at the center of the treads. The furnace and hot water heater are indeed enveloped with spider webs. He takes a handkerchief from his pocket and sweeps them aside. He feels around the top of the furnace and hot water heater and looks behind them. He opens the small door over the controls of the hot water heater. He feels along the top of the cinder block foundation. By the time Arroyo joins him, he is convinced there is nothing of interest in the basement.

He opens the small door to the crawl space, borrows a flashlight from Arroyo, and shines its beam into the space. The door is four feet above the floor to the basement. "I can't get my head and arm far enough in to see or feel along the wall to the sides. See if the woman has a step ladder but wipe your shoes before you go back up. There's some soot on the floor."

"Wipe them on what?"

"Your pants."

"No way. I'll put the coveralls on."

"You might not need to."

"I'm not wiping my shoes on my pants."

"Okay, be prissy."

"Yeah, and I see you're holding a handkerchief."

"Some of us plan ahead."

Maddox stands, slightly annoyed, while Arroyo pulls the coveralls over his suit, goes upstairs, and returns shortly with a step stool. "This will get you up a couple feet. I hope that's enough."

Maddox takes the stool and sets it in front of the crawl space door. With his handkerchief, he wipes the area around the entrance, holds up the handkerchief to study the dirt, and groans, "I think my suit's in danger too."

He steps onto the stool, leans into the opening, and shines his light along the wall to the left and right. "Box of something is eight feet down on the right."

Arroyo sighs. "Damn it." He replaces Maddox on the stool and pulls himself into the crawl space. A moment later, he sets a metal box in the crawl space doorway. Maddox takes it. While Arroyo backs out of the crawl space, Maddox walks to the side of the steps and places the box on the fourth step from the bottom.

Arroyo hurries to Maddox's side as the box is opened. Maddox takes out a plastic bag. "Bunch of photographs and a memory card."

Arroyo catches his breath. "Looks like the same kind of card we got from the kid's bag."

"You think? There are probably a million like it."

"Who's the babe in the pictures?"

"Looks like the picture at the top of our whiteboard."

"Yeah, Mrs. Mallet, but these aren't posed. Just snapshots, as if Covington was stalking her."

"Interesting."

They clean their shoes and ascend the stairs.

They find Arlene Covington in the living room. Inquisitively, she asks, "Did you find anything?"

Maddox sets the metal box on the coffee table, opens it, and takes out the plastic bag. "This was in the crawl space." From the bag, he extracts a couple of photographs and holds them out to Arlene. "Do you recognize this woman?"

"Uh, it's been a while, but I think that's Ms. DuChant."

"Any idea why a bunch of pictures of her would be in your basement?"

"N-no. No idea."

"Did your husband have an interest in Ms. DuChant?"

"Why would he?"

"I don't know, Mrs. Covington. I don't know."

The agents leave Arlene Covington looking worried.

Chapter Ninety-Two

"Did you gather all your FBI buddies in an auditorium to watch this and party?" Cathy is sitting at her desk at the back of the mattress store, staring at the agents' computer. Her face is flustered and looking angry.

Maddox protests, "We only showed it to our boss. We had to."

"But I bet you watched the whole thing. Where the hell did you get it?"

"It was hidden in Covington's basement crawl space."

"The bastard kept it."

"You knew about it?"

"Oh yeah."

***

The agents had been at the mattress store when Cathy unlocked it in the morning. She had been surprised to see men waiting for the store to open, especially two men in suits, not the clientele's usual dress.

Grimly, Maddox had quickly invaded Cathy's personal space. "Mrs. Mallet, let's go back to your desk."

Shit, she had thought, more cops ... can't be good.

The agents had escorted her, one on each side. Now at the desk, they tell her to have a seat and to take off her sunglasses. "With the low light in here, you won't be able to see what we have to show you."

Cathy takes off her sunglasses and looks indignantly at the agents. "That what you want to see?"

Arroyo protests, "No, we didn't know. What the hell happened to you?"

"The cure."

"The cure?"

"Yeah, I've been treated to remove the effects of Bleu Glo. Within a couple of months, most women in this country will be wearing sunglasses inside buildings and out."

"Gee, we'll try not to look."

"You do that. Now, what the hell is going on? I've talked to the police already."

Maddox pulls a manila envelope out of a briefcase and extracts photographs. He spreads them out over the desk. "We're FBI, and the police didn't have these." The agents hold up their IDs.

Cathy acknowledges them and then looks down at the photographs in bafflement. "What the hell are these?"

"Photographs of you."

"Hell, I can see that. Was someone stalking me?"

"Billy Covington."

"Really?" Cathy nods as if suddenly comprehending.

"You didn't know about them? You don't seem terribly surprised."

"Should I be? I'm pretty accustomed to men."

Maddox considers what Cathy has said and decides not to comment. He signals Arroyo to put a laptop on the desk. The man does and turns in on.

Cathy watches. Her face tires.

After she acknowledges she knows about the video, Maddox and Arroyo sit down opposite the desk. "Care to tell us about the video?"

"Not really."

"Do us a favor."

Her mind remembers setting up the camcorder and it all going

317

wrong.

"He used it to blackmail me."

"You look like you're acting in the video."

"I don't know, agent. You know what acting like this looks like?"

"It's not about me, Mrs. Mallet."

"You can turn it off now."

Arroyo gets up and turns off the laptop. Maddox sits watching Cathy and waiting.

She says, "I had second thoughts."

"Not in time, I guess?"

"No."

"You say Covington was blackmailing you with this?"

"Yes."

"For money?"

"No, for sex. He made me his slave. When he snapped his fingers, I had to come."

"You sound like you're angry about it, even after all this time."

"Wouldn't you be?"

"Sounds like you've been angry a long time, Mrs. Mallet. How angry were you at the time, Mrs. Mallet?"

"Very."

"Angry enough to kill him."

"Yeah, probably, but I didn't. Look at me, agent. I'm a mere 127 pounds."

Maddox sneers. "Soaking wet?"

Cathy's eyes flash. "Are you imagining things, Agent Maddox?"

Maddox flushes. "I repeat the question."

"Well, while you're imagining things, Agent Maddox, imagine me hauling the body of a two-hundred-pound man to West Virginia and burying him."

"Maybe you had help. Did Stanley Wigram help? Did you have something on him?"

"You do have an imagination, Agent Maddox."

***

The agents leave the store.

Arroyo asks, "Well, what do you think?"

"I think, if I were her, I might have killed him."

"You think she could have?"

"Don't underestimate a woman."

"Never. What's next?"

"Mrs. Mallet's ex-husband, this Leslie Warin, and what they were doing walking in the woods."

Chapter Ninety-Three

A little after two in the afternoon, Maddox and Arroyo reach the Bleu Regrets building north of Martinsburg.

"God," Maddox grumbles. "Twice to West Virginia in a few days. That's enough for a lifetime."

"And this place is a damn warehouse. Thought this was going to be high technology."

"A warehouse with a million doors."

They stop at the gate and hold up their badges for the guard. "FBI. We have an appointment with Leslie Warin."

The guard nods. "You're expected."

Arroyo leans across the seat. "What's this place, Fort Knox? How come all the security?"

The guard presses a button to open the gate. "Keeps the place from being overrun. Go to door 1."

"Overrun. Hell, it looks like the Capitol after January 6."

"Yeah, kind of feels like it too. We've been overrun, but you guys don't have blue hair, so you probably don't know about it."

"Blue hair? Heck, we're FBI. Blue hair's not allowed. A bulletin was put out about it. It's on every bulletin board in the Hoover Building."

The agents drive through the gate and find a parking space. Arroyo muses, "How come all the Mercedes Sedans and Cadillacs?"

Maddox proposes, "High-paid workers?"

Arroyo shakes his head. "More likely high-priced visitors. Heard they fix blue people here."

Maddox nods. "Yeah, the world is changing again. No more blue people. Let's hope it's for the better."

The men enter door 1 and find a young receptionist behind a desk.

She looks at the men directly—no foolishness. "May I help you?"

The agents display their badges.

The woman nods solemnly. "You're not clients."

Arroyo chuckles. "No blue?"

The woman grins. "No blue. At least none I can see."

"What's that mean?"

"It means that in this job, I've been exposed to more than you want to know. Anyway, you're expected. I'll buzz Mr. Warin's office."

Shortly after, a woman comes through a door to the right of the desk. Unlike the receptionist, she isn't young. She is extremely slender. Her hair is cropped short and beginning to gray. She looks efficient, very efficient. She doesn't introduce herself. For the agents, it isn't unusual. They are often treated as the enemy. "Please follow me, gentlemen."

She leads them into a vast bay filled with a one-story structure with many doors. Women with various levels of blue adornment are being led to the doors.

The agents follow the woman up some stairs. They enter a hallway lined with windows overlooking the bay and then enter a luxurious suite of offices. They pass through an outer office that is apparently the office of an administrative assistant, probably the office of the woman they are following. She knocks on the inner office door, opens it, and ushers the agents in. A man sits behind a desk at the far end of a large office with an entire glass wall overlooking the bay.

As the agents approach the man, he stands up, comes around the desk, shakes the agents' hands, and introduces himself. Then he leads them to an arrangement of two club chairs and a love seat. He motions them toward the love seat where they sit on the front edge.

They are surprised that Les Warin hasn't maintained a superior position behind his desk and hasn't made them sit in the two chairs in front of the desk.

Warin sits in a club chair, with his back to the window. The agents face the window. Perhaps, Maddox thinks, he's set us here to distract us.

Les studies the agents. He's come from behind the desk intentionally. He's changed his strategy. He wants the agents to think he has nothing to hide. "Yes, gentlemen, how may I help you?"

Maddox swallows. "We're here about a body found in West Virginia."

Les gives a tolerant smile. "Gentleman, we are in West Virginia, but I think I know what you are talking about."

"A fellow named Billy Covington."

Les has decided to take things head-on. After all, the agents don't know what he and Cathy said to each other. "Yeah, finding his body has been in all the newspapers around here. The guy once worked at the same hotel where my ex-wife worked. She knew him. Small world."

"Your ex-wife being Catherine Mallet?"

"That's right."

"Did you know Mr. Covington?"

"No, I didn't know any of the people my wife worked with. She and I kind of worked in different worlds. I was a chemist."

"We understand you and Mrs. Mallet went to where Mr. Covington's body was found."

Les nods. "Yeah, that was kind of strange. Cathy, er Mrs. Mallet, came here to be treated for problems she had due to using Bleu Glo cosmetics. She had phoned me ahead of time about an appointment. For old times' sake, I met her in the treatment room and then asked her up here to the office to talk. It was the first time I had seen her in several years. We had a lot to talk about."

"How many years?"

"Oh, six or so."

"You had a friendly conversation."

"Not entirely. Our interactions about the blue dye have not always been friendly over the years, but time heals things."

"Again, why did you go to where the body was found?"

"Cathy brought it up … that is, about the body being found. She said that she had known him … That his body being found was really strange after all these years. She asked me if I knew about the area where the guy was found. I told her no … that that was a different area of West Virginia. At least it seemed different, though in reality, it's not very far from here. She became animated about the subject … asked how to get to the place. I told her that if it meant a lot to her, I could probably take her there … just for an adventure. We agreed to meet the next morning at my house in Millwood and drive out there and take a walk in the woods … just a fling of curiosity."

"And you found the site blocked off?"

"Yes."

"But you later went in anyway?"

"Yes."

"Why did you do that when you knew it was a crime scene?"

"The policeman guarding the area left, and we thought the area had been reopened. We'd come a long way and decided to take a quick look."

"And you found a cell phone?"

"Yes, we turned it over to the policeman when he returned and asked us to leave."

"After that, what did you do?"

"Drove back to my house. Cathy came in, I gave her a drink of water, and she went on her way."

"Have you talked to Mrs. Mallet since then?"

"No. I have no reason to. We hadn't talked in years. I suspect we may never talk again. We no longer have anything in common."

"Just a body in West Virginia."

"Cathy and the body had something in common. They had worked together. I just went along for the ride. What she and I have in common is that we were once married."

"And you never met Covington?"

"No."

"Did Cathy talk to you about her relationship with the man?"

"Only that she knew him and that he had mysteriously vanished."

"To change the subject, Mr. Warin, we know you're being investigated by another office of the FBI. Does that have anything to do with Covington?"

"Agents Raby and Mant-something. No, nothing to do with Covington."

"They charge you with anything?"

"No, I suspect they're still working on it. Scheming and conniving, or some crap."

"Blue-collar stuff?"

"I guess."

"That takes time."

"Thanks for the encouragement."

***

Back in their car, the agents fasten their seat belts. As Arroyo starts the car, he asks, "What do you think? Seems like this guy Warin is flying high. Why would he get involved? It can only hurt him. He didn't work at the hotel and claims he didn't know anyone there. His only connection is that he was married to a questionable woman who worked there, and he hasn't been married or in contact with her for years. So why the hell would he go to the burial site? Why get involved? It doesn't make sense."

"Joy ride with his ex? Really? He's not thinking, or there's more to it than meets the eye."

"Well, he's put the trip out to West Virginia on Mrs. Mallet's back. Claims he just went along for the ride."

"We're in West Virginia."

"Damnit, I know. And you know what I mean."

"Still, got to keep places straight."

***

When the agents get back to headquarters, the results of the fingerprint analyses of the syringes are waiting. Prints have been found on the syringe with the broken-off needle but aren't in the database.

Another set has also been found on all the syringes. The database says they belong to a man named Chisholm. He's an ex-con. He was previously sent up for dealing. He lives in Alexandria.

Maddox looks at Arroyo. "Get a picture. Put it up on the whiteboard. I'll set up a raid for early in the morning. Go to bed early."

Chapter Ninety-Four

After the FBI agents' visit, Les sits with his feet on his desk, looking out over the activity on the floor below, but he doesn't see it. His mind is far away, thinking about his life and his future. We should never have killed Godfrey, but what would have happened if we hadn't? Life might have been very different, but it is what it is. Now I'm here in the process of becoming very wealthy, but that murder will always hang over my head, and I have to depend on an ex-wife not turning us in. I can't believe she will … at least I'm 90 percent sure she won't … maybe 99 percent, but there's always the one percent. There will always be that. And this conspiracy business, is that for real? Will it ever amount to anything? Maybe there's never any rest for the wealthy … always something in the past.

Berty comes in. He never knocks. "Blimey mate … are you sitting here looking over your kingdom … admiring your world?"

Les smiles poignantly. "Just thinking about the world—the world as it may be."

"Maybe? Mate, you know how it's going to be … limousines and yachts … the good life."

"Yeah, what if we're taken to court … charged with conspiracy?"

"Lord, that's going to sort. They'd have to invent a new crime to get you on that, won't they? All the courts in the land would throw it out."

"You think so? Lots of people out there are clamoring for our heads."

"Mostly your head."

Les sighs. "Thanks for the clarification."

"No worry, there are more people who want to be cured. They're not going to put you out of business."

"I can't help but worry."

"Don't. You need to stop worrying. Live your life. Get on the pull."

"Jesus, Berty, if that means what I think it means, I've done that, been there."

Berty hooted, "Mate, that's something where 'I've done that, been there' doesn't apply ... never will."

"I was married to the most beautiful woman in the world."

"Never saw her, but I believe you. There are things other than beauty. Besides, with a few million in the bank, I'm convinced there's more beauty to find in this world. You need to get your mind on other things ... buy a yacht or something ... move on."

"A yacht? I can't imagine anything more boring."

"Okay, just consider what you might buy ... or what you might do ... give to public radio ... build a cancer institute ... vaccinate everyone in Africa."

"Good ideas, Berty. Maybe I'll do those things ... maybe give some to Cathy."

"What? The woman who double crossed you? She wouldn't even appreciate it."

"Probably not, but she'd know how to spend it ... how to enjoy it. It would make her happy."

Berty shook his head. "Lord, help us. You can't forget her?"

"Cathy's hard to forget."

Chapter Ninety-Five

Eddie Chisholm is awakened by flashing lights reflecting from his bedroom ceiling.

"Oh, shit," he says aloud. He throws off his covers, jumps from his bed, and rushes downstairs to open the door. He'd been raided before. He's had doors bashed in before. He doesn't want it to happen again. He stands in the doorway, hands held high.

Two men from a SWAT team grab him and turn him toward the door. "You armed?"

"In my pajamas?"

They pat him down.

Chisholm looks back over his shoulder. "Satisfied?"

Agents Maddox and Arroyo come to the door and turn to the SWAT team leader. Maddox directs, "Find a chair for him to sit in and watch him while we search the place."

They move Chisholm to the sofa in the living room. Then half a dozen agents follow as they enter the house and are assigned areas to search.

Chisholm complains, "What the shit are you doing? I'm a normal guy with a job. I need to be at it by eight o'clock. You're screwing up my life. Where's the damn search warrant?"

Maddox flashes a warrant at him.

"Shit, you didn't give me a chance to read it. I need my glasses, anyway. Get me my glasses."

Maddox slaps the warrant on the coffee table in front of Chisholm. "Read it as best you can." He and Arroyo join the search party.

After a short time, the team assembles in the living room. The material they have found is stacked on the floor and the coffee table.

There's a laptop, four boxes of syringes, a bottle of alcohol, gauze 2x2's, rubber tubing, three boxes of latex gloves, a butane blow torch, and a small bag of white powder. Maddox sits in a club chair facing Chisholm. "You a diabetic, Eddie?"

"Maybe."

"Maybe? Where's your meter? What do you prick your finger with? You have syringes, but we can't find the insulin. You care to explain?"

"No."

Arroyo returns, wearing latex gloves and carrying several bags of powder. "Jeez. I'm afraid to touch this stuff. Don't know what it is, but it was hidden on top of a sheet of plywood laid on the rafters in the garage. Had to lean a step ladder against the van to reach it."

Chisholm growls, "You better not have damaged the van."

Maddox chuckles. "Then you better give us the keys. We need to take it with us so we can check it out. We need to check you out too. You have a cell phone?"

"Yeah, getting charged in the kitchen."

Arroyo says, "I'll get it. I'm gloved."

When he returns, Maddox instructs, "Give it to Eddie so he can call into work and say he's got other things to do this morning. When he finishes, add the phone to the pile of stuff we're taking."

***

At FBI headquarters, Maddox and Arroyo sit down across a table from Chisholm. They stare at the man for a minute.

Finally, Chisholm looks down and sighs. "I need a lawyer."

Maddox concurs, "Yes, you do. You have one?"

"Barry Tancredi."

"Really."

Chisholm smirks. "Yeah, I know. He's a sleaze … but he's my sleaze."

Arroyo laughs. "Best you can do?"

Chisholm glares at him.

Arroyo holds up his hands in defense. "I didn't say anything."

Maddox addresses the one-way mirror. "See if you can get Tancredi in here for Eddie Chisholm." He turns back to Chisholm. "We'll get word back on whether he's coming. Let me do the routine while we wait."

Maddox turns on the recorder and the camera and settles down. He specifies the time and the occupants of the room and reads Chisholm his Miranda rights. "Any questions?"

Chisholm grimaces. "Nah, I've heard it before."

Maddox nods. "Okay, while we wait for Tancredi, let me tell you about a few things."

"I already know what you found."

"Yeah, that will get you time in jail, probably big time. You've already got a couple of convictions for distribution."

"Marijuana."

"Yeah, but convictions, nonetheless. Now we've got you for the hard stuff."

"You've got nothing on me distributing."

"Yeah, but possession. Possession of a lot. It will earn you a few years, but it's not what I'm going to talk about."

"Shit, there's something else?"

"Maybe … probably."

Maddox reaches into a briefcase and pulls out the bag with the syringes, the memory card, and the notebook. He lays them on the table and briefly studies Chisholm's curious face. "I need you to think about this, Eddie, because it's a real mystery. These syringes here all have your fingerprints on them."

"Yeah, so what?"

"Don't talk, Eddie. Your lawyer's not here yet."

Arroyo intervenes. "We just want to give you some things to think about until your attorney gets here."

"Yeah, so what else?"

Maddox continues, "Well, it doesn't surprise us that your fingerprints are on the syringes. Hell, that's your business … your profession. What's surprising is the other things in the bag. You see, these things were all found together. There's a notebook with some coordinates written in it. You'll be interested to know that the coordinates are the location where the body of Billy Covington was found. We know that Covington was your former boss at the Pleasure Hotel. The syringes and the notebook are a strange convergence of information. But that's not all. The memory card is a video of another hotel manager, Stanley Wigram, in his office, skimming off cash from the hotel's receipts. As a result, Mr. Wigram is probably meeting with his own lawyers."

"I didn't skim anything."

"I told you, Eddie, don't say anything."

Eddie frowns and nods.

"That's a strange combination of items in one bag … a real mystery in and of itself. Now add this. We searched Covington's home and found another video on a memory card that looks very much like the memory card in this bag." Maddox takes the memory card from an envelope and lets Chisholm see it. While he studies Chisholm, he makes an assertion that he doesn't know is true. "It looks like both these videos are made with the same camcorder. You know what's on the second memory card, Eddie. It's a movie of Billy Covington and Cathy Mallet, aka Cathy DuChant, having sex in what looks like a Pleasure Hotel room. Funny, you don't look surprised, Eddie. I wonder why. I wonder if you didn't know about them having sex. I wonder what the connection is between you, Cathy DuChant, Stanley Wigram, and the deceased, Billy Covington. Someone is going to tell us. It's just a matter of who and when."

Chisholm sits, with his mouth slightly agape, breathing steadily but more deeply than usual. He stares ahead and looks deep in thought.

Maddox scrutinizes Chisholm's face. It's just a matter of time.

***

Maddox and Arroyo are excused while Chisholm talks to his attorney. They close the one-way window to the interview room for privacy and go to get coffee.

After half an hour, the agents are called back. Barry Tancredi offers to shake their hands. They are reluctant but do so, looking Tancredi up and down, taking in his two days growth of beard and rumpled suit. They wondered if he is sleeping in his office.

Tancredi challenges the agents. "You haven't charged my client with anything."

"True, but we will," Maddox responds.

"Seems like we need a charge as a starting point for a discussion."

"What discussion? Your client is guilty as hell."

"We don't agree with you on that."

"It's cut and dry. We have the evidence."

"But my client may know some things that will interest you."

"Is he going to tell us what they are?"

"Maybe. We need to discuss it."

Maddox bites his lower lip in contemplation. "How about I have a prosecutor in at two o'clock. Can you be back by then?"

Chisholm answers for his attorney, "Sure, we'll have lunch and be back by two."

Maddox chokes back a guffaw. "You'll have lunch, all right, but it will be courtesy of Uncle Sam."

***

When Tancredi reaches his car, he takes a burner cell phone from his glove compartment and makes a call Chisholm has asked him to make.

A woman answers, "Brenner Bedding."

"Cathy?"

"Yes, may I help you?"

"Message from Eddie. Get your ass out of town. Run."

He hangs up and thinks, Damn, another wasted phone. I need to toss it … The sooner, the better. No damn aiding and abetting.

Chapter Ninety-Six

Cathy holds the phone for a moment, her mind racing. Eddie? Eddie? Damn, Chisholm's the only Eddie I know. Chisholm, damn it, what's the guy on the phone saying? Telling me to run. Did Chisholm fold? Has he confessed? Damn it. Who was this guy who called? Does he know anything? Why the hell wouldn't he say more? What should I do? Wait it out? Play it safe and vanish? If it's a scam, can I ever come back? Damn, damn, damn.

She picks up the phone and punches in a number. "Hello … Yeah, it's Cathy at the store. I've got an emergency. I need to go … No, I can't wait … I'll lock up … Yeah, I'll be okay … No, no, you can't help … I'll let you know about it later."

She grabs her purse and heads for the door. How much money do I have? Less than fifty dollars … need to stop by an ATM … Damn machines only give three hundred … How am I going to survive on three hundred dollars? I'll think about it later.

She carefully locks the store. She doesn't want damage to the place by vandals or thieves added to her worries.

She hurries to her car, starts it, and roars out onto the road, with the car fishtailing as she straightens it out. Slow down, damn it. Don't you have enough problems?

She stops at a red light. She pounds on the steering wheel. "Change, damn it, change, change!"

The light changes, and she starts up. Where do I go? ATM first. Can I go by the apartment? Damn! Will the police already be there … waiting for me to roll up? Damn, I'd better not. Get my three hundred dollars and run … Run where? Go west … away from Alexandria … away from Virginia. I'll figure it out on the way. What do motels charge? Damn, I'm only good for two or three days. Shit, shit, shit!

She checks the gas gauge—half full. I'll fill up at the next station … use the credit cards before they use them to track me. Then the ATM.

***

Cathy drives west on U.S Route 50 toward West Virginia. It's a familiar route. A route she had never driven until after all the damage was done. It is the highway of her fate. She will leave it behind—leave it and its memories, forever.

When she goes through Millwood, she thinks about going to Les's house and hiding but realizes the authorities are bound to find her there. She and Les are connected, forever and ever. They are connected by Blue. Damn Blue.

She drives through Winchester and eventually through the now all-too-familiar town of Capon Bridge, accelerates out of town past the Jesse James Outlaw Bar and Grill, and approaches the exit to the dirt road where the bodies had been buried.

There's a police car sitting at the intersection.

Damn, it's the same police cruiser that was there before … still guarding the road. Hasn't he got anything better to do? As Cathy passes the cruiser, she keeps her eyes straight ahead. No eye contact, damn it … no eye contact.

After passing, she looks in the rearview mirror. To her horror, she sees the cruiser's lights flashing and watches it turn onto the highway in her direction. Shall I run for it? She knows her car has the power. She knows it can hug the road. But she knows the police cruiser is probably souped-up and that the driver knows the roads.

Cathy pulls to the side of the road and stops. The cruiser pulls in behind her and angles out toward the road. The cruiser's door opens, and the policeman gets out and approaches her car.

Cathy recognizes him. It's the same cop. What was his name?

Billops, that's it, Billops. She rolls down the window.

Billops leans down toward the window. A look of surprise then crosses his face. "It's you again."

Cathy pulls down her sunglasses. "My eyes are getting better."

"Yes, ma'am. Please get out of the car."

"Why? I wasn't speeding."

"Please get out of the car." Billops reaches for the door handle.

Cathy flips up her glasses. She has never taken the car out of gear. She takes her foot off the brake, and the car lurches forward.

***

Billops barely gets his hand off the door handle but still staggers and falls. He gets up, races back to his car, and follows Cathy.

She rounds a bend and is momentarily out of his sight. As Billops reaches the bend, he catches a moment of Cathy's car turning to the right. He knows the road loops around and comes back to the highway. He stops and waits for her.

He sees her car approach. Her car slows and veers to the left onto a dirt road leading past a farm.

Billops follows down the dirt road until he passes all the farm buildings. He knows the road is going into the woods, and that it's a dead end. He parks the cruiser across the road to block the woman when she returns.

He radios into his office to apprise them of his whereabouts and what is happening.

***

Cathy races on, struggling to hold the car on the road. The road begins to deteriorate, and a canopy of trees starts to envelop her as the road narrows and becomes rutted. The ruts in the road jerk the car to the side. A wheel drops into a ditch. She races the engine, shifting the gears forward and back. The car is stuck.

In frustration, she gets out, slams the door, and heads off into the woods, staggering through the underbrush that thrashes and tears her clothing.

After running and staggering a few hundred yards, she turns her ankle. The pain shoots up her leg, and she falls. She lies on her side, clutching her leg. Damn, damn, damn. I'm in the middle of nowhere and can't walk.

Tears come into her eyes as she crawls to a nearby tree and sits up against it. She clutches her ankle and sobs. She finally rolls back on her side, breathes heavily, pulls off her eyeglasses, and bites down on them in pain and hopelessness.

Time passes, and Cathy feels her life will end. She almost wishes it would. Her mind whirls. That damn Les Warin and his Blue. He's going to get away with it. I thought I had him set up. They're going to get me, and he's going to laugh. Damn him. Damn him.

After a half-hour or so, she hears thrashing coming through the woods. She lies there, still waiting as if an ax is going to fall.

Finally, Billops staggers out of the underbrush. He leans, his hands on his knees, and struggles to catch his breath. In one hand, he holds his weapon.

Cathy raises her head and looks at him. "Did you bring aspirin?"

He gasps between breaths. "Advil's back in the cruiser."

She groans. "Lot of good that does."

"What did you do?"

"Broke my damn ankle."

"Broke it or sprained it?"

"How the hell do I know? It hurts. It's killing me."

Billops holds the hand-held radio he's carrying up to his head. "I'll phone in for an ambulance."

"Get a damned helicopter."

"They can't land in the woods."

Billops calls in his location, gives Cathy's condition, and asks backup to hurry. He listens for a minute. "She did?" He disconnects the radio.

Cathy rolls herself back up to her sitting position against the tree, wincing and moaning as she does.

Billops holsters his pistol and sits down beside her.

Cathy looks at him then down at his weapon. "Snap your damn weapon back in."

"What?" Billops looks down at his holster. "I thought I might have to use it."

"Well, if you leave the holster unbuckled, I will grab your gun and shoot you."

"What? You wouldn't do that."

"If I could walk, I would. It might distract me from the pain."

While Cathy talks, Billops is frantically buckling his holster and shifting away from her. "Would you really shoot me?"

"What did they tell you over the radio?"

"That you are wanted for murder."

"See."

"Damn, you killed someone?"

"It's a long story."

***

The medics arrive with a stretcher.

Cathy speaks between chattering teeth, "Did you bring the Advil?"

"Percocet."

"Thank heaven and all its angels. I may survive."

The medic gives her the narcotic and a drink from a canteen. The other medic checks her ankle.

Cathy screams, "Get your hands off that, or they'll hear my scream back in your hick village!"

The man stops touching her ankle, looking as if Cathy's scream is all in a day's work. "Just looks like a sprain to me."

"Just a sprain! Damn, man, you act like that's nothing."

"It could be worse."

"Yeah, are all the ligaments still in place?"

"Time will tell."

"So what's next?"

"We carry you out of these woods and drive you back to Winchester."

"Back to Virginia?"

"Nearest hospital, but I understand you're going back to Virginia anyway."

"Damn, that's convenient."

"Let's load you up."

"Be careful of the damn foot."

***

The medics put her on the stretcher. She grips the sides, wanting to scream and cuss aloud.

As they carry her through the brush, the branches slash at her. "Damn, guys, take it easy. I'm not Sheba, queen of the jungle."

She thinks, Damn, what an undignified way to be captured. Where are my sunglasses? I probably bit through them. I need to cover these bloodied eyes. I wonder if reporters will be waiting with cameras. Hell, do they even have reporters in Capon Bridge? They might in Winchester.

They transfer her to the ambulance stretcher at the ambulance, roll it into the ambulance with a bump, and close the doors with a bang, with her eyes shut tight the entire time and her breath held.

One of the medics sits beside Cathy, looks down at her, and

ruefully comments, "You sure got yourself in a heck of a place … no turning around. We have to back out of here through all the ruts in the road. Good thing you don't have a broken back … you're going to bounce."

Cathy closes her eyes, bites her lip, grips the sides of the stretcher, and hangs on.

When they are finally back on U.S. 50, she begins to relax. The Percocet is kicking in. She starts thinking about the future. She knows she is going to trial. They will hear my story … every bit of it … of the awful rape and abuse. It was all in self-defense. God, I hope my eyes have cleared up by then. I want to look good. Maybe I'll even be on crutches with a big cast. I'll prop it up so all the jurors can see.

Printed in the USA
CPSIA information can be obtained
at www.ICGtesting.com
LVHW091514310124
770461LV00001B/36